REQUIEM FOR BARBARA

Books by Branka Čubrilo

Requiem for Barbara
Dethroned
Fiume - The Lost River
The Lonely Poet and Other Stories
The Mosaic of the Broken Soul
Three to Tango and Other Tales

REQUIEM FOR BARBARA

Branka Čubrilo

SPEAKING VOLUMES, LLC
NAPLES, FLORIDA
2023

Requiem for Barbara

ISBN 978-1-64540-927-4

For Lora, Althea, Barbara and me.

Acknowledgments

Many thanks to Irina Dimitric-Stojic and Althea Kuzman.

Table of Contents

LETTERS TO TED

My mother has died. For days after her burial, I did not know where to turn to. I am eighteen years old. I only had her; she died believing so.

She left me a small apartment, furniture, paintings on the walls, a computer desk and the computer on it.

My first thought, my first impulse, was to sell all her belongings, to liberate myself from the unbearable pain. The pain sat on my chest and shoulders and in each moment, it seemed to me that mother was going to step into the living room from her study, deprived of sleep. The pain never lessened, but I understood that all that around me was what was left to me after her passing away. Whatever I looked at, it spoke of her.

Soon after her death, I sat at her desk in her study.

My mother was a writer, and that was the way she tried to make our living. I always believed she was the best writer in the whole wide world . . . but she didn't have much success. She published several short stories in women's periodicals, a collection of poetry . . . she was far ahead of her time.

Sitting there at her desk, I started to pull the drawers out to examine their contents. The contents in the drawers were in perfect order—which was not typical of my mother. She was not the victim of any kind of order.

In the lowest and widest drawer, I found a cardboard folder tied up with a yellow ribbon. On the folder was written *Letters to Ted.*

So, it looked like—she still remembered Ted.

It was quite a thick folder as it contained numerous sheets of paper. I started to read the papers in the order they were placed.

Hi Ted,

It was raining on the day you walked out. Miserable, it looks like rain accompanies all separations. I can't even call it separation, you left without a word. Lora came in and asked me what was written in the letter I was holding in my hand. I said, "Ted's gone". She fell silent. In her angelic eyes, I saw sadness. She did not cry, her petite, narrow face battled with a wild storm of emotions. Then, she said quietly, "He's gone for good." She knew that you had gone forever this time. I nodded my head. I could not utter a word, I was afraid of my own voice.

She never cried for you, Ted. You coached her how to handle her emotions. After a while, they called me from her school. They told me her marks had dropped; her eyes were red and teary, often. I explained that her father had left us. Her father, Ted. You (who would doubt it often), you are her father.

There were too many discrepancies between us, Ted. (So, you left.) Ted Donoghue . . . her father . . . you left.

I heard about the wicked illness of your family. Incest. You went mad on this deserted island.

Well, the late Aurelio Milich was my cousin. To your wicked mind, it was unnatural and incomprehensible why we would hug and kiss every time we met. Your superior arrogance towards other people, to people who migrated to your country. We all were primitive in your eyes, for we displayed our emotions freely (I could never grasp what was primitive about it). Aurelio Milich's father and mine were brothers. When I tried to explain that to you, you waved your hand, and a small cynical smile would appear on your face. Yes, a cynical smile. Before I met you, I lived with Aurelio. He was all I had in this faraway and strange land. He helped me a lot; he loved me with the same kind of love with which he loved his younger sister. She would never let herself into such a grand adventure intuitively, knowing that heavy were the dawns when you woke up looking at an unfamiliar sky . . . she knew it intuitively, yes intuitively . . . but I was the one who left (intuition deserted me . . .) . . . you never asked—why?

To forget. Yes, Ted, to forget Dado.

When I married you, I thought I loved you (as if you can think up love; how naïve, childish or sorrowful—to think love is a matter of the mind). It could be that I thought I could learn to love you with time, but you were so aloof, so cold. You were suspicious; you would not let me see Aurelio, oh, those horrible insinuations of yours . . . Much later, I learnt about your unusual family history. Your ancestors were criminals. Alcoholics. Incest—is in your family. And you, you were a chemist. The intellectual one in the family. (The only one). You never introduced me to anybody so you could build your false history. You said your ancestors came from England, but they were rather Irish, Ted. You told me that your grandfather was a high-ranking officer in the Queen's Navy. Lie; I learned it was a lie.

You lived with lies, Ted.

When Aurelio died in a car accident, a strange grimace played on your face. After that you asked me why I was crying. I loved Aurelio, but with a different kind of love to the one Allan loved Margaret. Don't you remember Allan O'Donoghue (later you got rid of the O, so just Donoghue remained), he was your father's relative; he left Margaret with a child, and a child she was herself—the child of his own sister? I know that you do remember, for something like that should be hard to forget . . .

When we got married, I was already pregnant. I conceived a child with you.

When you left, I did not know whether that was better or worse for Lora. We were teaching her different things, constantly. The things that were valuable and honourable in my culture and tradition were unimportant and cheap to you. You had contempt for tenderness, calling it weakness; you mocked sincerity, calling it indiscretion. The things she had to hide from you she would whisper in my ear at night when I would come into her room to tuck her in. You would say, "Why are you covering her five times every night? You will spoil her, make her weak. Let her toughen up." Why did you allow her to walk the streets barefoot in winter? It used to horrify me. It used to horrify me!

You never asked me anything about my country nor about my past. (Why? Were you afraid I might ask you the same questions?) It all was below your interest, below your level. And so, my own past was suppressed in some strange liminal space where I had sealed the doors tightly shut. (They were sealed with padlocks one thousand tons heavy, a thousand tons of silence, a thousand tons of concrete . . . with padlocks that seemed as if they would never be unlocked, or broken, with padlocks rusted like the ones in the stories of locked princesses . . . like the ones in the stories with a tragic end, because the main protagonist fell ill of a rare illness that came from a silence weighing one thousand tons . . .)

But look, now I want to tell you: I had my country and I had my past. Even though it looks like a dream now, dreamt long ago (which I dreamt when I was very young), but the one I still remember. You hid your past, for you were not proud of it; it was not 'good enough' for you; therefore, you narrated a different one. I could not talk about my past because you were not interested in it (as if it were shameful). But I was proud of it.

My first and only love was a painful affair. I left because of him, believing (still too young to understand) that I would forget him.

His name was Davor, but everyone called him Dado.

He lived in an old building with colossal dark corridors, with marble stairs built during the Austro-Hungarian Empire. My hometown is very old.

I remember a big, thick wooden door on the first floor; I could not reach the doorbell nor the door knob yet. I would knock with my tiny fingers at the door and call, "Dado, Dado come out to play!" I would stay there and call for him until someone came out to open the door. Usually, it would be his grandmother coming to the door, and each time I heard her coming, I would call for God's assistance—'Please, kind God, help me; let it not be the old woman.'

She would open the door, just a tiny bit, she would say with a frown, "Go away, Dado is not going out today. Do not knock again." She would slam the heavy door in my face. (I measured the heaviness of the door by its sound.) I would sit on the cold stairs waiting for Dado to come out, the whole morning. Sometime around midday, from the open window in the corridor, I would hear my mother's voice calling me for lunch. When I came home, my mother would be angry with me while touching my thighs and little bottom frozen from sitting on the cold marble in the damp corridor of Dado's building, in which the temperature never changed regardless of the season.

Often, Dado would jump on the garage roof below his window, then down onto the street, calling me, "Let's run, Barbara!" He would be in a panic, afraid that his grandmother would stop me in the corridor and hold me there hostage.

Dado lived with two grandmothers. One was the 'Good Grandma'; the other was the 'Bad One'. It was difficult to get the 'Good Grandma', for she was of fragile health, often ill and would rarely open the door. Her existence was confirmed rather by her name than her persona. She lived like a ghost. If she, on the very rare occasions, was the one to open the door, she would say with a quiet almost surreal voice, "Wait a little, I'll tell him you are here, but please, do not wander off too far; be around the building so you can hear us when we call." The 'Bad One', would always slam the door in my face (the heavy door whose weight I measured by its sound) while saying, "Go away and leave him alone." She was more real than the other one, and her heart couldn't be changed, ever. I would sit on the cold marble stairs full of childish pride believing that sitting there, in that coldness, was a sign of revenge—'I will wait for him the entire day!' Passing-by neighbours, stroking my hair, would ask me, "Are you waiting for Dado, again?"

My mother was concerned about it; she would say that it was not a nice picture—to see a little girl, sitting in front of someone's door. I never listened to her remarks. Never. I would say, "But I love him."

Dado didn't have a mother. He did not even remember her, nor did I. His father worked in Germany, and because of that Dado had the best toys in the neighbourhood. But nobody was allowed to play with his toys, so he would smuggle them under his T-shirt, or under the tea-towel in which his sandwich was wrapped. The 'Bad One', the worse grandmother, was his father's mother, and the 'Good Grandma' was her sister. Dado was always overdressed, even in the middle of summer (only old women overdressed kids), all his clothes smelled of mothballs. When we played hide-and-seek, just by his scent, I could easily find where he was hiding. Later I believed that first love smelled of mothballs.

Rainy days would be spent in my mother's kitchen. She was cooking or baking and we were playing underneath the table. Right there, underneath my mother's dinning-table, he solemnly declared that he would marry me when the right time came. It was 1966, we were five years old, and we loved each other to death. All the kids in our street knew about the intensity of our love (is there a need for any stronger proof?), all their parents knew it, too. My parents knew it as well. Everybody respected our love, considering it as the real thing; everybody except the 'Bad Grandma', who would always slam her (heavy) door right in my face (the heaviness of the door was measured by its sound—a strange, hollow sound. It seemed to me that the sound was not strange and hollow because of its movement or its sound, but because of the old woman herself . . . her personality . . . strange and hollow . . . it seemed as if she did not like children, so she slammed the heavy door before them!)

So, Ted, that was how my first love started. You know, Ted, in my country people are born in the same house for generations. We are proud of it. My mother and Dado's father were school friends. My mother liked Dado even more because he had no mother. He would often dine at our place and when my mother would buy chocolate bars, there was always one for him.

It is 13th of June 1987 today; six months have passed since you left. Lora has never asked about you. Since you left, she has been very quiet, her self-esteem has been very fragile. She has completely lost interest in the violin. When I ask her, what would make her happy, she only shrugs her shoulders and says, "I don't know."

That's how the first letter my mother wrote to Ted ended. I did not know were these copies of the letters she sent to Ted, or were they letters Ted never received? Letters never sent.

My mother was unhappy. I understood that from the first letter. Anyway, I always felt her sadness. (She carried me inside her!). I believed that her sadness came from Ted's departure and the difficulties of finding a publisher for her novels. But I was wrong. She was not sad because of Ted's leaving. I was sad because of it.

I felt that in these letters, all her life was contained—the history of her hometown, her family and the history of one love.

I put down that letter and with trembling fingers, I took another. It said:

Hi Ted,

We celebrated Lora's birthday yesterday. She turned nine. Comparing her to me at that age, it is just impossible—she is so mature! She is a responsible and modest young girl. She always puts others' needs before her own. Even when I asked her on her birthday, "What do you want to do today?" she replied with another question, "What would you like to do?"

"It's your birthday, you decide."

"Maybe we can go to the cinema, what do you think?"

We went to the cinema and after that we ate a cake in a little cafe. Even though I didn't have much money, I borrowed some and bought her a bicycle, knowing how much she wanted it. From her father, she did not get anything, not even a birthday card. That was one more reason why I was determined to get her a bike. Her silence grieved me much.

Oh, if I only compare her ninth birthday with mine.

Twenty kids came to mine. All from the same street, all growing up together. My mother baked cakes, a big birthday cake, and auntie Zlatka (Aurelio was named after her) brought sandwiches from a hotel where she worked. Two big platters of colourful sandwiches, and precisely those sandwiches from Hotel Continental were the ones the kids liked best. We believed that their taste was unique and unrepeatable.

How many gifts! Surely, Dado's gift was the dearest to my heart. A big red heart was on the cover of the little book he gave me; and there, on the first blank page he wrote, 'To Dear Barbara, for your ninth birthday from you best friend—till death do us part. Dado' On the last (blank) page he had written, 'Love forever, Davor.'

Then, on my ninth birthday, he disclosed to me for the second time his undying love for me. This was much more serious than when he said it underneath my mother's dining-table some four years ago. Often, kids were teasing us, and I would be angry at those who teased me, but there he was, just like a knight defending my good reputation.

We celebrated Dado's ninth birthday in his apartment. Only once a year, on Dado's birthday, were kids allowed to enter their apartment. The year before Dado's ninth birthday the 'Good Grandma' died. He was left with the 'Bad One', but luckily for us, on Dado's birthday, his father would come from Germany, a real celebration for all of us. His father drove a big black BMW, and it seemed to me that it was the biggest and the nicest car I had ever seen. And it was, indeed, for all other fathers drove little cars, or many of them had little motorcycles.

On his ninth birthday, Dado got a real guitar from his father. At first, I was glad he got a present he dreamed of, but as he started to spend all his time with his guitar, I began to hate it. It stood in between us. If we ever argued, it was because of the guitar. He started private classes for classical guitar; Saturday and Sunday afternoons he spent locked in his room with his guitar.

'He cares more about his guitar than about me,' I thought.

Lora doesn't have friends from her street. The kids she grew up with. We moved four times, and four times she changed kindergartens and schools. Kids never invited anybody to their homes, and rarely did anyone have a permanent address.

When I told Lora that there were fifteen or twenty kids at my birthday party, she would laugh, "Did you invite a whole class?" No, they were simply friends from the street. We all knew when everyone's birthdays were, and all of us assumed we were invited, we never needed a formal invitation. Often, parents would compete to see who would organise the better party and for how long it would be the talk of the neighbourhood.

Do you remember our promise to Lora when she was seven, that we would take her to Disneyland the following year? For her eighth birthday—you had already left. I never knew why you left. Why we never talked about it? That damn silence of yours. Eternal silence.

I took the bus the other day downtown, and a young boy and girl came on. They sat next to each other, opposite me, in utter silence. Not a word. He stared at one spot on the floor, whilst her eyes circled around the bus. Silence. Then, I thought, maybe they did not know each other, maybe by chance they sat together. After a good ten minutes of silence, he asked without lifting his gaze from the floor, "Did you take the ciggies from the table?". She nodded her head looking nowhere in particular. We were riding for another half an hour, they never uttered a word. All of a sudden, he said, "We're getting off." They took off without a word. I looked at them through the window. He was walking in front of her, with his hands deep in his pockets; she dragged her feet twisting her head right and left as if she was searching . . . not knowing for what. (Or as if she was searching for lost words, as if she was searching for the lost page ripped off from her childhood where somebody was meant to give her a lesson about conversations or how to use words . . .)

When Dado and I used to enter a bus, I would give him money to buy tickets for the both of us. We would sit next to each other and chat about the day at school, about homework and the things which mattered and really did not matter. We would talk about our plans for the day, where should we go, who shall we invite to the playground, what kind of games should we play . . . Dado would talk endlessly to keep me entertained. When with me, he was never silent; with him, I was never bored.

Your silence looked as if you were worried endlessly. You gazed into the distance, into your past or future, far away from the present, far away from me, far away from the plans and the chatter which makes a marriage alive.

When I met you, your silence looked to me rather like wisdom. Wise people are silent. You lived in your past, and I did not know what kind of past you belonged to. I could only guess. You went to a Catholic school. I remember the scandal linked to that school.

We went to school together—boys and girls. In your school, there were only boys and priests. Two, or three of them were sentenced, they abused, raped the boys. You never talked about your high school. When the scandal came out, you would turn off the television; your neck and face were bright red, disgust on your face changed your features. When I used to ask, "What's wrong Ted? Why did you turn it off, let me hear it . . ." you would take your car keys and leave in a hurry, without a word.

Silence. Damn silence, heavy as a marble tomb. Silence which keeps a secret. You owe me an answer to the secret, Ted, if not to me then certainly to Lora—Why did you leave without a word? I forgive you for leaving us without money, but I can't forgive your silence. What was I to you? Just ether? Lora is your child (do you owe her words?)

Persevere in your silence. Barbara.

I slid my fingers down the sheet of paper. All her letters were written on the same date—on the second day of June every year until the last one. Every year on my birthday, she wrote him a letter about me and about her. And about Dado.

Why did she do it?

The third letter said:

Hi Ted,

It is your daughter's birthday today. I bought her a coat. I found a real Italian coat, nearly identical to the one I got for my tenth birthday. My mother asked me:

"What would you like for your birthday?"

"A coat," I said. So, she bought me a coat, a red one even though she tried to convince me to buy the same one in blue. But I couldn't give in, so we came back home with the red coat.

I saw such a similar one in the city, and I asked Lora:

"Would you like a coat for your birthday? A pretty red coat? Like Little Red Riding Hood?"

Lora laughed, Little Red Riding Hood was no longer her idol, but she liked the coat very much. The biggest surprise she got for her birthday was her grandmother's visit.

My mother came to visit me. You never met my mother. You probably would not like her, for she is so soft, kind and loving. Lora loved her.

She learned my language with her. I am very proud because of it, she speaks three languages now.

My mother stayed for one month, and I saw Lora's happiest face. My mother is a born entertainer. What a pity she never worked in the theatre or circus. She is so creative and does not have any inhibitions when it comes to being silly.

She was a child psychologist. She never worked while I was little, only when I started school, she went back to work. She wanted to dedicate all her time to me.

Lora took her out downtown and to some places out of the city. Can you believe, they wandered alone, Lora is so independent and capable. She was proud to show her grandma how independent she was. My mother said that she was too gentle, too sensitive a girl.

I told my mother how you had left; she did not say a word.

There were some topics she would avoid talking about. (About things she believed still hurt me). Like, about Dado. She never mentioned him, not once. (She never mentioned what she believed might hurt me). I did not ask about him, either. I was afraid I might hear something particular. (I would never admit to myself that it could still hurt me). I wanted to remember him the way I knew him, the way I loved him.

For my tenth birthday, I got an album for my stamp collection from my father, and Dado got a new guitar, better than the one he had got a year before.

Ted, it has started raining, I have to pick up my washing from the line; oh, I can't stand these domestic duties. Was that perhaps the reason why you left? No, that could not be possible. Barbara.

Why did she write these letters? Did she ever send them away? Did he read her letters, did he ever reply to any of them?

Barbara was sad. Her sentences were heavily coloured with cynicism. I never knew her being cynical. If she did not love him, why did she reproach his departure so much? Wounded ego? Or was it because he left her without any money? Or was she so sad because of me?

Tears were rolling down my cheeks while I picked up a new letter. The letters danced in front of my teary eyes. (Barbara's letters were dancing on the sheet of paper, so it seemed as if she were happy whilst writing them).

Hi Ted,

It is one of these days when I should be the happiest if only I could stay under the covers. It rains, and it is too cold for this time of year. Lora's at school. Once again, she is a very good student; they say one of the best. She studies a lot. It looks as if she is over you leaving. She never mentioned you any more as if you never existed really, but I saw that your leaving had hurt her badly, like a little snail she withdrew inside. Now again, like a little snail she is emerging from her shell. Her ringing laughter is back; again, she calls me 'Bombi'. You gave us both this nickname. I said "Bambina" and you said, "What? Bombi?" When she heard it, she laughed hard, but the nickname stayed the same for the both of us.

I'll make a gourmet lunch. Dishes she loves the most plus a birthday cake. After lunch, I will take her to the theatre. She will spend the day with me, even though it seems to me that she would rather be with Louise and Marianne, her school friends. She said she'll go downtown with them on Sunday. She said she'd like to go with them to the Art Gallery and have ice cream in the Gallery café.

I asked her: "Why Louise and Marianne, why not, let's say Peter or John?" She laughed, her laughter still was a child's ringing laughter.

For my twelfth birthday, I had already gone out with Dado. Can you believe we went to the cinema and watched 'Splendor in the Grass'? Oh, how much I had cried, Dado gave me his handkerchief; he hugged me and comforted me. (He comforted me . . . I remember his words of comfort . . . nobody gave me that kind of comfort ever, not even my mother . . . and, I cried more and more, all out of my need to hear his sweet words; they were like beautiful music which I wanted to carry within me forever . . .) When the film ended, he promised, he would never leave me. In his wholehearted attempt to dry my tears, he was ready to promise anything, he was willing to give up his guitar and the time he was spending alone with the guitar. On our way back home, we held hands. I wished that the road to our home never ended, and that my hand stayed in his for eternity, and that he kept on telling me his sweet words of comfort (I still remember these words of comfort . . . nobody comforted me like that ever, not even my mother knew such words . . .)

In front of my building we let go of our hands, I smoothed my hair and wiped my eyes. When I entered the apartment, my mother asked:

"Who did you go to the cinema with?"

"With Dado."

"Just the two of you?"

"Just us. Why?"

"Barbara, you are a big girl now, you should know . . ."

"Please mother . . ." I did not allow anybody to say a word against him or against our friendship. It was sacred.

At twelve he had changed already. When eleven, he was still a young boy, but at twelve his eyes were quite different, his hands stronger. And his sentences were stronger, more meaningful.

For my twelfth birthday, I got David Bowie's Long Play record from my mother and from my father a beautiful fountain pen, rimmed with golden circles; for his twelfth birthday, Dado got a bicycle from his father, and Lora, she got an Anthology of Worlds Poetry and twelve yellow roses from her mother.

Good luck, Ted. Barbara.

I took another letter which always started with the same opening:

Hi Ted,

This year, for Lora's thirteenth birthday her grandparents came to visit. My mother is deeply unhappy, for I live so far away (a mother always finds a reason for unhappiness); she is unhappy because she can't see Lora more often. We were waiting at the airport and Lora was so excited, she imagined what her grandfather would look like. A photograph is one thing, a real person is something else. She was keener to know his personality rather than his looks, for she had already seen him in photographs and video tapes.

You never wanted to meet my parents, Ted. Only once, I said that it would be good if they came to see us, for they really wanted to see how I lived here. But you quickly replied that there were not enough spare rooms for guests. After that, they never offered to come again.

But, perhaps, you would have liked my father. In your small way, you were always impressed by 'important people'. My father was a judge, the chairman of the Supreme Court. Impressive, isn't it? Because of his name, I was privileged in my town, I never waited in queues; because of him, I was enrolled in the best schools; because of him, I enrolled in University, which never interested me really. What kind of a lawyer could I possibly have been? I was free as the wind. I could not be squeezed in any templates. I always had my own rules and my own games. My hometown was just too small to overlook or ignore the rules of 'the best opinion and the best behaviour'. It was too small to allow me the rules of my own logic, and my own heart, which would change according to need. (And the logic which ruled the city was opposite to mine). In an environment like that, I could live by my own rules only because I had such an influential father. If he sold potatoes at the market place, then, like many of the other free-thinking girls whose fathers were fishermen or labourers, I would have been declared a 'weirdo' or 'not properly adjusted' or 'poorly brought up' or 'unscrupulous' . . .

But I had my father.

More importantly, I had Dado. Because of him and only for him, I wanted to be 'the craziest one', 'the weirdo', 'different or unique', original, mine and his. Dado had known me only like this. And he wanted me just like this.

But you had never really known me, Ted. You never wanted to know me. Could it be because you had never known yourself? Maybe the reason for your long silence was because you had never known yourself. You were searching for the answer which was lost in the past.

For my thirteenth birthday, Dado had bought me shoes. Can you believe it, he bought me a pair of shoes when he visited his father in Germany? He brought shoes wrapped in a nice box, and I thought it could have been a doll. I thought he was mocking me. But when I unwrapped the present, my jaw dropped: a black, patent-leather pair of shoes with a small heel, and a little black bow in the middle.

"Dado, you are mad!" I screamed and jumped on him.

At that time, he was thirteen, but he looked like he was fifteen—he was taller than his peers and very different to all of them.

My mother gave me a knitted scarf, mittens and a little hat in the same colours and my father took me horse riding.

For his thirteenth birthday Dado got 'The Count Monte Cristo' from me and a golden chain from his father.

From her mother, Lora got a painting of three women sitting in a café reading some papers (that was what she wanted, she hung it above her desk).

From her grandparents, she got a golden ring with a little white pearl.

She was extremely happy for her thirteenth birthday. We cruised with my parents around the harbour on a big cruiser, and she was delighted that she could teach my father the things he never knew of. He used to tell her things she never heard of, and she believed he was the most learned man on the planet, but when she told him some historical facts about her hometown and he did not know it, she was delighted to teach him. They both were very proud, my father of his granddaughter, and Lora was proud of herself. His company was so beneficial to her, it strengthened her self-esteem.

Take care Ted, Barbara.

She was presenting these memories as if she was putting together little pictures on a screen and these little pictures started to materialise in front of my eyes. I remembered some of these little vignettes she was painting.

It was so lovely when my grandparents visited. They were both pretty unusual people. My mother had a very strange relationship with both of her parents. She was capricious all the time trying to show them her self-sufficiency. She would claim that she could do anything by herself, that she didn't need any help.

Grandma would let her do whatever she wanted, grandpa tried to reason with her, but my Barbara would always do exactly as she wanted, what pleased her at that moment.

I said to myself, 'Let's see what happened on my fourteenth birthday.' I had already forgotten.

Hi Ted,

Time just flies, the years are racing. Is it true that a year has already passed since my last letter to you? In this last year, Lora had changed so much. She is not a child anymore; she is fourteen. But, she is neither a woman yet. Often, I see her confused for she doesn't know herself, whether she is a child or a woman. She likes looking at her image in the mirror. She is so pretty, reminds me of you. She inherited your hands and your mannerism. Her fingers are unbelievably long, her movements slow and measured (like those of a chemist). It is better to be like that, my movements are quick and nervous, my fingers are much shorter than hers. Long fingers would be an advantage if she decided to write, even though her clever head would be of better advantage. She has a pretty face, big blue eyes, Ted's eyes. Her hair is the colour of wheat, it is a little bit darker than yours, but a little bit lighter than mine. She shows little dimples in her cheeks when she smiles, the same ones which used to be seen in my cheeks when I would smile. I do not smile often any more. Lora is often away; she is at school or attending some after school activities, so I am left with plenty of time for writing. Still, I am the happiest when writing (still, I am avoiding reality), but I am still nervous and tense when trying to present my work (presenting it to someone, I feel as if I am squeezed in some other reality). For so many years, I had been told what great talent I posses. I do not believe in that any more. Regardless, I am still writing, for there are too many voices within me crying and begging me to let them out, to give them life. When I liberate them from that cage, from my chest, when I make them alive, strong waves of happiness course through my body. I feel thunder and lightening in my head, I hear music which Lora says isn't there. And this is my reward. Only that. That music. Celestial music. Then I hear words, words, words . . . I hear them everywhere, I see the words, I see them as frescos, I see them as memories, I see them as music, I see them within me and out of me, I feel I am made of words, that I am a word itself . . . and this is my reward.

Nobody wants my stories.

Even you did not want my stories. When I used to tell you the tales of my past, you would turn your head to the other side. Why did you never care about my stories?

Today is Lora's big day, mine too. Her birthday.

On this day, we spend a lot of time together; we talk a lot. (Her tender soul likes the tales we weave). We spend days and weekends together, but we mainly do our own things. Lora studies and I do some chores like cooking or washing. When the evening comes, I write. Three years have passed, and I still can't find a publisher. I have written several novels and I am still writing even though none of them have been published. Maybe one day Lora will publish my novels.

You know, Ted, sometimes I feel that I am going to die young. That's why I look forward to each of Lora's birthdays, she gets a year older. I want to see her, at least, get to eighteen, so she is not a child any more. It would be horrible if I go while she is still a child. She doesn't have anyone, not even you ask about her.

Fourteenth birthday, that's something! Even Lora is excited, she says, "Can you believe I am fourteen already?".

When she comes home today, I will take her on a boat. We'll have dinner there. We will have plenty of time to talk. We talk just about everything (her tender soul likes our tales). She never asks about you, Ted.

On Sunday, she is going out with Lucy. Lucy is an introverted girl, maybe because she is a little bit chubby. Lora says that Lucy has a heart of gold. Lora has a gift to notice human weaknesses and virtues.

It could be to her advantage later in life.

I did not spend my fourteenth birthday with my mother.

On that day, I still remember, my mother woke me up with music. At that time, I was listening to Queen, and my mother gave me their new Long Play record.

Dado used to like Queen.

He was taking down their songs and tried to play them on his guitar. It was finally time when his grandmother could not send me away any more (I was not listening to the hollow sound of the front door). Dado did not need to ask her permission to let his friends into his room. His room was as big as a soccer field. In two corners of his room, there were two big speakers, and he was so proud of their size. He said, "Marshall, the best in the world".

I loved Dado's room. A mirror of him. In his room, there was partial order and partial disorder. In perfect order was everything that was important to him. His Long Play records were organised in a perfect straight line. Daily, he would take the dust off them, change their order alphabetically or by the musicians. He would take the dust off his speakers and his guitar several times a day.

Music books and sheets of music were on the spare shelf, and they were put in perfect order. Above the books there was a poster, his idol—Crazy Charlie, 'The Best Guitarist of all Time'.

On the other shelf, were 'all the other books' where disorder prevailed. Majority of the books in his collection he had received from me. Often, I would buy him a book for a certain occasion and more often without any particular reason. I would read a good book and think, 'I have to buy this one for Dado.'

On that shelf, he kept other things like: models of small automobiles, little flags, funny pictures from previous birthdays and one wooden pipe which nobody ever smoked even though that particular year, around his fourteenth birthday, he started to smoke. I was angry because of it. He wanted to be 'different from all the other kids', and I told him that because of it 'he was just the same as everyone else'. At that time, all of the kids started to light their first cigarettes, they tried to look older.

So, that shelf was a dusty shelf, nobody had ever tidied it up, nobody ever cleaned it. His grandmother was not allowed to enter his room anymore; therefore, all responsibilities regarding its cleanliness and order were solely on his shoulders. His school bag was thrown on the floor, next to his desk, and his school books were scattered everywhere, underneath the table, underneath his bed and just randomly on the floor. In this room, Dado kissed me for the first time. It was a serious kiss. We would say, 'the way they kiss on the silver screen'. That 'cinema screen kiss' was absolutely different to all the other kisses and touches. It completely and forever cemented my belonging to Dado.

Just after his fourteenth birthday, I was sitting in his room, holding a big fury dog with red boxing gloves on its front paws. The whole afternoon, he was trying to play Iggy Pop's song, and after many attempts, he threw himself on the bed next to me, saying:

"Horrible, I will never amount to anything."

"C'mon, you are awesome."

"That's what you think; if someone who knows anything about guitars heard me, they would pass out laughing."

"But, Dado, I love the way you play. For me, you are the best in the world".

When he turned toward me, I saw his eyes, which were not the eyes of a little boy. He kissed me for the first time, and we kept on kissing the whole afternoon in his room lost in time, lost in the sweetness of our kisses. My mother came knocking on the door with a worried look on her face. She did not like that we spent whole afternoons, or sometime days, alone in his room. I said to her:

"We study together, when we finish, he plays to me."

It stayed that way, nearly every afternoon. Sometimes Dado would come to our place for lunch but not as often as before, when we were little kids. My mother loved him.

I think Lora still doesn't have her own Dado. Sometimes, I ask her is there someone she fancies, she just waves her hand, she doesn't want to talk about boys yet. She is shy. I did not talk to my mother about Dado either, but our story was different. He was a part of my history and a part of my family history.

This year, I said to Lora, there will be no birthday present. The present could be dinner on a boat. We are saving money, for we want to self-publish one of my novels. It was Lora's idea.

For my fourteenth birthday, I got from my father a collection of Dostoyevsky's books. My mother said:

"It's too early for Dostoyevsky," but my father nodded his head and lifted his index finger up.

From Dado, I got a nice picture frame where he had placed one of his pictures with a cowboy hat on his head, and Dado got from me a wooden box with black and white chess figures.

If you think about Lora, Ted, what would you give her for her fourteenth birthday?

Barbara.

My fifteenth birthday, I remembered quite well; it was exactly the way Barbara wrote in her letter. I was more interested in what happened for her fifteenth birthday. Hers and Dado's. It said:

Hi Ted,

Another year just flew away. Lora ended up in hospital, nothing serious, they took her appendix out, she feels much better now. She was in hospital just for a few days. I saw so many ill kids and devastated parents, so it made me very grateful to God. I could not wait for her return to make her delicious Mediterranean soups (we say they heal the soul). My mother wanted to come, but I told her not to. At that moment, I didn't have much money, so I couldn't afford any luxury. In fact, her visit wouldn't have cost me a cent, they always paid for everything anyway, but it would have been insane letting her see in which circumstances we lived. Anyway, whenever they rang, they were repeating the same words:

"Barbara come back home, what still keeps you there?"

She knows exactly why I am not coming back (the corridors and the smell of dampness; the smell of damp memories, the corridors which no longer smell of my childhood, nor of my spite . . .) She knows that I know it, too. Maybe she hopes I will find a good excuse, but I doubt it, she knows me too well . . . at least she knows my spitefulness . . . (spitefulness has defined me as a person in the last few years; can that ever turn out well, I ask myself . . .)

Plus, a long time has passed; I don't even know what I would do there. I don't know where my friends are, the war destroyed friendships, there is high unemployment, the city is full of people who don't belong there. This is not the town I used to know, I don't belong there anymore.

For Dado's fifteenth birthday, I had written a short story. Just for him. I typed it on my father's typing machine; I rolled it and wrapped it in coloured paper, tied it with a red ribbon in the middle.

When he read the story, he asked:

"What is it?"

"A short story, do you like it?"

"It's great. Whose is it? Where did you get it?"

"Guess."

"I don't have a clue."

"It's Barbara's."

"Barbara, who?"

"You are funny. I wrote this story just for you."

He looked at me still smiling:

"I can't believe it, Barbara. You did not write this story yourself."

"Why do you think so?"

"It is so mature, so wise; it is taken from some novel, from some experienced writer. You could not write something like that."

"You are an idiot! Give it back!" I jumped on him all red in the face, trying to take the sheet of paper out of his hand.

"Give it back to me right now, you moron!" I was screaming at the top of my lungs while trying to jump up and get the sheet of paper he was holding high above his head. I was kicking his chest with tightened fists, I was kicking his legs with my feet, I was trying to scratch his face, then his extended arm in which he was holding the piece of paper on which I had written my short story. He held it high up while laughing

heartily, I was screaming and screaming, and all of a sudden, I burst into tears.

Then he stopped. He put the piece of paper on the table and hugged me.

"Don't cry, Barbara. I was joking. Fine, I believe you. You have written this story just for me. Sorry. I accept, I am an idiot, I am a moron, but my intention was not to make you cry."

I solemnly promised:

"Never again, understand, never again will I dedicate a word to you."

"But Barbara, I was joking with you; I didn't know that you would end up so offended and sad."

Once again, I solemnly stated:

"Don't you ever again play with my emotions and belittle my writing, never again, Dado."

My voice was so serious, Dado said:

"Look, Barbara, I love you."

In that moment, all was forgotten.

And Lora, too, got a short story for her fifteenth birthday. I simply called the story —'Lora'.

When she read it, her eyes were full of tears. It moved her deeply. What made her sad was that I could not find a publisher for my stories, so she said:

"Barbara, you are the best writer in the whole wide world."

I hugged her:

"Your opinion is very important to me. When we publish the new novel, I will take you to Europe. I'll take you to Paris, then to Cortina D'Ampezzo, it is the place where my father used to take me skiing, a long, long time ago. (It sounded like a lie but it was not a lie . . . it

seemed so far away, so distant, hence so surreal that it could only be seen as a lie.

I never published that novel. I didn't have six thousand dollars to publish it myself. At that time, I met a man from my country, and somebody told me that he might help me. (At that time, I still believed in a pure human heart, free from malice and envy.) As soon as I saw him, I thought:

"I should not have agreed to see this man. He is shady." (I could not describe this feeling of him being 'shady'. I just felt a very strange atmosphere around us, there was a hot temperature in the air, it came from inside of him, from his poorly hidden haughtiness and envy.)

He extended his hand. The feeling was as if I had taken a damp, dead fish into my hand. His hand was damp from the cold sweat and it was soft from his soft character. He quickly removed his fingers from my hand and said (with a wispy voice):

"Let's sit down."

When we sat, he had a little smile on his lips, I kept quiet. He asked:

"What are you writing about?"

"Well, it really varies, often my memories take me back to my hometown . . . actually, I am trying to find the meaning of our existence."

We agreed to be on a first name basis; we found out that we were the same age, and the same language was the only connection between us, so we agreed to talk in 'that language'.

Without apparent reason, he leaned closer to me and with a voice full of conspiracy (which sounded like the voice of an old woman) he whispered:

"I am gay, you know?"

"Beg your pardon. I did not understand."

"I said, I am gay."

"Ah . . . I see . . ."

"What I want to say, being gay is not my problem; I accepted myself for who I am. It is, I would say, your problem if you can't accept me for who I am . . . then it is entirely your problem. I want to say . . . I am clear about it . . . but if you are not, then it is really your problem . . ."

I cut him short:

"Bobby, it is not my problem, don't worry about it. My problems are of a different nature. I have financial troubles, I can't find a good publisher . . ."

"Yes, yes . . . but you know, sometimes people say 'this' or 'that' . . . but that's their problem, not mine. You know, I am OK. I live in this great city where I could be the real me, you remember in our country people were full of prejudices, double standards . . ." and it looked to me that Bobby was turning on and on the same old broken record. I stood up, I did not extend my hand (I could not stand once more the dampness and softness of his palm), and I simply said:

"I got to go and pick up Lora from school."

"Lora? Who's Lora?"

"My mother."

"I see, she works at school?"

"Let's say so. Bye-bye, Bobby."

I never heard from him again, I could not stand his elongated sentences, his trembling, nasal voice (it was trembling from insecurities). I never wanted to be exposed to his smell, for he smelled like an old woman, he smelled of lilies. Plus, he played endlessly with his unlit cigarette, I had the urge to smack his fingers . . . but, instead I left.

There were some other people who wanted to 'help' me. (Not because I was a single, pretty woman . . . no, to help me as a writer . . . but, in my encounters with these people, I discovered over and over again the truth of how small a human heart was, full of envy and pride . . . and a big human heart, the one my mother used to talk about—it looked like I was never destined to meet.)

But that story doesn't really matter anymore. Do you know what I got from Dado for my fifteenth birthday? He took me to David Bowie's concert in Trieste. We slept at his cousin Alfia's place; she was a student at the school of medicine. She hid us in her room, for we could not legally sleep at the university campus.

David Bowie's concert was the one I remembered for many years to come.

My father said:

"I think she doesn't need to go."

My mother said:

"All her friends are going. Three of them will sleep at Alfia's (she counted Igor, who was Dado's best friend and vocalist in his band).

My father would always say, "If other kids are going, she can go too."

He rang Dado and lectured him about proper manners. Dado was patiently listening to his tirade, but we behaved as all teenagers did. We went crazy, we got drunk. That was the first time I got drunk. I was so drunk I could not even remember what I drank that evening. The next day, Alfia was curing me with some teas and soups which she brought from the campus canteen. When I came home, I was exhausted and pale; I threw myself on my bed and my mother stared at me, and in her stare it was written, 'Everything's so clear'.

I did not feel like a little girl anymore. I had a boyfriend who came over regularly, I went to a concert in Trieste with him, I got drunk . . . I survived the next day . . .

For Dado and me, the wild times had just commenced.

Till next time, Barbara.

I could not help but laugh. My mother was a wild teenager, too. I could just imagine her, with her fierce temperament and her flamboyant character, just twenty years younger.

Later in her life, she became quite nervous, but always patient with me. She had so much creative energy, and when she wasn't writing, she would be dispirited or irritable. Sometimes, she was so absent minded that she wasn't aware of my presence. But whatever she touched, she turned into art. The way she decorated our apartment, the way she selected her sentences, the way she dressed herself . . . her artistic soul was visible in her daily life. She had a unique imagination. Our relationship was art itself, our conversations were theatre roles.

What am I supposed to do with her novels?

What happened for her sixteenth birthday? Mine I do remember, it was just two years ago.

She wrote:

Hi Ted,

Our girl is already sixteen. I can't believe it, it seems as if she started school yesterday. Do you remember those first days and her insecurity? She was always thorough and pedantic. Too much, as if she were not my daughter. I was surrounded with disorder, whilst around her, order prevailed. She is still like that, a real little pedantic lady. She inherited your sense of order. Order irritated me always.

In the city where I was born and grew up, its people were obsessed with law and order. Everything needed to have a proper name and to be in proper order. Everything was shaped by the family you were born into. I learned that when I was about sixteen. Before that, I did not notice such things.

Dado was a fan of the Sex Pistols and the Clash, he was the 'first punk in the city'. My parents' friends were shocked by 'what company Barbara kept, the daughter of the respected Mr. Milich'.

I loved Dado and his friends and I loved his guitar. Yep, I grew to love it.

For his sixteenth birthday, he got an electric guitar form his father. He was so excited, he rang me, stuttering:

"Barbara, come over, you've got to see it . . . you've got to see it, fuck . . . you won't believe it . . ."

I ran down the stairs. When I flung myself, breathless, into his room, I froze seeing the scene: the little table (which usually stayed in the middle) was pushed in the corner of the room, and in the middle of the room a big blanket was outstretched, on the blanket (like on some altar) was a black electric guitar of an unusual shape.

I put my hand in front of my open mouth and said:

"Wow . . . what the fuck is that?"

He stood next to me, he hugged me; full of sweet ecstasy he lit his cigarette and in an altered voice, he asked:

"What do you say?"

"Speechless! Is it from Carlitto?"

"Yeah Carlitto, who else?"

His father's name was Carlo; we called him Carlitto.

For my sixteenth birthday, Dado with his band, organised a concert for me in his garage, just two streets down from mine. What a show, what a commotion! We shook the whole neighbourhood, the police came. There was too much noise, too much alcohol, the neighbours were yelling at us, after a while someone called the police. They came so serious and theatrical, full of authority with threats on their lips and their eyebrows (we were too excited and too drunk, so they appeared even more comical in their uniforms, which asked for obedience.)

They asked for our IDs and as we were minors we didn't have IDs. Igor earned a slap on the face, Dado was yelling at them, "Why aren't we allowed to play? Is this a country of free people?" I held back his arm, for I knew he could get a slap as well and blood could run down his nose. Then the policemen turned to me asking what was happening, and I told them it was a birthday party. They were abusive and called us 'a wild mob', 'junkies', 'street kids'. Only then did Dado react, swearing at the police officer who was shouting 'slut' in my face.

They took us all to the police station. They took our details. When they learned who my father was, an awkward situation took place.

They called him at home. Told him his daughter was in the holding cell. They let us go home afterwards, all of us.

When I walked in, Markie (his pet name) was silent. We were all silent: Markie, mother and me. Then he gave a signal to my mother, nodding his head, which meant she should leave the room. After some unpleasant silence, he said:

"So, Barbara, how can you explain it? The police called me; you were taken to the station. Who are your friends, my daughter?"

I did not say a word.

"Barbara, you are out of control, is this the way a sixteen-year-old girl behaves?"

"They insulted us, they smacked Igor's face, they called me 'a slut', so Dado reacted . . ."

"Listen Barbara, this boy, Dado . . . it is all far too much. He grew up without any control. His father has been living in Germany for years, doing God knows what, the old woman has no authority over him. While you were kids, I understood that friendship, but now, what do the two of you have in common? Please, end your friendship with him. And who are those boys? Are you the only girl among them?"

I was speechless, and Markie continued:

"From now on take care of your company and your behavior, do we understand each other? I don't want to hear one more word about that boy, whatever his name is. If he rings the bell, I will talk to him. Am I clear enough?"

Yes, he was clear enough. But he could not know what I was thinking. I was thinking, "You are not going to boss me around. You can't stop me seeing Dado."

I could not stand his voice full of authority, it only provoked disobedience in me.

The whole district was talking about us: about the noise, the drunkenness and the way everything ended when police arrived (with their uniforms, their eyebrows and heavy words on their lips . . .)

What did we do wrong? We played loudly? The boys drank a bit too much? I wanted to scream loudly that everybody could hear me—"Is there anywhere in the world where sixteen-year-olds are not too loud and do not drink too much for their sixteenth birthday party? Where is that place where sixteen-year-olds are taken to the police station because they are too loud . . .?" Markie could not answer these questions . . . these were the kind of questions he never wanted to discuss, let alone answer. His kind of answer was punishment, always.

The next day, he took me to school. He wanted to talk with my teacher. I never knew what they were talking about. The defiance grew in me.

During recess, I talked to Dado:

"It's a mad house at home. My father went ballistic. He forbade me to see you, he thinks it was all your fault."

He lit his cigarette and asked:

"So, what now?"

"Look, let's cool down. You can stop playing in Igor's garage for a while . . ."

"Are you sane? You want us to stop playing in the garage . . . no way."

I stood up, but he took my hand. He said:

"OK, for a while. But what then?"

"We better stop seeing each other for a few weeks until everything settles down. Markie went to see my teacher today. I will write you letters." I propped myself on the tip of my toes and planted a kiss on his lips. He was already so tall that I could hardly reach his neck with my hands.

"Everyone is against us. They don't like our music. What does he want—a better boyfriend for his princess?"

"Please Dado, don't make it even harder. Just let's be quiet for few weeks and it will be forgotten."

"I love you, Barbara, nobody is going to stand between us."

"Don't be silly, just be a good boy for a short while."

He smacked my bottom and left.

That afternoon my mother entered my room. She wanted 'a chat'. She said I was wrong being angry at Father. She said this was not the way how a girl from a respectable house behaved. She talked about Father's reputation and my expected behaviour because of that. She never mentioned Dado, so I asked:

"So, Dado, he is not good enough for you two?"

"Barbara, Dado is a child who grew up without anybody's care."

"Oh really? He has been coming here his whole life, since he was a little boy. Never before have you said a word against him, but now when you know that we love each other and that this kind of love is different than the one when we were five, now he is an animal without proper manners."

"Barbara . . ." my mother would always start her sentence with my name in a very calm voice ". . . for Christ's sake who said that he was a wild animal. But can't you see the way they dress these days, the way they comb their hair, and that loud music . . . everybody's talking about them."

"And WHO is everybody that is talking about them? I do not care about 'everybody', about 'them'. I couldn't care less about that surreal 'Somebody' for whose sake we always have to be dressed properly, combed properly, polite and quiet . . . the way that 'Somebody' is expecting from us. I want to be me, regardless of whether "Mr. Somebody' likes me or not."

"You are still a child, full of spite, but you'll see, Barbara, all we have been doing is done for your best."

"What? What? What is it that you were doing for my best?"

"Calm down, think a little, and then we will talk later."

She stood up and was about to leave my room, but then she turned towards me and innocently said:

"Ah yes, nearly forgot, your father said that no more visits to 'Tennis' after school. After school, straight home."

"Fine," I thought, ". . . you want a war, you'll have a war. OK, no more 'Tennis' after school, no more going out with Dado and friends, but you will not stop me loving the one my heart had chosen. A long time ago."

I started writing him letters. I wrote to him every day. Through Igor, Dado sent his messages and short notes. They stopped playing in Igor's garage. He said he was able to do just about anything for me, even to smash his guitar if I only wanted. I knew how much Dado loved me, and there was no Markie or police squad who could stop our love.

Dado had replied that my letters were so good that he could cut his veins because of them. The letters were full of a child's pain and very brave ideas. I loved Dado so much, and it seemed to me that every day spent without him was completely meaningless and entirely empty.

In one of his notes I received through Igor, was written, "I live thanks to your letters. I will love you till death do us part. He would always say that he would 'love me till death do us part', and I believed him.

That particular year, the whole year, Dado and his band did not play in Igor's garage. All that just because of me. The boys were telling him that he was a softy, that he was a punk with no balls, but his philosophical stand was—no Barbara, no playing.

Nothing can last forever, so everything came back to normal. Markie was once again the same old Markie, and Mum asked here and there:

"Is everything well now?"

She knew that we were writing letters to each other and smooching during recess on the schoolyard bench. She knew, she asked me:

"You did not eat your sandwich again?"

"Oh, I forgot," I replied muddleheaded, and she just smiled.

Once, when we were sitting on the bench, he said:

"Your letters are mad. Do you remember the story you wrote for my birthday? You were mad at me for saying you could not come up with something that good, that you copied it from some book. Barbara, you are

great, you got to continue writing. Write lyrics and I'll come up with the melody, we can make something great."

We lived often, we lived a lot, in the clouds. The future always belonged to us together; we never thought that he could have his own future and me mine. It was unthinkable. There was no Markie on this earth who could separate our futures.

For her sixteenth birthday, Lora asked me to buy her a little dress. I nearly laughed when I saw the dress, it was almost ridiculous. I thought it was ugly, just a cheap rag. She said:

"Mummy it's in; all the girls wear a similar one."

Then I remembered how I used to dress myself at sixteen. Whoever would meet me on the street would turn their heads after me with an open mouth. Older women would stop and stare at me until I turned a corner, where their gaze could not reach me anymore. When it came to dressing, Markie never said a word. He would ask: "Is that what other girls are wearing?" and when I said it was, he would reply, "Then wear it yourself."

Afterwards, when Lora put the dress on, she asked me, turning herself around in front of the mirror:

"How does it look?"

I said:

"It looks sensational. What a beautiful dress!" and she laughed, she laughed.

But, Ted, in that dress, she looks like a grown-up girl, not a trace of this little Lora you used to know. Barbara.

Two tears dropped on the sheet of paper, I cried again. I never knew Barbara like that. I knew she was different, not like other mothers at all. We were friends. She never asked suspiciously; she never preached. Whatever I would say or suggest, she accepted and agreed. She would ask:

"Would that make you happy?" and if I said "Yes," she chirped:

"So, let's do it."

What made me saddest was her writing. How many times she had tried; on how many doors she had knocked! She received fantastic reviews, but . . . no publisher. Language was the problem. I really did not know what was happening in her country, she used to say that those were the times of blackguards, sycophants, mediocrity, and nobody in her country wanted to publish her books, for she was not considered suitable with her ideas and opinions. She would say that nothing has changed, that they can change the government, but the problem was that the consciousness stayed always the same.

For the translation, we didn't have the money. That was the reason why I never liked it when she bought me anything new, when she gave me pocket money, or when she took me out for dinner. I always wanted her to save that money. But Barbara did not know what the word saving meant. As she was a nervous person, she handled money nervously. She never respected material things. She would say it wouldn't make her any happier if she had a bigger apartment or new furniture. She told me that happiness didn't come from the outside world—buying a house, clothes or furniture. She told me that happiness came from a full heart, and her heart was not full, I knew it. That's why none of the furniture could make her happy.

Barbara was not happy, that's why I was crying again.

Often, she would hug me and whisper in my ear:

"You are my happiness."

I knew that I was her only happiness, and that fact put a lot of weight on my shoulders.

She used to spend day after day in front of the computer screen and write. For days, she would go without any food. She would make me lunch and when I asked her had she had hers, she would only nod her head.

Barbara was always skinny. She had a little girl's face. Often, I was asked if she was my sister or my friend. She never looked like a mother. Nobody's mother, particularly not mine, for I had strong bone structure, just like my father. When I was sixteen, I was much taller and heavier than her. Her face was wrinkle-free and her eyes were like a child's eyes. Sometimes, I would see shadows in her eyes, and then I would ask myself whether this is my Barbara or someone who belonged elsewhere.

At sixteen, I was not as carefree as my girlfriends were. I had unexplainable concerns about Barbara. Every day she looked more far away, as if she was about to go somewhere, but I did not know where. (And I did not know where; I did not know that she was going on a voyage from which she would never come back, for I never knew that mothers could die. Not my mother, that happens only to others . . . in other stories . . . not in the story of Lora and Barbara . . .)

Her last letter was written last year, a birthday I clearly remember. Before she wrote it, she just came back from hospital. She told me she had pneumonia, now I know it was not true. Barbara was really parting away from me (from me who thought that her mother could not die, that it happened only to others . . . in some other stories . . .)

The letter said:

Hi Ted,

One more year and Lora is going to come of age, I am looking forward to it very much. I can hardly wait for that to happen.

She is seventeen now; if you could only see what a beautiful girl she turned out to be; I am so proud of her. Even though I think sometimes that I do not know her well enough, my own child. It seems like she does not belong to me and my family. She has a very strange nature. Maybe yours, I can't distinguish it anymore. She is so stable and mature; sometimes I fear that she is far more stable than I am. Her decisions are not like mine—instant and mood-driven. Before she decides, sometimes it takes her days to think about the right decision. These characteristics are a good foundation for her future, I suppose.

Did your decisions, Ted, brew for days as well? Before you left us, Ted, how long did this idea brew inside of you? Or was it a quick, moody decision? Well, I know it wasn't, because we regret moody decisions and you never regretted yours. If you ever did, you would have at least called Lora.

You never rang Lora—Ted!

You never rang!

It seems like I am reproaching you, but, I really—am not. I'd like those letters to be a mystery, an enigma for you just as your leaving was wrapped with eternal ambiguity.

It looks like I am going on a voyage. One from which we never come back, the one on which we go alone.

I am heartbroken when I think of Lora without me. She is so bound to me. I bound her to myself daily and consciously. I could not have imagined that she would leave me even for a day, but look what a fatal mistake I have done—now, I am the one leaving her.

What will I leave her, Ted? Unpublished novels?

She is seventeen now, the last year of school. I wanted to educate her further.

At the end of our lives we turn to God. I had never turned to God, for nobody taught me how. In my country, we believed in something else, but it was all a Grand Lie. Because of it, I don't know whether God himself is just a Grand Lie. When you go, it means simply that you are not here anymore, you are nowhere, you do not exist.

Lora is reading books about guardian angels as if she foresees something.

I read very similar books at her age. Of course, I got it from Dado, he bought it in some second-hand bookshop. There, on the cover of the book, stood the face of a beautiful young girl, and he said:

"When you were seven, you looked like her. A real little angel."

And when he was seventeen, he had a real, heavy, macho band. They played 'things with balls' at various cafés where alternative music was played. Dado was the frontman; he wrote the music, I did the lyrics.

At that time, I took the craft of writing very seriously, and all my spare time I dedicated to it. My father bought me a typing machine. At that time, I believed that my destiny was charted—destined to be a writer. Dado could not wait for me to finish my short stories; he would read them several times, nodding his head:

"You are a genius."

That year, I found in a youth magazine a competition for the best young writer in the country.

That whole summer, I spent alone, locked in my room: no swimming at the beach, no concerts; only later in the evenings, I would go to Dado's just to see him, give him a kiss and promise that I would make it up for lost time—but I needed to finish my novel. When I finished it, I was so excited. Well, the short stories were not the same as my own real novel. I named it 'I Knew Jane Eyre'.

The days were full of anticipation, and they dragged as if they were years while I was waiting to hear the destiny of my novel. To shorten this painfully long time, which made me sick in the stomach, I sat down and wrote the sequel 'Looking for Jane Eyre'.

Dado was really convinced that I would win the contest and earn the title of the best young writer in the country. We were told that the best novel would be published. He would yell:

"Yes, yes, yes, my Charlotte Brontë is going to publish her novel."

After my patience was nearly all used up, the long-anticipated letter arrived. The letter from the editor. I did not dare open it; with trembling fingers, I dialled Dado's number and said in a low voice:

"I got a letter."

"What letter?"

"From them. I'll come right now, I can't open it alone."

He was standing at the open door, I ran to him, I heard David Bowie's sorrowful voice from inside of his room, and hearing his elongate cry 'Sorrow', I felt shivers along my spine and anticipating something horrid, I said in a nervous voice:

"Take it off, take it off, at once!" He took the record off the record-player, and silence sat in between us.

We sat on his bed, and he opened the envelope.

On the sheet of paper, among some sentences, there were three names written in order. The first name was, by all means, the name of the person who won first place. The second name, my name, was the name of the person who received second place, and the third name, I hadn't read.

Dado cheered:

"Yep, yep, we are second!!!"

And me? I was sitting there as if lightening hit me and was staring at the piece of paper. Dado continued to read, ". . . and expressed in sport jargon, we could say that you had lost the race at the last second . . ." I could not wait for him to finish reading; I remembered some bits before I took the letter from his hands and ripped it into small pieces. I remember they said something about my novel 'being mature, but the plot was too complicated;' I remember they suggested to 'find a young, but more experienced, writer who would help me simplify the plot . . .' It just infuriated me, so I tore it into little squares which were now lying on the floor.

Dado looked at me thunderstruck, he kneeled and started collecting the little pieces scattered on the floor, telling me:

"You are mad. You are beyond normalcy. You are mad, mad, mad!"

I was crying.

He tried to convince me that it was a grand achievement.

"You were awarded the second prize in the entire country, who knows how many people participated . . ."

I said:

"Do you know, man, what that means? Second best? It means, my manuscript didn't win first prize, and if it didn't get first prize, it won, just as all the others did— second. They must have sent exactly the same letter to the rest of us. I don't want or need second place."

I went home bitterly disappointed. My self-esteem as a writer was smashed. I took both novels, 'I knew Jane Eyre' and 'Looking for Jane Eyre', went down to the meadow next to the basketball court, lit a fire and threw them in. While the fire was swallowing my novels, I said into the smoke:

"Adieu, Farwell Grand Authoress."

So, that was the end of my writing career, which did not even commence.

For many days to come, I didn't want to talk to anyone, not even Dado. I told him I don't want to write lyrics for his songs anymore:

"Find somebody who knows how to write."

"Why are you so theatrical and miserable Barbara? You know how good you are, you know you were awarded an award as the second best young writer in the whole country."

"I don't want to be the second. Can't you understand, I do not want to be second best!"

Only Dado could understand me. He never liked being second best. He was first in everything. That was the reason why he was not liked. They did not like him at school; the average, so-called nice guys did not like him because all the average and so-called nice girls did like him.

In my time, in my country, individuality and originality came with a very high price.

Exterminate him, he is different to us!

He is a threat; he doesn't think like we do; he doesn't dress the way we dress, and he doesn't laugh at the jokes we laugh at. Or, on the other hand, he does laugh just at everything, his laughter is somehow mean, provocative, is he mocking us?

And I was a girl. A girl quite different to all other girls. I was myself, I loved Dado. I loved to laugh at everything he laughed at—stupidity and mediocrity.

During that time, the police would often visit Dado, but he never could figure out why exactly. His father lived in Germany, so officers would ask him what he did when he went to visit his father, where did they go together when in Germany. They checked his new stereo systems, his expensive guitars, they asked about receipts as a proof of purchase. Even though Dado had receipts, and he could prove where the expensive things came from, they never left him in peace. They called him by abusive names, laughed at his looks, asked him where he bought weed and who supplied him with it.

Dado as Dado, he would only say:

"Bloody tyrants, I do not care what they say, I am not afraid of their threats a bit."

And then Aurelio had appeared to take on a more prominent role in my life. At that time, I did not know that he played the role my parents asked him to play.

Aurelio was eight years older than me. So, back then, I was seventeen and he was twenty-five. He had a car and he knew all the 'important' people in town. All the 'important' people knew him, so to speak, he was an 'important' guy. But his 'importance' did not really have any foundations. I could never grasp why he was so 'important'; he was of average intelligence, his occupations were plain, average, but wherever he appeared, people would treat him like an emperor (a Very Important Person). He drove a brand-new Mercedes, his father bought it for him. He was studying to be a marine engineer. The first year of his studies he passed all his exams, but he stayed in his second year for almost five years.

His mother worked at Hotel Continental, which was a gathering point for 'posh' youngsters. My hometown at that time was divided into three separate groups of young people. There was a group of outsiders—young people without an image, nobody knew them, nobody noticed them as if they really did not exist. They didn't have an image, any stance, any great idea, they were like ghosts.

The other group of young people were the post-hippies—the cool guys, punks, rebels, the youngsters who studied at the university of philosophy, psychology or fine arts. An alternative scene. They still listened to the Beatles, Bob Dylan, Leonard Cohen, Tom Waits or the Sex Pistols, Iggy Pop and The Clash. It was said that they smoked marijuana, that they swung their hips to the rhythm of tranquilizers, and that they read decadent books. They always alternated between mild depression and rebellion as a result of frustration with the way they lived and the world in which they lived.

By force, everyone wanted to squeeze Dado into that group. Everybody would say that 'Dado was the first punk-rocker in town'; they said that he was always 'as high as a kite', but it wasn't true. (Everything is just an image, just a little snapshot). But he could not care less; he never cared about the gossip small minded people spread. He lived in his own world, so the rest did not exist. He had his guitar, his books, and me—his girlfriend, Barbara. What was happening outside of that world, he did not have a clue.

The third group of youngsters were—the 'posh people'. This group was made of children who belonged to 'finer families'. Children of distinguished and successful families and all those who wanted to look like them, copy-cats and plagiarists, they were higher in number.

There was a group of people who used to stand in the piazza, underneath the arcade of the town tower. They were those who wanted to look like the 'posh kids', the imitators. They were young people who never worked, not a day; they had quite a lot of money. They were petty thieves pretending they were not. They talked about themselves with an air of importance trying to make others believe that they were 'Very Important

People'. They acted like real charmers, but they had no foundation for their pretences. They would stand there, under the arcade of the old tower with their hands in their pockets and malicious comments on their lips. They used to lie endlessly, never tired of their own lies. They would claim to dine with respected judges, distinguished lawyers, with renowned doctors and their children. Their stories were all made up, purely showing off, and only they pretended to believe one another.

Aurelio belonged to that group.

There was one funny, significant episode which happened at that time.

Once he took me to his favorite discothèque (for him: a very important place, full of very important people), (for me) a boring place full of pretentious characters unable to enjoy the music or dance. They were all just looking around, evaluating others. While I was standing there, (Aurelio went to buy us a drink) a young man approached me. He came all puffed up, like a little peacock, wearing a superbly cut silken suit, and his hands were in his pockets (maybe I saw him once or twice standing underneath the arcade of the old tower), and he started telling a story I didn't care about in the slightest (he talked about himself . . . how important he was for this city, how influential he was, how reputable he was; he said that he never paid entry-fees anywhere—all doors were open to him; how he bought the best, the most expensive jewellery for girls . . . how he, how he . . .) I did not want to talk to this little puffed up peacock; what could I have possibly talked about with a man like him—I knew he never read a book. On his way back, Aurelio met a 'Very Important Man' and stopped to greet him. Then the little peacock put his index finger underneath my chin, lifted it up and asked:

"What is your name; I have never seen you here before?"

"Hey, can you leave me alone?" I replied nervously (for he was lifting my chin with his index finger!)

"Do you know who you are talking to? Answer my questions. Have you got any clue who I am?"

"I know who you are," said I irritated, "You are a plain idiot."

Then he grabbed my wrist tightly, his eyes nearly fell out of their sockets, his shirt unbuttoned from his already puffed up chest (oh, how painful it would have been for his ego) and said:

"I will smash your bloody mouth. I will smash your bloody face, you, bloody peasant. You, you, simple cow, I know you should be one of those . . ."

"Hey, you fuckin' idiot, leave me alone, I am not afraid of you."

At that moment, Aurelio came running toward us:

"What, what is happening? Gigi, she's my cousin! What's wrong with you?"

"Cousin!" he let go of my hand and started straightening his silken jacket while breathing heavily (his ego was still screaming inside his chest, so his movements were still jerky, and his voice sounded like he was going to sing in a high-pitched tone):

"So, Aurelio, tell your cousin then, that if she doesn't hold her tongue I might pull it out."

"Listen, you bloody idiot, I will find out who you are."

Never before had I threatened anybody with my father, but I was so irritated that I said:

"My father knows idiots like you . . . be assured, he knows you . . . be assured you will pay for this."

Aurelio stood in between us, he pushed me away with one hand and him with the other one. The little peacock tried to reach my face, my hair. Then the security guard came to him, whispered something into his ear, I heard my father's name mentioned. After that he looked at me for the last time, straightened his silken jacket and walked off taking his wounded ego with him.

Aurelio said:

"You are absolutely wild. Do you know who he is?"

"I don't know, but I think he is a complete idiot. Yeah, tell me who he is, I will ask Dad if he knows him."

"Hey Barbara, calm down. What the hell does your father have to do with it? He is a fine guy, just a bit short-tempered, but otherwise, a fine guy."

"Look Aurelio, I won't come with you, ever again, to places like this. Look at the people here, they are all pretending to be something they are not. I know some of these girls, they go to my school. They are not what they want to portray . . . take me home."

Aurelio always attempted to introduce me to the 'right crowd', telling me that the times of childhood had passed and I needed to know 'better people'. His sentences often had a double meaning (as if I could not grasp what he was trying to tell me):

"It is not right that Barbara of Marko Milich goes around with some losers. When I see you sometimes with some of your characters, I am just speechless. I can't really understand what you have in common with some of those people you hang with."

"Hey Aurelio, stop bullshitting please. You know what Dado and I have in common? We have in common our entire life; we have our books in common; all the films we watched together; all the concerts we went to together; we have in common the love we share, and we both have a free spirit that we share. Never again make me meet any of your empty-headed friends, they have only one concern—how they look in their expensive suits. They talk only about what they bought or how much their jewellery costs. I know, whatever they have has mostly been stolen.

They are like leeches, never worked for a day in their lives, some of them who belong to 'better families' live off their parents' money and reputation and they think that life owes them a living. I do not have time for such kind of crap."

All these characters with masks on their faces. Nobody could replace Dado. The time spent apart from him was time lost. He knew all the right words; our imagination would take us back to our childhood and further—on some planet achievable only to children and lovers. When he held my hand, I did not need anything else. We shared all our moments together; there were no secrets between us. He laughed heartedly when I would retell him about my outings with Aurelio. We both knew what Aurelio's aim was, and it really entertained us.

That same year, Aurelio went away and he wasn't seen for quite a long period of time. I received a postcard from Sydney.

His father was a merchant navy captain. He worked with an Australian company. I missed him when he went away. As I didn't have a brother, he was a surrogate brother to me, more than a cousin. He sent me a letter from which I learnt that he liked Sydney, that he worked and earned a lot of money. I could not figure out what he could possibly do in Sydney, for he was still a student stuck in the second year of his studies, and he never had a day of serious work.

I looked forward to his letters, his postcards and little parcels in which I would find nice silk scarves, little hats, oddly shaped pencils, sometimes notebooks with a hard cover and funny picture of Garfield on them, Larson's funny books and his cards, sometimes T-shirts with funny sayings and similar knick-knacks.

When Aurelio left our hometown, Dado was glad. He never told me that, but I knew he could breathe easier.

By that time, all the people in our town knew that I was Aurelio's cousin and Marko Milich's daughter.

I was protected like a rare, exotic animal.

Because of this 'untouchable' aura around me, I felt trapped. It looked to me like there was not enough air to breathe in this small town of mine, full of, to me, incomprehensible rules.

But what always angered me the most, was the notion of the famous 'Imaginary Someone'. The entire town was under the oppression of this 'Imaginary Someone'. Because of 'Someone', girls my age needed to behave in a particular way, they needed to dress in particular clothes. Because of 'Someone', they had to apply makeup every morning. Because of 'Someone', one always had to be in good spirits, civil and kind, because of 'Someone', one was never allowed to be in a bad mood, have a bad day or be late or to show your real emotions.

"What would 'Someone' say?"

You could not define this 'Imaginary Someone' or point your finger at them. In other words, this 'Imaginary Someone' was society as a whole: neighbours, relatives, school teachers, parents' friends, friends of relatives and friends of their friends. This 'Imaginary Someone' was ever-present. 'Someone' was always on the look-out.

'Someone' would always snitch on you to your parents, neighbours, relatives. There would always be 'Someone' ready to report you to the police, to the council, to the tax office.

"What would 'Someone' say?" – the whole town was under such a threat. Because of this famous 'Someone', everybody played roles assigned to them by others; therefore, nobody knew who they really were, indeed. Everyone was 'Someone' to somebody, and it could be heard everywhere:

"Watch out, 'Someone' might hear you, might see you."

'Someone' was spreading paranoia throughout the town; nobody knew where 'Someone' might be at any given moment, they could appear behind any corner, so be careful of your deeds, of your words; be watchful of what kind of mask you are wearing, for 'Someone' never sleeps.

I hated Mr. Someone from the depths of my soul.

I would say even to my own mother:

"You are always paranoid because of 'Someone'. Let me live, let me be myself, I don't care about your 'Imaginable Someone'."

She would twist her head, saying:

"Where did you learn all of that Barbara? You did not learn that attitude in our house."

"Who do you think taught me to think like that? Dado? It wasn't him. I couldn't care less for others, especially for your famous 'Someone'."

Those were the times of conformists.

We were all 'one', all dedicated to the 'same' idea, and we were all 'Someone', but an individual wasn't 'Someone', an individual was—no one. If an individual wanted to be separated from the oneness there was, in an instant, a collective 'Someone' was ready for a lynching.

And I, even though I loved Dado, did not know who I was. I always wanted to know who I was, so that I could fully be myself, that I could freely live as myself. Sometimes in my sleep, an unusual dream would come to me—a man would come to visit, with features similar to Dado's but much older, with longer hair, with sadder eyes (I thought it might be Dado in his late thirties), and he would whisper in my ear: "Write Barbara, write. You will find yourself only through writing. Write Barbara, write . . .")

Aurelio's postcards smelt of a strange fragrance (the fragrance of sadness . . .? At that time, I wasn't familiar with such a fragrance . . .).

Larson's jokes were addressed to 'Someone, Everyone and No-one' and for me, that was the pinnacle of freedom. You could laugh at 'Someone, Everyone and No-one', and we were not allowed to laugh, especially not at 'Someone'. We laughed, yes, we did, but, sorry, not intentionally; not maliciously, sorry, not to you, not to you sir; not to your stupidity; no sir, you never say stupid things, we are the ones who are stupid, we little people, us, 'No-one' we are prone to stupidity; sorry, we only laugh at our own stupidity . . .

Like spineless reptiles.

For days, I could talk with Dado about topics which were not of interest to the famous 'Someone'. Only with Dado. Dado could not care less about 'Someone' or about 'No-one'.

(His stories were completely different to any other stories. The places where we would go were inhabited by love and goodness. When love and goodness abide in a heart, there is nothing 'Someone' might say that could darken a heart like that, for there is pure light in there. The light of love and goodness.)

When I would tell him about my concerns, he would say:

"Why do you care Barbara? Do what pleases you. Why do you light as easy as a fire? This town of ours will live by these rules for another hundred years, and after that another hundred years, it is a matter of mentality. Do you know, Barbara, what real democracy is?"

"I don't know."

"Don't flare up, my little robin. Do you know the reason why my father never came back from Germany? When the right time comes, we'll go there too."

"I don't want to go to Germany."

"You like it better here, around your daddy."

Dado had much more insight into everything than I did, but rarely did he express his thoughts. (Later I understood: the more you know, the less words you need). He played his guitar and listened to his kind of music, those were his words, he didn't need other ones.

Barbara liked to fight with windmills.

You never knew this Barbara. Take care, Ted. Barbara.

Nor had I known this Barbara. She was a nervous kind; it looked as if she was always ready to fight with windmills, but every day she looked to me more and more tired, as if she was giving up on her fight. (Like someone who hurried towards death. Only, I wasn't fully aware of that though, for it was buried deep down, suppressed in my subconscious).

The next letter addressed to Ted, was the last one. It said:

Hi Ted,

A few months ago, we celebrated Lora's eighteenth birthday. I couldn't write to you as usually on that day, I left this letter for the end.

This is the last letter I am writing to you.

Because of sadness and unfulfilled dreams, in my stomach black flowers grew. They started slowly to wither away; a long time ago I noticed them starting to wither away and eat away my insides.

Lora has reached her eighteenth birthday. For her eighteenth, I gave her all that belonged to me. I signed all my belongings into her name.

I never told her that sadness and unfulfilled dreams had eaten me; I never told her that I was dying. I could not tell her. How could I have told her that?

Night after night I cried; I cried my eyes out. How to tell her such a truth? All my strength ran out of me. There was nothing left, not even that little which would allow me to tell her, "Goodbye Lora, I am leaving, my dearest."

I could not tell her . . .

And I, I could not read Barbara's letter any further. I threw myself on the sofa, buried my face in my palms, and I cried, cried and cried for hours, calling my late mother's name. It was twilight when I sobbed my last sobs. The first dark tones sneaked into the room like a deep sadness did into my heart. I brewed the tea, Barbara's tea, I gazed into the wall. After a while some strange peace fell upon me, like Barbara was there and brought it with her, and it gave me the strength to continue with reading, reliving her and my pain, which was intertwined and tied up in a knot like our destiny that was intertwined, never to be separated.

I could not tell her Ted, I hated myself, for I couldn't tell her the truth; I call myself a coward, but . . .

Do you know what had happened one year after Aurelio's departure?

I celebrated my eighteenth birthday. I had already enrolled into Law School; my father wanted me to study law. That was not my wish. They told me that nobody made a living by studying literature and writing books. Yeah, I know now, they were right, once again. I did not live of it, I died of it. With this kind of mother, Lora barely survived.

Oh, Lord, what have I left to this child, piles of worthless papers . . .

(I shall never see Christ's face. Never.)

I said to my father that I did not like law; he said I would like it when I understood it better. I did let him down, didn't I?

For my eighteenth birthday, Dado gave me a golden chain with a pendant. On its back, engraved were the words 'to Barbara with love—Dado'.

When I saw it, my eyes were as open as parasols:

"Wow, why did you buy it? How much did it cost you?"

He smiled:

"I bought it because it was beautiful, because it suits you, and because I love you."

Then he added:

"Promise me something, Barbara, for your eighteenth birthday."

"I will never leave you Dado."

He smiled:

"I know . . . I want you to promise me something else."

"You want me to promise something that I don't know."

He nodded his head, and I said without blinking (I could promise him just anything):

"I am promising whatever . . ."

"You promise me that after your eighteenth birthday you are going to write again. I like the way you write, I like you when you write . . ."

I kissed him:

"I promise, tomorrow I will start writing again. I will be relieved as well, for all these words are constantly playing in my head . . . it looks as if I have been living others' lives, the stories want to get out."

"I know. You are more and more absentminded. I like it when you are present, here with me. I love you so much, I have never loved anyone as much as I love you, and I know, I will never love anybody the way I love you. Even when we have our children, I will love you the most, more than our children".

That year, Dado and his band played some very serious stuff. They earned the reputation of 'a very promising band'.

Then Dado's birthday came.

It was Monday, it was cold, the windows clouded by mist. The presentiment was that snow will fall soon. (Or there was a presentiment of unknown misfortune coming, presentiment of some future looked through misty windows.)

That morning, Dado did not ring. (He would ring after waking up).

If it wasn't his birthday, it would be strange that he did not ring. Eleven had passed, he always rang around ten. I thought, because it was his birthday, he expected me to ring first. I didn't want to ring. I wanted to surprise him. I took the present. I bought him a black skivvy, and Davidoff, eau de cologne. I wrapped it in red paper, a card was glued on it. It was in a shape of a heart where I had written, 'I love you. B.' I rang the bell. Once. A second time. A third time. (By then some presentiment touched my heart . . .) I heard very slow steps (slow, slow steps), his grandmother was dragging her legs and armor of her age on her back. She opened the door and let me in without a word. The door of his bedroom was closed. I knocked on the door, (still) with a smile on my lips. I wanted to be the first one to kiss him for his day. The eighteenth birthday was the most important day in our lives. Coming of age, we thought we would gain sweet freedom. I didn't know what kind of freedom we dreamt of, but we often said, 'when I finally turn eighteen, I can . . .' I had my eighteenth four months before him. There was nothing to be heard coming out of his bedroom, so I thought he was still asleep. I opened the door and walked in.

He was sitting in the corner of the room with his forehead leaning against his knees. He did not lift his head. I screamed from the entrance door:

"Happy birthday, Davor!" I called him Davor only when I wanted to tell him something very important.

He did not raise his head. What kind of game was he playing with me? I came closer and I messed his hair.

He raised his head and in a quiet voice he said:

"Sit next to me, Barbara."

Because of the way he said it, I felt something uncertain, a thought came:

'I shall never see Christ's face. Ever.' (What a funny thought, it came from nowhere.)

His voice was strange; it did not belong to Dado. His eyes were strange, neither them belonged to Dado any longer. Some unexplainable fear grabbed me; I was waiting for the next sentence like a defendant waiting for their impeachment. He looked at me with red, teary eyes:

"You better hear this from me, for you are going to hear it from the others anyway."

He tried to hide a tremble in his voice, a tear in his eye. I was already crying. I did not know why I was crying, but I knew that what he was going to tell me would bring tears and chaos to my soul. (It was not bringing Christ's peace!) He said:

"Do not cry, I can't stand your tears."

How banal!

He was crying, I could not stand his tears, either. Then he said again:

"I don't deserve you, go away."

"I love you, Dado."

"Don't love me any longer, I am a coward."

"But, what happened?" I asked him, hoping that these tears were in vain, that my fear had no basis, my presentiment was wrong. But he prejudged:

"I had a birthday party last night with the boys. We were alone, just the boys, so we got drunk. When we were very drunk, much later, Vera came . . . I don't know how I got so drunk . . . (then silence fell upon us . . . long, long, too long a silence fell upon us) . . . I found her this morning, here, in my bed . . . naked . . ."

I felt an incredible sharp pain in the lower part of my stomach. I felt as if somebody's fist with all its might hit me and all my insides exploded. I felt as if I lost the last breath, as if I lost my heart . . .

I do not remember how I left his room.

I do not remember where I went. I was, perhaps, roaming the town streets, maybe I was walking along the sea shore, I do not remember whether I met the 'Imaginary Someone'.

I was running around like an empty soul, while tears were running down my cheeks like a wild river.

Everything around me lost its colour; sounds disappeared. Wherever I looked, I saw greyness and I had a horrible noise in my ears. That was the pain of first parting. That day, I could not soothe that pain with anything.

Roaming around, I met Ina; she took me to her home. I told her I left Dado and I cried inconsolably. She brought me several glasses of water and in the end, she gave me two tranquilizers saying:

"Have these, these will calm you down."

They did calm me down. I fell asleep and slept at hers for several hours. When I woke up, Ina was sitting next to me. I wanted to go home; she asked if I was feeling any better. I said, "Sort of," then she said, handing me a few more tranquilizers:

"Take these for later, you might need some. These are my mother's, they save her sanity; I take them sometimes before an exam."

I grabbed the whole box and said:

"Give me all of them, I need them badly."

She gave me the box of tranquilizers and told me to ring if in need.

I was not in need of anything. What could ease the pain of first parting?

I knew we parted forever.

On my way home, I took two more of the tranquilizers Ina gave me. There was nobody home. It was better that way. I don't remember how my brain was working; all I knew was that my heart was not working any longer. I opened my father's cabinet, and took a bottle from it. It said on the bottle—Hennessy. On my mother's side table, I found some more pills, some were painkillers and some were different tranquilizers to ones Ina gave me. I put the bottle on the table, the pills Ina gave me, my mother's pills (as I can recollect now, I think it said valium on the box), then I put David Bowie's record on, the one Dado lent me a few days ago . . . 'Sorrow', I opened the bottle where Hennessy was written, I looked myself in the mirror and said to the image of my face, "Farewell".

I swallowed all the pills; I drank half of the bottle (Hennessy was written on it). Across the mirror, with red lipstick, I had written, "Goodbye, Dado"; I increased the volume of the music to maximum . . .

After that, I didn't remember anything. I woke up in hospital. Above me, with ever flowing tears, my mother was standing (she looked like an un-named saint who knew all the sufferings of this world). When I opened my eyes, she uttered through tears:

"My beloved child, my beloved child . . ."

Markie came closer, he hugged me, saying:

"Everything is going to be alright."

I swung my head from left to right, which meant: "Nothing is going to be right ever again."

I felt sorry for my teary parents because now, the 'Imaginary Someone' really had 'something to say', but in their eyes, I saw that this time they did not care 'what Someone was going to say.'

When I came back home from hospital, my parents took time off work, and they tried to be 'natural and relaxed'. Tension could be felt in the air. Nobody ever mentioned Davor's name, just like we never mention long dead relatives we were never proud of.

Aurelio called inviting me to visit him in Sydney for several months. My father liked the idea. Mother supported him.

So, I gave in. Aurelio looked after me as if I were a little girl. He used to bring me ice cream, every day. He would bring me comedies to watch and funny cartoons.

He lived in an expensive area; he rented a very expensive house; he drove very expensive cars. He told me not to ask what he did, he said it didn't matter; he said that what mattered was that he was making a lot of money. I never asked him what he did, it was not important to me.

Because I had often splitting migraines, I frequently went to a local pharmacy to buy painkillers.

It was there where I met you, Ted.

I saw so much kindness in your eyes; there was so much peace in your voice. Your movements were so measured like a chemist's movements.

For six months, I was buying different kind of things in your pharmacy. Except for painkillers, I would buy toothpaste, sunscreen, different kinds of teas . . .

Each time I would enter, you welcomed me with your broad smile. It left the impression that I was the most important costumer of the day, as if you were waiting just for me to come.

One day, you simply asked:

"Are you working somewhere?"

"No." I replied.

"I need an assistant, the current one is about to leave. Would you like to work in a pharmacy?"

I wanted to work. I felt entirely useless sitting all by myself while Aurelio was out the whole day. Even though my English was almost perfect, I didn't seek people's company which later brought loneliness. So, I said:

"I'd like to work, but I have no experience at all."

You said:

"I will help you, no worries, this is not really difficult. Can you come next Monday?"

Thank you, Ted, you did help me a lot. You helped me to come back into my body, you helped me to understand what happened, you helped me to see life around me once again.

I was just a few months short of my nineteenth birthday, you were thirty-five. It seemed to me, at that time, that there was nothing you did not know; it looked that your heart was the seat of deep, profound peace; it seemed that all the goodness of this world stood in your calm eyes; it seemed as if you were my friend and my father. (And that was all I really needed, only that . . .)

I worked at your pharmacy for five months and my working visa was valid for another month, so I told you I couldn't work for you any longer. That was when we started our relationship, and you already started objecting my living with Aurelio.

Do you remember when I told you my visa was valid for only one more month? We sat on the shore of the lake in Centennial Park feeding the ducks and pelicans. A piece of bread dropped from your hand in the water, you looked at me all surprised:

"I thought you were living here permanently."

"No, they extended my visa once and that was the last time. I have to go back now."

You took both my hands in yours and said:

"Barbara, marry me."

I replied:

"I can't make a decision like that in haste."

And you said:

"Well, think about it . . . and tell me when you decide."

And you continued to feed the ducks.

I felt immense tenderness for you at that moment. I wanted to hug you, but I could not for some reason, so, I too, continued feeding the ducks and pelicans. I wanted to tell you something but did not know what; you already started a new theme with your calm voice. You talked about the Dalai Lama's visit to Sydney. You promised to take me to one of his talks. You knew so much about the Dalai Lama, about Tibetan Buddhism, I had never heard about it before.

When I decided to marry you, I was already pregnant. Don't you remember, we made love for the first time at your place and that first time I fell pregnant? You were so astounded. Immediately, you wanted me to move in with you; the idea that I would be still living with Aurelio wasn't acceptable to you anymore.

You would be surprised if I told you that Aurelio was very happy for us. He simply said:

"Ted is a fine man."

Maybe he was happy believing that I had forgotten Dado.

Aurelio was not invited to our wedding. Neither were any of your relatives. You told me that you were not close to your family, that there was some family feud. I was not particularly keen. I even did not want a wedding dress. We got married in the same park where we used to feed the birds every Sunday.

I thought you loved me. You used to say so. Then Lora was born, and I stopped working in the pharmacy.

Aurelio died that year; he fell into an abyss while madly driving his car. I was so young, inexperienced and nervous; I didn't have any help from anybody.

Then one day, you simply left and you never returned.

From my letters, you could have had insight into how we managed to live. I wanted to write to you for all these years; I wanted to keep you informed about Lora at least in this way. I felt it; I knew that I was going to die young—empty are those unfamiliar dawns . . .

You might wish to know now if I had thought of Davor all these years. Where was he, and what had happened to him? You might want to ask me if I still love him.

I do not know what happened. I had never heard anything from him or about him. That day when I learned he woke up in his bed with another woman, I tried to kill myself. But I did not kill myself though I killed something else in me. I killed grief. All these years I never grieved for him. I thought if only I killed that unbearable grief within me, it would go away as if it had never happened. But grief was still there masked with a different name—horror. Sometimes, I would feel pure horror towards myself because I deprived myself, like the worst tyrant, of my grief. I had never asked anybody, 'What happened to Davor?' I had never asked softly, with concern. Softly, with a heart full of respect for our days. I just couldn't. I couldn't . . .

My life has come to an end. I do not know if Lora would like to meet you, we never talked about you. You vanished; you did not exist any longer.

Goodbye Ted. Barbara.

EPILOGUE

These were all her letters written to Ted.

I was sitting on her chair and crying.

I called her Barbara, for she never wanted me to call her—mother.

Barbara was a rebel. I did not know her well. I knew her as a kind, sacrificing mother ready to take life as it comes. She taught me that. She used to say:

"Lora, do not knock your head against the brick wall, the world is like an old tortoise shell." She taught me patience, love and forgiveness. She taught me to respect people and things worthy of respect. When we would come across someone hostile, brutish or arrogant, she would say: "Ignore those kinds of people, seek peace and purpose within yourself, seek the company of noble people, there are many, take notice of them . . ."

Now I learned that Barbara was a teenager, too. We never think that our mothers were teenagers, at least not when we are at that age.

I learned about her love and about her pain.

After my mother passed away, nothing was left there. The world became empty and silent. What pain! There were no tears which could wash out this pain, and there were no words of comfort which could ease it.

'My Barbara is no more.' That was the only thought which was left in my mind.

I loved her hands. I loved her long, slim fingers. They were nervous from all the typing. They were dancing on the keyboard, and it looked as if she was composing music while writing; she would only move her lips barely noticeably, and slowly she would nod her head. Nothing bothered her: noise from the street or in the building, or my conversations on the phone. She was in another world; with her eyes half-closed, she would listen to the stories told to her by an invisible narrator. I would often look at her clandestinely. She would put her palms on her chest as if in prayer, lowering her head as if she was bowing to the Invisible One.

My Barbara died believing that there was just one secret. The secret was—why did Ted desert us. But she died with two secrets. The other one I shared with Ted.

2.

So, Ted left in the spring of 1988. He left a letter for Barbara, but in the letter, he never said the reasons for his leaving. He wrote:

This is not a good life for us. I tried to make it better, but whatever I did, it wasn't good enough. I am tired, so I am leaving. I know that you will be the best mother to Lora. Goodbye, Barbara. Ted.

This letter, as well, was in Barbara's file among the others. I don't remember any longer what I felt when he left, I was only eight. But I clearly remember, that all of a sudden, I felt much older. I lost interest in the things I used to love; everything lost meaning—the games I liked to play looked stupid, my friends irritated me, and I felt empty and alone.

I think this is the right word. I felt empty when Ted left. I never mentioned his name to Barbara, for I feared that mentioning his name could hurt Barbara. I feared she was in pain. My own pain I tried to hide from Barbara, but I can't say if I was very successful at it. I could not play my violin any longer. Ted would sit in his favorite armchair, put his legs on an ottoman, fill his pipe with tobacco, close his eyes and say:

'Lora, it's violin time.'

He was my audience. Barbara was locked in her world writing, she would not hear anything, but Ted enjoyed it very much; the scent of his pipe and the sound of my violin.

A day before Christmas holidays, I got out of school. There were several fathers waiting for their kids. I walked down the path in the schoolyard when I noticed a man standing, leaning against the entrance door. There was no doubt—it was Ted. I ran toward him, he squatted and spread his arms. When I came close to him, I stopped running and I looked at him (I looked at my father with eyes full of sadness). He put down his arms, then he stood up. He was standing there for a while, just a few seconds, and he looked so tall to me, like a giant, and in a calm voice he said:

"Come, Lora, come."

I came closer, and he put his hand on the top of my head:

"You are growing fast, aren't you? You are so tall."

We sat on the bench. From his pocket, he took out a long woolen thread. He tied it around one palm, and with fingers of the other palm he started to form a 'star', and he stretched the star toward me. I took his star and with my fingers I formed four horizontal lines, and out of these lines he made with an easy movement of his fingers something that would resemble two intertwined squares . . .

We ran out of ideas and everything started to repeat itself: a star, four horizontal lines, two intertwined squares. Then we laughed. Ted folded the wool thread four times and put it back into his pocket. Then he said:

"Would you like an ice cream?"

We walked to the nearest corner shop and bought an ice cream. He did not ask about Barbara; before leaving, he only said:

"Would you like me to come again?"

"You know the answer . . ." I said lowering my eyes.

Then he mapped out the destiny of our future get-togethers:

"Shall we keep this as a secret, Lora? I really do not want your mother to know that I am seeing you. I can come sometimes after school . . ." He took both my hands in his and squeezed them tightly; I nodded my head.

Happily, I walked home. When I turned my head, Ted was still standing on the same spot looking at me. We waved to each other.

I never revealed this secret to Barbara.

He came every week. Sometimes, it would be only once a week, but more often it was twice or three times per week. Our get-togethers were short, just a few minutes. Every time he would pet my head, and when I was about to go, he would say:

"Go fast and be careful when crossing the road."

We continued to see each other in this manner for ten years. Every week, except for school holidays. Sometimes during the holidays, I would sneak out and run to the pharmacy just to see him for a few minutes.

He would often ask me about school, about homework or if I needed anything.

I did not need a thing. I had Ted again.

He never asked about Barbara, I never mentioned her. I never knew that she was writing him letters.

And he knew it, too, that I did not know it.

He never gave me anything, not a single present, not a penny. I did not need anything. All I needed was to see him a few times per week, for five minutes. Again, I had my father.

I took a deep sigh. My chest was heavy, my throat tight, I felt as if I were choking. Would Barbara ever be able to forgive me for this deceit? Would she be glad had she known that I was meeting up with my father?

After the pile of letters, the *Letters to Ted*, there was one more, the very last one. It was in an envelope and on the envelope, with her fine handwriting, was written *'For Lora'*.

Her last letter said:

It is 12th of September today; I just came back from my doctor. I have written the last letter to Ted and this one is for you. The doctor told me that I only have three months left of my life.

Forgive me, my dearest, I could not tell you. There were many things which I could not do any more. I could not look at your angel eyes and tell you that I am leaving you all alone in this world. I could not afford a better life for you. So, my dearest, forgive me that as well. I was writing, for my soul was burdened with a strange, unknown suffering and I believed that that pain God only gives to chosen ones as a peculiar present. When I did not write, it would choke me, threatening my life. Certainly, I couldn't be a bank clerk, but I should have afforded you a better childhood. Ted left, and he never helped us. I never wanted to call him, to ask for alimony. I did not want to owe anything to anyone. But I should have thought more about you than about my pride.

All I gave you was love, was that enough?

My dearest little soul, it seems now, at the end, that I know everything. Everything seems now simple and easy. Make your life easy and honourable. Simplify it as much as possible, for then you will hear the music. Then you will enter into a world which cannot be seen by the naked eye, but it can be seen and felt by your heart. Listen to the music of your heart, abide in the world of simplicity, do not fight in uphill battles, you are not born for that. I could never figure out what your soul was striving for, it is older than mine.

My sweetest little girl, in this life I had learned so much from you. You taught me how to care, you taught me how to love, how to forgive; you taught me patience; how to laugh and how to be happy. You were all that to me. You were the air I breathed, the food which sustained my body, and you were the dreams I dreamt at night.

At night they used to come, my own demons, and they would tell me:

"Get up, Barbara!"

I would switch on my computer and listen to their terrifying voices.

You never read my novels. Maybe you will one day when the pain of losing your mother subsides.

I will be fine, do not worry. Nobody taught me to believe in God. I never needed Him. The whole country where I was born never needed God. They took Him down from that part of heaven; they threw Him into the mud, with cudgels they beat Him to death never to resurrect in that part of the world.

I met a man called Deva. He taught me to listen to my heart; he said that God speaks to us through our heart. When I started to listen to my own heart, the Almighty came to me in His full beauty and might. I saw Him in the simplicity of life; I saw Him in forgiveness. I had forgiven Dado, I had forgiven Ted, I had forgiven myself and life itself. When I learnt to forgive, when I learnt to listen to my heart, black flowers grew in my stomach and started hurriedly to multiply; it was too late for God.

You know, I belonged to that land. There, too, black flowers were sown, the flowers of evil, and there, too, nobody had listened to God's voice communicating through people's hearts.

Ah, Lora! What am I leaving to you? All my belongings, which are few. This apartment was not mine. It belonged to Aurelio. You never met Aurelio. His foot was always on the other side of the law. After only two years in Sydney, he acquired two apartments and five luxury cars.

How was that possible? I never asked him. One of his elegant apartments he had signed over in my name, as he would say, 'not to draw attention'. That was how I came into possession of such a nice place. The rest, I bought myself.

Writing could not provide a good life. As you remember, I had private students teaching them Italian and French. Both languages I learned myself having private tutors. Markie wanted that. It proved to be very useful. Some of my stories I published . . . I could have published even more if only I were smarter. I never wanted advice. I never wanted to write what publishers suggested; I wanted to write my stories, in my own way.

I am leaving you my novels, all are dedicated to you.

I am leaving you my heart and the promise that I will look after you if there is anything after this life. I will see that only when I leave.

I was made of desires, and nobody could help that. I always desired the things I could not have. Whatever I had or acquired, I wanted something else. I wanted to live in some other country, in some other city, in some other district . . . I wanted some extraordinary hero in my life . . . I found him in my stories; I wanted peace, love and harmony for this world . . .

In this letter, I won't leave you a single piece of wisdom, a recipe for a good life. If I knew one, I would have followed it myself. As you can understand, I was led by my desires, never-ending desires, some were really confusing, some completely surreal. I knew it, but nevertheless, I wanted them even more. As I told you, I was made of my desires, and as they made me, they dissolved me in the end. My own desires.

Maybe the secret of life is in silence. Maybe, honestly, in the simplicity. Maybe it is in the acceptance of everything. But that was not me. My soul, at one moment, longed for deep peace, as deep as a mountain lake, and at the other moment, it longed for turmoil like a whirlpool on that peaceful lake which swallows its peaceful surface and everything on its way. My soul was like the wind . . .

In the end, all my desires met in you. I would hide what a possessive mother I was, but I knew you felt it all the way. Seems like it was like that because I was scared that I would not have you with me long enough.

Let the Heavens bless you my child.

Thousand kisses from your Barbara.

I finished reading my mother's letter. It seemed to rain over Sydney, and out of nowhere I heard verses, verse by verse of *Prevert's 'Barbara'. Remember Barbara it was raining unceasingly on Brest that day . . .*

"... And I ran into you on Siam Street
You were smiling
And I smiled too
Remember Barbara ..."

TED'S STORY

Twilight had long crept into my room and stuck to the walls, objects darkened and the darkness crept into my thoughts.

I never really knew Barbara! That thought played with my mind all the time. If I tried to think about something else, the same thought would come back again (so stubborn as if the thought was alive).

I heard a doorbell. Who could that be? It rang again, but this time longer. I went to the door and heard little coughs in the corridor.

"Who is it?" I asked.

"Ted."

I opened the door. Ted hugged me and pressed my head against his chest. He caressed my hair while I was crying. He led me inside, and we sat on the sofa. I buried my face into Ted's hands and wailed like a little dog. Ted was silent. I do not know for how long we sat there. I thought that I had used up all my tears the past couple of days, but it looked like they could never run out, like a heart that could not run out of all its desires. Like Barbara's heart, full of unfulfilled dreams.

When I stopped crying, Ted said:

"I only heard about it now, I was away. Why didn't you call me? You know I would have been here at once if I had known; you know I would have been with you, dear child."

I know, Ted was at Lorraine's. She is his friend, they say so. Maybe she is Ted's real love, I don't know. She lives elsewhere, he often goes to see her and even more often she would come to visit. They've known each other for three years. He mentioned her several times, but as I had never expressed any interest in meeting her, he stopped mentioning her altogether. I did not want to ask at the pharmacy for her phone number. How did he learn that Barbara had died?

He had waited for me in front of school. As I had never appeared, he went to ask where I was on that day. He was told that I had been absent for several days, as my mother had passed away. He ran to me. He hadn't been here for ten years. I asked:

"Is everything the same as it was ten years ago?"

"Nearly everything . . ." he said with a little smile, and I thought "Nearly everything . . . but there is no Barbara anymore."

"I'll make a cup of tea. Are the teacups up there, where they always used to be?"

"Yes, right there."

He made us a pot of tea and brought it to the living room.

"What did you eat today?"

"Nothing. I am not hungry."

He reached for the telephone and asked:

"What would you like to eat? You like pizza, don't you? I'd like one as well."

I shrugged my shoulders, I didn't want to eat anything. While we were waiting for pizza to be delivered, he went out and came back with a bottle of red wine. He was agitated, vividly.

We ate pizza and Ted drank two glasses of wine. He said:

"Barbara has died. I am so sorry, but now we must think of you, Lora. Have you thought what's next for you?"

"I did not think of anything; I don't know what's next. I have to finish school; there is one more term left. Barbara always wanted me to go to university. I wanted to study archeology before. But, now, I really do not know, since she is not with me anymore all is different."

"I am your father, Lora. Barbara used to say, 'my daughter', 'my Lora'. She was a possessive mother, she never wanted to share her love for you, she wanted you all for herself. But the fact is—I am your father."

He fell silent, then he drank a little bit more of his wine and after a short pause he said:

"You know, my dear, as your father, I was supposed to have responsibilities toward you. I did, I used to come and see you as often as I could. Me and Barbara, we never met again. She was a proud and stubborn woman. She never wanted anything from me. In order to protect and to carry on with our meetings in front of the school, I never gave you a present or any money. You were anyway too young to be given money. On the other hand, it would not be fair toward Barbara. She wanted to have some sort of control over what you were buying, eating, drinking et cetera.

So, in 1988, I opened a bank account in your name; for each and every birthday of yours, for every Christmas and successful completion of a school grade, I deposited money on that account."

He reached in the pocket of his jacket and took out a little blue bank book. He opened it and said:

"You see, this is the last deposit on 2nd of June 1998. There you have a nice sum of money which can secure you a good education. I thought about your future. Now you have only me, you don't have to worry about the future. The only thing you need to worry about now is how to go through these difficult days ahead of you. I am here, anything you need, just let me know."

He caressed my hair once again and put the bank booklet on the table.

'Kind, the kindest, Ted,' I was talking silently to myself.

Loudly, I said:

"Barbara left me this apartment and with everything in it; she has left me all her novels, the last one was unfinished."

"She was a good writer, wasn't she? Do you want to talk about her?"

I nodded my head, my eyes were full of tears again. I said to him:

"I found the letters she wrote to you."

For a long period of time, he did not utter a word (we heard the ticking of the wall-clock). The sound of wine pouring in his glass was heard. He took out his pipe and it took him a long time to fill it with tobacco. The well-known aroma of his tobacco started spreading through the room. This smell led me into my childhood, reminded me of my violin. Carried by the aroma, I said:

"When you left, I stopped playing the violin. Once this aroma of tobacco disappeared, with it went my desire to play the violin."

"I know my leaving hurt you. Now you are a big girl, now we can talk about it. You read the letters your mother sent me; every year one letter. Unusual woman, unusual letters; I could never understand why she wrote me those letters. She had the immense need to tell her story. She was a lonely soul. But that was her choice. She preferred to be alone. She never acquired friends, but she never tried, never made any effort. In the company of other people, she would become tense and nervous. Barbara was often ill; I consider that her illnesses were self-made. Only ill could she deliver such stories. Her stories were strange, full of unusual, unpredictable characters and bizarre plots. She hated ordinary things and people without imagination. For ordinary people, she would say:

'There is no personality there at all.' There were only few who could follow her. It looked to me as if there were several characters within her which often changed their places. She had so much energy that I thought she needed several characters to use up all the energy stored within her. She was the happiest when writing. I never knew where she wandered to when writing. She would not eat for days or utter a meaningful sentence. She smoked too much, and smoking only enhanced her nervousness."

He stopped and rested his eyes on the rim of his glass. His eyes sank into the past, into a time when he used to know Barbara. It looked to me that a little gentle, or melancholic, smile was oscillating on his face; it seemed as if he carefully searched for his words not to harm me with any.

"When I met her, she looked completely lost. She was painfully thin, just her eyes like two turquoise glow-worms were constantly oscillating. I was looking at her eyes unable to answer whether those were real eyes or just coloured contact lenses. When she was pregnant, I hoped that you might inherit the unique colour of her eyes, but it seems that those turquoise eyes were meant to be only Barbara's.

She would come to the pharmacy and sometimes it seemed to me that she was so confused not knowing why she came. She would search through the shelves moving her lips frantically. Seeing her so thin and absentminded, I even thought that she was on drugs; she would look for pills. To end my suspicions, I came to her and asked if she needed any help. Without lifting her eyes, she asked which tablets were the most effective painkillers. She was always buying painkillers. I could not figure out why she needed so many painkillers, was she really having daily headaches? I looked at her eyes and they were clean and healthy. She spread around her some sort of sweet aroma, there was some sort of irresistible urge to hug her, she looked to me like a helpless child. I caught myself at each and every sound of the doorbell hurriedly rushing towards the door in the hope that it might be 'the thin girl with turquoise eyes'.

What happened next was that the pharmacy assistant who worked for me three days per week went back to university. I offered Barbara that place, she accepted it.

She was often absentminded (as if she had forgotten something a long time ago). I never knew how to get closer to her, for the doors of Barbara's world were tightly closed. Which road led to Barbara? I was determined to find the road to her heart. But in her heart, there was not a place for me, for that place was taken by somebody else, a long time ago. I understood that, but anyway, I tried everything to get closer to her heart. We started going out together; she liked my company, she said I was interesting. This city is my hometown; I used to take her to places which Aurelio had never even heard of. She trusted me; she appreciated me, I knew that.

When she told me that her visa was about to expire, I thought that it was a sign from above. I offered her to marry me; she accepted. The same year, you were born."

I didn't know how much those memories meant to him. Even though he was telling me the story as a matter of fact, it seemed to me that I was reading pain on his face; I did not ask anything. We both were silent, between us, Barbara's reflection was dancing.

After a short silence, he continued:

"Did I try everything that was possible to save our marriage before I decided to leave? I do not know anymore. I thought I tried all I could have possibly tried in the eight years of our marriage. The most difficult part was the fact that I was leaving you, Lora. Barbara was not happy being my wife; from day to day it was more and more obvious. She reproached me silently, without words. I could not help her to find a publisher. I tried to organise her life the way she wanted. The way she would be the happiest. She wanted to be a stay-at-home mum, to be with you, to write. She got that. Then, she wanted something else; she wanted to 'get out of these four walls'. I offered her to work at the pharmacy; she didn't want that either.

A good friend of mine, a museum executive, offered her a job in the museum, but she said if she accepted it, then she would not have time for writing. She hated boring housework, so I hired a woman for all domestic work. She wanted to travel, so we travelled. Often, she would say that she did not know herself what she wanted; she was deeply unhappy. Only much later, I understood that this was her nature. She was born like that. Could it be that on the day she was born all newborns were given the gift of discontent? I do not know.

Then, the time came when nothing was good enough anymore: this country, its people, this city of ours, her marriage, her life . . .

In her heart, there was only place for one person, only for you, Lora.

Everything was better in her old country. People were more cultured, friends were more sincere; food was tastier, the sun shone warmer and her heart was fuller. Daily, she complained about something. She was so agitated; she used to smash her hands onto the keyboard while saying that it would be much better for her if she only was a potato vendor in the market place."

He sighed deeply, then carried on:

"I blamed myself. I thought, I wasn't a capable man, I was not a good provider, I was a weakling and I did not know how to become the hero from her stories, the hero from her dreams.

One day, I simply left.

She asked me later, in her letters, whether my leaving was thoroughly planned or was my decision governed by the whim of my moods. I did not know her discontentment was a heavy load for me, too. Towards the end, I started fearing what mood I would find her in when I came back home. I would search daily on her face some signs to figure out her particular mood, or fearing she might be ill again. I would carefully choose the tone of my voice when addressing her, or I was careful of a certain expression on my face when talking to her. Oh, how much I loved her! I adored her and would give anything to once again see that old Barbara of mine—the kind and softly-spoken woman, who was almost like a little girl when I met her for the first time in my pharmacy . . . But every day that kind and softly-spoken girl was further and further away from me, until she had finally disappeared. She tortured me with her silence and aloofness. There were days when we would not exchange a word. Initially, she wanted to talk about her family and her country. But I told her that she was selective in her memories, that she remembered only the good things. After that, she talked less about it.

I imagined her father like some exceptional character, her country like an ideal place. It did not feed my esteem, it diminished it.

Later, in her letters, she often reproached me, my background. I never told her that my family wasn't, actually, my family. I never knew my real family; I was adopted. I never told her about my days in the orphanage. I was ashamed. So 'my family' (the one she knew), adopted me.

He stopped there, he fell silent for a while and with a changed voice, he continued:

"I do not want to go into lots of details even though I think you should know more about me and your mother. I do not wish to say something that might sound like the truth seen only through my eyes. We should (only if we could) hear what Barbara had to say about it. For me, 'Barbara's head' was always a mystery. I would often ask myself, 'What thoughts is this little head churning around now?' She had a rich, complex personality; it was difficult to please her. She could not settle for average, but I was an average man; I was not some unusual hero with extraordinary intelligence or a man with some rare gift."

I was silent for a long time; my heart was full of compassion for Ted. I know he loved her a lot. When I come to think of it, it seems to me that whoever encountered Barbara, loved her very much. Any person, whoever met her. She would attract people with some unusual charm of hers. But it looked like she was never sure of it. She would always check everything suspiciously, feelings and emotions of others.

I asked myself silently, 'Did Barbara ever love herself the way others loved her?'

"And? You, finally left?"

"Hmm, Lora. I knew you were going to ask me that question one day. And I have never prepared an answer. I let time and circumstance answer it.

I do not know, even now, what to say. Yes, I left in the end. I left you, too. My steps were heavy, my soul was split in three parts—you, Barbara, and me. My heart was heavy all those years while I was coming in front of your school, hiding, just to see you getting taller, getting older . . . I felt like a thief, like somebody who was sneaking around without any right to peep into the intimacy of your life, intimacy of your home to which I did not belong any longer. Barbara was not waiting for me to come back. I knew that. I knew if I went away, there was no returning, ever again.

I hated the idea that she would find somebody else, that she would remarry. But she never filed for divorce. She stayed Barbara Donoghue. My Barbara."

I found myself crying again. He wiped my tears, his eyes looked glassy as well. One tear rolled down his cheek, he didn't wipe it off. I asked him through the tears:

"Did you ever cry for us, Ted?"

"Many nights I cried for the two of you. I would say to myself that I never deserved Barbara, so weak and weepy. She searched for a hero, somebody who could dry her tears forever. Oh, Lora, my one and only child, if you only knew how many tears I had cried for the two of you! And what was it all for? Our hearts were heavy from that pain and I am asking now, what was all that for? Or was it all meant to be just as it happened?"

"Do you believe, Ted, that everything is written in the stars?"

"I do not know, my dear. I have been asking myself the same question. In the stars or elsewhere, but people spend their entire lives searching for the answer to that same question. We do not know while we are here; on the other side . . . well I do not know what's there."

He took his handkerchief, wiped his eyes and blew his nose into it, then he asked:

"I expected to find her parents here; did they not come for the funeral?"

"They didn't come." I gazed at a particular spot, hoping it would ground me:

"I came back from school and called her name. She did not reply. I came to her desk and to my surprise the computer was turned off. I called again and again, and then I started looking for her throughout the apartment. I peeped into every room even though I could not believe that she would be in her bedroom at this hour. But she was there. She was sleeping; she looked as if she was dreaming the dreams from which she would never come back. My Barbara fell asleep, forever. I knew that at first glance. I did not know how I knew it, maybe you can sense death by just the smell in the air. Or maybe it was the sixth sense. Death was seated next to Barbara, I felt shivers along my spine from the strange smell and the cruel coldness which had spread through the room. I said, 'Mummy, Mummy, wake up,' and passed by Death, sat next to my dead mother and repeated the whole afternoon:

'Mummy, wake up.' But she did not. I did not call anybody and nobody came. Then it grew dark and on my hands and knees like a little stray dog, I crawled to the neighbour's door. Susanne still lives here, so she opened the door. When she saw me on my knees all in tears, she panicked:

'Lora, what happened to you?'

'My mummy died.' I howled.

That night I slept at Susanne's, a doctor came and gave me some sedatives. Whatever I did the following days looked like somebody else was doing it, not Lora. It looked to me that that 'somebody else' was far older and much more mature than the Lora prior to mother's death. I grew up in twenty-four hours. I knew it was not me anymore, and I knew that I would never be the same Lora again; I knew that a new Lora was born, and while 'new Lora' attended all the duties around the funeral, 'old Lora' looked at her speechlessly.

The next day, I called my grandmother. When she answered my call, I said:

'Granny, I got to tell you something,' I felt trepidation in her voice when she asked:

'What has happened, Lora?'

Calmly, I said:

'Barbara has died.'

There was no answer from the other side. There was a long, long silence, and I was silent myself. She did not say a word, I heard her crying and I was crying too, then the line dropped.

She rang immediately, and through the tears, she asked:

'What happened Lora?'

'Barbara has died.' I said once again.

She tried to talk to me, but she could not talk, for she cried bitterly. Once again, we cried together and once again, the line dropped. After a few hours, the telephone rang again and this time it was Annamaria. She told me that she was the daughter of my aunty Zlatka and that she was Aurelio's sister. She asked the same question as grandma—what had happened?, and I said again:

'Barbara has died.'

She asked:

'How is that possible?'

I said:

'I do not know.'

She asked when the funeral was, and I said that I still did not know, but I would inform them as soon as I found out.

The following morning, I rang my granny, but Annamaria answered the call. She said:

'Is it you Lora? Your grandma is not at home.'

'Where is she?' I asked and she said:

'She went to hospital. Your grandfather just had a heart attack. It is his second. After he received the news about Barbara's passing away, he just fell down on his knees.'

Nobody came for the funeral. They did not come, and you were not there either, so I thought it would have been best if I had ended up next to Barbara and had closed my eyes forever, but upon that thought I heard a little voice in my head which told me, 'this is not your destiny now.' I didn't know 'what my destiny was' just as I do not know now, but I knew that I was lost without my Barbara. Once again, I grew up hurriedly in twenty-four hours, and right now I feel tired and old."

Ted did not utter a word. Only his face was pale, so pale that it seemed to me that it could have lit the dark room.

"Why did we not know better . . . why didn't we do any better . . . (Why could we not do it, know it any better?)" he was repeating like a broken record.

"In the last letter she wrote to me, she said she was ill. I never took it seriously. She liked to be dramatic. She lived in a world I could never understand; she played with death often and I thought it was some other message she wanted to send me . . . I never knew her well. Often, I would think that she was not 'the real Barbara' that somebody else knew 'the real Barbara', not me. She would half-disclose some mystery; she would tell half of a story leaving me with unanswered questions. She would move on, open another chapter, write a new story. She never searched for the protagonists of her stories, they would come to her offering themselves gladly, she would take as much as she needed, then she would disappear into her world again.

But she was a dedicated mother. When she gave birth, it looked as if nobody ever did it before her, as if a miracle happened. You were her icon. She would tell incredible tales about you; she would say how special a child you were, or you were a child coming to this planet with a special mission. She would say that you were born with three gifts, that you will be a very important soul for this country, for this planet. I would be at odds listening to her stories and looking at her so carried away with her tales. I asked myself if every mother was so in love with their child, or was it just Barbara? Whatever she did, she did it because of you; later, I assume, she did even more. Often, I would think: 'If she only gave me a little piece of that love, it would be a love of enormous proportions.'

Well, it looked like Barbara was a woman capable of loving only one person at a time; she wasn't able to love a few people simultaneously. The love she had for you was so intense and there was nothing left for anybody else.

Sometimes, I would tell her that she was strange. It would aggravate her mood. She never liked the word 'strange'. She told me that this epithet of being 'strange' followed her everywhere, but it came only from average minds. She was not 'strange', she was herself; a woman who understood the world in her own unique way and acted in the same way. So, there was no place for anything unusual or 'strange', she knew herself well and lived according to who she was. She used to tell me that her hometown was a 'a place of the rules'. Everybody followed certain rules but nobody knew who mapped out these rules. Regardless, everybody followed the rules obediently never asking—why? God forbid, if you only earned the label of 'a strange one'. The town rules were often in discord with the ethos of the soul or the notion of common sense. Barbara followed the ethos of her soul and practised common sense, and would use each one depending on the occasion. It was much harder to live that way. I wonder, was that the reason she departed so early? Maybe she has found a better world where she can live according to the ethos of her soul and where she can follow her common sense."

"She would not leave me here alone, Ted."

Ted shrugged his shoulders and started slowly to fill his pipe with tobacco, again.

I loved the scent of his pipe . . .

We spent the entire night putting together little stories about Barbara, crying sporadically.

That night, he talked about Lorraine as well.

She was the absolute opposite of Barbara. Lorraine was a woman who liked to cook; she liked picnics and parties. She liked to laugh and make others laugh. She was the kind of person anybody would like to befriend.

"In simple words" Ted said, "a simple woman."

She never cared about important questions, the questions about the meaning of existence and the meaning of death. She never felt others' pain and suffering; she never asked where the soul journeys and what would be its purpose on this earth. She never cared about social injustices, never cared about poverty and wars nor about abandoned children.

She was a sensual woman. She enjoyed good food, good wine; she loved to laugh, laugh a lot.

When I heard that, I thought that Barbara could not put up with a person like that—not even for a few minutes. Ted said, "She has a pure heart and good intentions even though she is a very, very simple woman."

I said to him:

"In her last letter to me, Barbara told me that all the wisdom of this world is in simplicity."

"It could be. If that was Barbara's last conclusion about life, I appreciate it. It seems to me that all her life was organised that way—to teach her that simple truth. She reached it. And me too, the further I go, the more I understand that all the wisdom is in simplicity. Simplicity of living, simplicity of expressing one's thoughts, simplicity of acting . . ."

"But, what about love, Ted?"

"Maybe love, too, is simplicity. Barbara simply loved her Dado—just simply loved him. Full stop. It looks as if, after that love she tangled herself into life. She lost simplicity and spontaneity."

We went to rest before dawn. I slept in my bed, and Ted slept on the sofa in the living room. When I woke up, the sun was up high. The smell of fried bacon and eggs woke me up. Ted brought breakfast to my bed; he was already dressed and shaved.

While I was eating, Ted asked me:

"So, what are you going to do next?"

"I shall go to my grandparents. I have never been there, I want to be with them right now."

"When the school finishes?"

"No. I won't wait. I am going as soon as I buy a plane ticket. I can't go to school right now; I know I will catch up with school later."

Ted agreed with me. We called a travel agency and booked the flight for the following week.

All this time Ted was with me. He helped me to pay the bills: the late ones and the future ones. He helped me buy what I needed and pack my bags.

I called my grandma and told her I was coming. She was happy to hear it.

I needed to get away from this city; I needed to go there where my Barbara's spirit had probably returned.

So, I let myself go 'in search of Barbara.'

EPILOGUE

To understand where I belong, I needed to understand where Barbara belonged. But there were things I was confused about. Barbara was displeased with life in her hometown. She never liked the rules, as she would say, by which the town played. She never liked the 'comfort of the mediocre' and obsessively hated the Imaginary Someone.

She longed for freedom.

Freedom from stupidity and prejudices. Freedom from lies and cajolery. She longed for freedom of expression, freedom to create. Freedom of the soul.

I wanted to find out what was binding her, I wanted to know what was hurting her. I wanted to learn what she loved, what she longed for, and what she grieved for in her hardest times.

When she finally got her freedom, in the city where nobody knew her as Barbara Millich, in the city where the Imaginary Someone was not in play, it seemed as if she had lost herself. It looked as if she did not know what to do with the freedom she longed for so desperately. She didn't know where to start from. She started with writing. I took with me her novels ready to read them in her bedroom. I wanted to see Davor's window from her bedroom window, and wanted to imagine what she was feeling while waiting at the window to see Davor, coming out and waving his hand at her.

I wanted to find out what kind of freedom she was dreaming of, with which chains she was chained; were these chains the same ones she did not know how to break in her freedom? When the Imaginary Someone disappeared, it seemed that all her revolt disappeared, all her need for freedom and individuality. There were no witnesses, those who could tap her on the shoulder or criticise her.

Freedom became her prison. Barbara talked about apathy with which she was surrounded. They were all indifferent, nobody cared what you were doing, who you were, what kind of stories you were writing and what you carried in your soul.

Instead of stupidity which she fought all her life, she was surrounded by total indifference. Indifference which gnawed at the soul.

2.

Ted took me to the airport. He said:

"Now, you really are a big girl; you are travelling to Europe. If you need anything, please let me know."

We exchanged hugs and kisses and off I went, it seemed, into the complete unknown. I looked back. Ted was waving his hand, and it looked to me as if he was waving it in front of my school where we would meet in secret. I turned back several times. He stood at the same spot looking at me and waving his hand. I yelled at him:

"See you next week!"

He laughed:

"Send me a postcard."

There was not any particular feeling in my soul. There was no anticipation or excitement; the grief for my lost mother did not give space to any other feeling.

When the plane took off, I saw my hometown. How beautiful it was, full of green vegetation, parks and bays.

"... A man was taking cover on a porch
And he cried your name
Barbara
And you ran to him in the rain
Streaming-wet enraptured flushed
And you threw yourself in his arms ..."

IN BARBARA'S WORLD

Annamaria and Tiyana greeted me at the airport. I had never met them before; I never even saw their photos, but as soon as I laid my eyes on them, I recognised them (there was something in the way they carried themselves) whilst they walked towards me.

Uncle Niko Millich is my grandfather's brother. His wife is Auntie Zlatka; they had two children, Aurelio and Annamaria. I knew of Aurelio's existence, Barbara mentioned him many times, but she had never mentioned Annamaria. My grandmother mentioned her for the first time when they visited. Annamaria had two children, too—Tiyana and Nino. Tiyana was three years older than me, she was twenty-one.

When they came closer, Annamaria simply hugged me and said:

"Welcome Lora," then she started to wipe her teary eyes. Tiyana said:

"It's OK Mum, please not now." Then she extended her hand to me, and said:

"I am Tiyana, your cousin."

Tiyana looked like Annamaria. Annamaria looked like Barbara, only she somehow had a fuller face and stronger bone structure. She didn't have the same eye coulour as Barbara, nobody had eyes like my Barbara. Annamaria carried my suitcase, Tiyana and I walked along without a word. When we came to the car, Annamaria told Tiyana to sit in the back seat, and I sat next to Annamaria. I did not know what to say, but Annamaria rescued me from the awkward silence:

"Are you tired?"

"Yes, I am. It was a long, tiring trip."

"I see, you speak well. It is so good that you learned the language."

"It probably is not the best version, but I now have the opportunity to better it."

We talked about the flight, about the weather, and she asked if I had taken winter clothes. I was in a summer dress and sandals; we maintained quite a boring conversation. On the back seat, Tiyana was quiet; she did not say a word. Then Annamaria said:

"Why are you so quiet back there? Say something."

She asked:

"How was your flight, Lora?"

"It was OK" I repeated for the second time.

She felt silent again.

I was very tired; the day grew dark quickly. I closed my eyes. When they woke me up, there was a man in uniform standing next to the car. We gave him our passports. He examined my passport thoroughly and asked me many (for me unusual) questions, like: Where was I going? Who will I be staying with? How long did I intend to stay? What were my grandparents' names? How long had I been living in Australia? What was I carrying in my suitcase? (as he was such a thorough investigator, he thoroughly examined my suitcase). Some of his questions and my answers he had written in a little notebook, and after one, for me very exhausting hour, they let us into their country.

I was very taken aback by that. Why and what for were all those questions? Annamaria showed a little, tired smile and enigmatically said:

"Welcome home, Lora."

Once again, I fell asleep in the car, and once again Annamaria gently stoked my arm telling me:

"Wake up Lora, we have arrived."

There was my grandma standing in front of the car. I recognised her when my eyes adapted to the light. From the sudden rush of excitement, everything fell from my lap: my purse, passport and some papers I had been given. She came to me and hugged me tightly, and embraced we cried together. In her soft arms, I could freely cry just like I used to cry in Barbara's soft embrace.

Annamaria put her arms around our shoulders and said quietly:

"Let's go inside."

I had never seen buildings that old. Their building was so beautiful, the architecture seemed as if it was taken from a beautiful picture book. The sky was low, it looked as if I could touch the stars. (Even the stars looked different here). The scents were different, everything around me smelled like Barbara, it smelled of her hair.

We entered a very big apartment with nicely organised rooms. In the living room, in the big armchair was my reclining grandpa Marko. He attempted to stand up, but my grandma stopped the attempt with words:

"Do not even try!" I came closer and hugged him. His embrace was warm, but it was not as tight as I remembered it from few years ago.

"How are you?" I asked, and my eyes filled with tears. I could not look at his teary eyes (who can look at the tears of their own father or grandfather?), therefore I turned my head to the other side. Tiyana was seated at the table, she was looking up at the ceiling while humming (I did not like her eyes). When I turned my head to avoid my grandpa's tears, our eyes met, then she quickly looked away (knowing probably that I didn't like her dark eyes?). There was an expression of utter annoyance on her face, and she didn't even try to hide it. She said:

"Shall we go, Mum?"

"Let's stay a little bit longer, I'll get tea and cakes. We won't stay long, Lora is probably exhausted."

Nobody mentioned her name. Barbara. I said:

"Did she grow up here, in this apartment?"

"Since she was born."

"I would like to sleep in her room."

My grandma hurried into the kitchen, grandpa coughed a little, and Annamaria took out her handkerchief. Tiyana was disinterested; she was playing with a pattern on the colourful tablecloth, following the lines with her finger.

In silence, we drank our tea. We didn't have anything to say to each other as if we were complete strangers. Only Tiyana was openly showing that we were strangers and there was nothing much to talk about. She stood up and said:

"I am off, Mum; if you wish you can stay longer, see you later," then she walked out.

Annamaria said:

"Well, it is about time; it's getting very late. I will come by tomorrow or the day after, when Lora gets some sleep." Before leaving, she kissed me.

When they walked out, I sat next to my grandpa. I asked him again:

"How are you, Grandpa?" and he said:

"How are you, my dear child?"

"It is hard Grandpa; I do not know what to do now."

The he said:

"You ought to be very tired; it would be best to go to sleep now."

Grandma helped me carry my suitcase into Barbara's room. In this room, too, everything smelt of Barbara. For a long time, I looked at everything in the room: the walls, furniture, records, books, toys.

"Is everything the same as it was when she lived here?"

Grandma nodded her head.

The room was not large, but there was room for everything a young girl needed.

In the left corner, next to the door there was a bed, above the bed were paintings of horses and olives, next to these paintings a window (which looked like it could have been a nice painting on the wall itself), on the other side of the window on the opposite wall there were two masks: two clowns—one laughing, the other crying. In the other corner was a wardrobe. Just a plain wardrobe made of very thick wood, for the doors were very, very heavy. There was a big bookcase next to the wardrobe. There were a lot of books on the shelves; there were soft toys there. Above it, there were another two paintings; one was Barbara's portrait on which it was written *Pierre '79*, beneath the portrait a picture of a little angel with big, black round eyes, which resembled the olives in the painting above the bed.

On the other side of the room, in the corner there was a table and on it there was an old record player and a pile of long-play records next to the desk. Above the table there was a hung puppet, next to it a straw hat and a few dry flowers caught in between two square pieces of glass a long time ago. On the other side of the desk there were two rubber dolls—'Stan and Ollie.'

There was a big colourful carpet on the floor, and in front of her bed there was a small dark red carpet. On the ceiling, there was a very beautiful old fashioned chandelier and on the bedside a lamp with a dark red shade, and around its edge some golden crystal beads were hanging.

Grandma was seated on the chair next to the bed, observing me attentively. She said:

"Everything is ready; you can have a shower now and go straight to bed."

When I finished the shower, it looked as if I had washed half of the tiredness out of my body. I wished them good night and went into Barbara's room.

I could not fall asleep that night. I felt as if her spirit was there. Everything here belonged to Barbara; I touched each and every book; I looked at the first page of each of them. In some books, there was written a little dedication, *'for your birthday, from Dado'*. So, Dado was real, he didn't reside only in her imagination; he resided in her neighbourhood. There were some other written dedications (with old dates on them) on her vinyl records, *'to Barbara from Dado'*. I put on some music quietly, the first *Roxy Music* LP. I had never seen that one. In the wardrobe, Barbara's clothes were hanging. I even found a new pair of shoes; they looked as if they had never been worn. Inside the shoes, it was written *Trussardi*. I smelt her perfumes, they smelt right after all those years. There was *Rive Gauche*, the one she always used to put behind her ears. I opened it, smelt it, and the feeling of Barbara's presence intensified; I turned around and saw my reflection in the mirror.

In the last, the largest and deepest drawer of her desk, there was a small typing machine. In other drawers, I found some documents, some photos and a large number of written sheets of paper. I knew those were her stories, which I intended to read whilst here.

In some of the photos, I saw Barbara with a wide grin on her face. I never knew that kind of grin; it was the grin of a cheeky teenager. There were photos with some boys, and I wondered which one was Dado. There were no photos of her and just one boy. There were always six-seven boys and Barbara. Looking attentively at one of those faces, in one, particularly nice photo, I thought, 'He could be the guy with these big black eyes.' I turned the photo but on the other side only the year was written.

I opened the window. The coldish wind blew into my face. Underneath the window, there was a nameless tree. The street was quiet and poorly lit. In some houses the lights were still on; I did not know which one was Dado's house and wondered whether he still lived at the same address. The air outside smelt of Barbara's hands or of Barbara's bosom.

I was very tired; I went to bed. There again, I started to cry. 'Why did she have to die, my Barbara?' I addressed that question, time after time, to a speechless, heartless, invisible someone. Deep down in my heart, I hoped that there was someone who might hear my cries and give me some sign, some indication . . . Someone who might take pity on a child's broken heart (I felt like a little, unprotected child).

2.

I slept an uneasy sleep, Barbara visited my dreams. In the dream, she appeared as the old Barbara, so familiar, so mine; the one which was always telling me how much she loved me and cared for me; the kind, loving mother. But, then, she would appear as completely unknown to me; a young girl who combed her hair in front of the mirror while singing songs I had never heard of. I touched her hair, I wanted to comb her hair, I wanted to kiss her soft hands, the hands of a young girl, I wanted to kiss her eyes, her turquoise eyes of the same colour as the sea which could be seen from the window in grandma's living room.

I woke up very early; it had just dawned. I could not sleep any longer, my bosom was full of anticipation, my breathing was heavy, burdensome. I felt as if someone very heavy sat on my chest and pressed down with all their might.

I looked at the chandelier.

Was this how Barbara would wake up?

The room was quiet and pleasant.

The morning gave a golden glow to a treetop which I could not see properly last evening. It was autumn. My first autumn in Europe. At that moment, it seemed to me as if I had always belonged here—in this apartment, in this room with the view of a tree whose name I did not know, to this autumn . . . It looked as if dormant memories had woken within me. Dormant memories, as if they peeped out through my eyes and saw the world in a new light. It seemed to me on this morning that I lived this life once before, that I knew what was going to unfold. It seemed to me that I was not Lora, that I was somebody else, just slightly resembling Lora until she completely forgot where she came from. I was not Barbara either, but I was someone who just returned home.

I opened the window and breathed the fresh, chilly air. The leaves on the tree were coloured in a few different pastel colours.

Even these leaves smelled like Barbara, they smelled like Barbara's words, they rustled like Barbara's words.

The fact that Barbara had died was so surreal in here. The fact that Barbara lived here was surreal too, just like the fact that she was my mother was surreal. Here, the fact that she had written letters to Ted was as unreal as Ted himself.

While I was looking at the building opposite ours once again, I wondered—which window could be Dado's. I looked at each and every window hoping I might see him, I might recognise him.

So, the days passed: some too fast, some too slow. Life here moved at a much slower pace. People would visit each other; they used to have morning coffee together. But sometimes, I felt that time was just galloping; I could not understand the mentality. So much was happening in such a short amount of time, so many new faces, new customs, new convictions and views. I felt like Alice in Wonderland.

Grandma was a kind and soft soul, full of compassion and love. She would often call me 'Barbara' not even noticing. Sometimes, she would be aware of it and then quickly would correct herself 'pardon, Lora', but more often than not, she was not aware she was calling me by the name that was not mine.

(I did not know if I were made of my name, the name Barbara gave me . . .When somebody called me by that name of mine, which should have represented me, I would think, 'What if I do not answer?' Just like when Grandma would call me 'Barbara', I would think 'What would happen to me if I answered to that name? Would I, by some great mystery, turn into Barbara herself?')

Annamaria and her mother, Auntie Zlatka, visited regularly. I liked going downtown in the mornings with Annamaria. It seemed like everybody knew her. They would stop us, greeting her, "Good morning Annamaria, how are you? Shall we have a coffee together?" During only one morning, we were invited for a cup of coffee several times. She would say, "I am in a hurry, there are things I have to do," but nobody really cared. Her friend would take her under her arm and say: "Nothing is so important that it can't wait, we'll have a cup of coffee first." She would shrug her shoulders in surrender, telling me:

"Let's go to the café."

She presented me to her friends. They all were about the age of my late mother. She would say:

"This is Lora, my cousin Barbara's daughter."

They all remembered Barbara.

It seemed to me that eighteen years were like an eternity; it was the entirety of my life.

But everybody remembered Barbara as if she had left this town only yesterday.

Everybody had a good word for my late mother, I was glad people liked her. Was she aware, back then, how much people liked her in her hometown?

Once, I was sitting in a little café with Annamaria and her friend. She asked him:

"Do you know who this young lady is?"

"I don't," said Marino.

"Do you remember Barbara? Barbara Millich?"

"I do. My God, I remember Barbara. We went together to high school. There is not a soul who doesn't remember Barbara and Dado."

"Lora is Barbara's daughter."

Marino stood up, took my hand in his and planted a kiss on the top of my hand.

Then, three women came in. All very tall, with distinguished features, very stylish. They looked to me as if they were going to the theatre rather than to buy some food and to have a coffee. When they saw Annamaria and Marino, they greeted them; they hugged and kissed each other. Annamaria said:

"Join us, girls."

When they sat at our table, they started teasing Marino, telling him that he never missed the opportunity to take Annamaria for a coffee . . . they said that old love never died. Marino smiled and went to fetch some coffees. Annamaria said:

"This is Lora." Then she introduced each woman by their name. We shook hands. One women asked:

"Are you Tiyana's friend?"

"No, she is Tiyana's cousin. Do you know whose daughter Lora is?"

They did not know, so Annamaria told them:

"Lora is Barbara's daughter. My cousin Barbara."

They did not speak, then one of the women said:

"You look like Barbara. Where is she now?"

Annamaria lowered her head and said:

"Last month, she died. She died in Sydney."

All of them repeated simultaneously:

"Barbara died?"

I saw tears in one woman's eyes. Then silence fell upon the table. When Marino came carrying a tray with coffees, they changed the subject. The woman who had tears in her eyes said to me:

"Barbara was a very good friend of mine. She was a beautiful soul. I am so shaken by this news. I'd like to invite you to my place one of these days," then she said to Annamaria:

"You've got to take Lora to our place, I want Miro to meet her."

They all talked about politics. It was so unbelievable to me. Literally everybody talked about politics: politicians, policemen, TV presenters, housewives, vendors at the market place, neighbours, school teachers, office workers, people in buses, in coffee-shops, families at the dinner table . . . Politics was set in every pore of society; little children in primary school talked about hot political issues, they knew the names and the roles of every politician . . . Just unbelievable. Politics on the streets was not loud words, but whispered ones. That was the first time that I understood what Barbara wanted to say when talking about the Imaginary Someone. Political issues and topics were whispered on the streets and in the *piazzas,* for 'Someone' was still alive, even more alive than before while Barbara walked these streets and fought the ghost of the 'Imaginary Someone'.

***

Tiyana introduced me to the bizarre world of stupidity and emptiness.

(Dark-eyed Tiyana, whose eyes never shone with trust. She could have had different eyes only if she had not tried to cover her fear and uncertainties with haughtiness. In her shallowness, she thought it would be easier to cover real emotions with false ones . . . but she really could not hide it, I saw it in her eyes . . . pretentiousness gave her eyes that cold mist of distrust . . .)

She lived a fake life. She was somebody else, never herself. I never asked her why she was pretending to be someone else (was there something crucial missing from her soul? Was she hiding something deep down; was she ashamed of it?)

The war drastically lowered the living standard in the country. War was accompanied by crime and deception. Majority of people lived on the edge of poverty, barely surviving; it was so obvious, even to me. The minority, the ones who robbed the majority, lived well. Again, it was so obvious even though people would not talk about it openly. They were only muttering it. Their faces were grey from deceit. The faces were grey from empty promises.

Tiyana belonged to a wealthier, middle class family, which went completely broke after the war. After her father, Ivan, lost his job and money, he soon found a new job in Morocco as an architect. It made their life much easier but still, it was hard to meet all their needs. Annamaria was a bank employee, she told me that her wage couldn't afford them weekly groceries. I was shocked:

"You're kidding, aren't you?" and she said:

"I wish I were kidding."

Ivan worked illegally, so they feared one day he would be caught and sent back home (if not deported for good). One of the reasons why Ivan went to Morocco was because Annamaria and Tiyana had to keep the image and standard of a wealthy middle class family at all costs. Even with him working in Morocco, it was impossible to keep the standard they once had, prices were sky-rocketing; it was unbelievable for me (again, like Alice in Wonderland, I was astonished by the high prices, by their way of life, by everything I saw . . .)

Annamaria and Ivan had two children: Tiyana and Nino. Nino was twenty-five and unemployed. Tiyana studied at university.

Nino was a down to earth young man but in the war, he saw meaninglessness and lies, plunder, cruelty and death, so he withdrew into his own world. He rarely spoke. He locked himself in his room listening to music and smoking all day long. He smoked so much, just like all the other people there—everyone smoked too much. Not only did they smoke a lot, but a lot of people drank far too much. 'War habits' I was told. (It all looked like some surreal American movie, the ones Barbara didn't allow me to watch . . .)

Tiyana did not live down to earth. I did not know where she lived, in which world she resided, but certainly she behaved as if she did not belong to the time and circumstance of her actual reality. She behaved as if her father was an architect in the richest country in the world, and as if her mother was the director of the richest bank. (Her mother too, as if she were in some old movie . . .) Her clothes were worth more than all the clothes, furniture and jewelry which belonged to me and Barbara, combined. She had countless shoes; every season she just had to buy several pairs of shoes—winter and summer collections, then the handbags which should match the shoes . . . She would change coats twice during the winter. Everything had to be first class, the most expensive and with a designer label.

"Why?" I asked Annamaria in dismay. She said:

"She was always used to that." (I was not happy with the shallow answer).

"But these times have gone; she can't afford it anymore."

"Oh, poor Tiyana, at least she can afford beautiful clothes if nothing else."

"Is that at all costs? Is there nothing else except the latest fashion trends? Can't she be happy with reading a new book?"

Annamaria shrugged her shoulders while lifting her arms in the air:

"I do not know how long we will last like this. I simply don't."

One afternoon, Tiyana invited me to come over (it was not her wish, she wanted to please her mother). She said we would go out with her friends, whilst looking at me with that particular look in her eyes; the one of indifference or disdain. She said:

"Don't you have anything better to wear? I can't take you with me dressed like that. My friends will laugh at you, and me, too. Look at yourself, aren't you aware of how silly you look. Is that what you wear over there? When people come from these overseas countries, they all look like little ridiculous clowns. Please, go and get changed. Put on something decent, we are not going to the carnival."

I said to her (even though I should not have):

"I brought a suitcase full of clothes. I know that you would not like any of my dresses. Well, there is no need to go and change into something similar; all my dresses are of a simple make, they are not designer dresses, they are much cheaper. My mother wasn't the best paid writer in the world. We spent our money on different things. She bought me a violin; she paid for lessons; she took me often to the theatre and to the Opera House. Barbara used to buy me books, recently she bought me a new computer . . ." my eyes were filled with tears and I nearly started crying (I was not hurt by the tone of her voice, I was not hurt by her insolence and her shallow persona, but I was hurt by my own weakness to stand up to her and say, 'Sorry, I can't go with you today.')

Tiyana said:

"What? Are you going to cry now? We do not dress like that here; look, you don't even have a proper bag. Fine, I will lend you some of my clothes, but be careful, they are fine clothes, do not ruin them."

She sized me up with her eyes while opening the sliding doors of her wardrobe. She was standing in front of her built-in wardrobe in her underwear and bra looking at the meticulously arranged clothes. Next to the wardrobe, there was a big mirror on the wall and often she would glance at her reflection out of the corner of her eye. In front of the mirror was a small side table and on it, there were many bottles of expensive, good smelling, perfumes. She picked some clothes, threw them on the bed, saying:

"Try this; I think this will suit you well."

I tried it on without a word (But I should have told her something. Something which would define me as Lora. Barbara would certainly say something . . .)

What I tried on was a short dress and a little jacket. Inside it said, *Chanel*. I knew what *Chanel* was, but I really did not care.

She said:

"It suits you well. Be careful wearing it."

Still observing me, she said:

"What are we going to do with your hair? It just hangs down, looks like spaghetti. First of all, go and have a shower, what will we do with your hair . . . we'll see later. After that, I will apply some makeup on you."

"I do not like makeup. I like when my hair falls naturally; I like my face without any makeup." That was all I said, but I should have said something different. I wanted to say something else, but . . . I did not, I just suppressed it . . .

"Yeah, yeah, a face without makeup, what a plain Jane! Today, you are in my hands."

When Tiyana finished her work of 'improving' my looks, a new hairdo and makeup, I looked at myself in the mirror. That was not me. That was some cover girl from *Cosmopolitan* magazine. I laughed a little covering my mouth with my hand. Proudly, she said:

"You see; you are pretty, why wouldn't you want to show it? In your silly dresses, and without any makeup, you honestly look as if you were skipping around with kangaroos."

I was astonished at how makeup could change one's looks, but regardless, I still didn't like that Lora who was looking at me from the other side of the mirror. That wasn't me. It was a false self.

It took hours for Tiyana to get ready. She said we were going just for a drink but she polished herself as if she was going to the *Metropolitan Opera.* When I told her that, she commented:

"You never know where you can end up. Who knows, we might even end up at the *Metropolitan Opera?* Before we left, she generously poured perfume all over us (I feared a headache!)

When Annamaria saw us, she said:

"My Lord, Tiyana, what have you done to Lora!" (It must have been so ridiculous).

Tiyana said:

"Finally, this creature looks like a woman . . ." ('but what kind of woman,' I wanted to ask).

Annamaria laughed, winking at me, she said:

"Look after her, Tiyana; you know what the boys are like here."

"Do not worry Mum, she is not the type my friends fancy." ('Not even this disguised?', I wondered).

I was not to the taste of her male friends. Neither her girl-friends. But they were not to my taste either. Nobody behaved naturally, and nobody was really what they pretended to be.

A big lie. They all had masks on their faces (I thought they should have felt exactly like I was feeling with all this heavy makeup on my face, and only I knew who was underneath it).

They had three topics.

The first topic was—daily politics. The second topic was—wardrobe, and the third was—who shagged whom the night before. I could not understand anything.

So, as I said before, a war happened in that country. I could not understand why a war happened in the first place, even when I was told 'the reasons', even when they explained it to me many times. I thought that war was led by hatred and greed, actions governed by the lowest of urges (I could not believe that war could be born from the highest of urges. How superior was one ideal that people willingly wanted to die or kill others for it? What kind of high urge could justify plunders, killings, arsons and other brutalities which come with war?)

People who had been living here for generations spoke the same language, they behaved in the same way, their custom and dress code were the same, and the food they ate was the same. How did they recognise the 'enemy'? I could not grasp that; they were all of the same skin colour and birthplace. Tiyana was right when she told me, 'You, the Australian, you do not understand a thing."

I thought that one can't understand war.

They went to war with a song on their lips and flags lifted high above their heads.

They came back from the war with a song on their lips and flags lifted high above their heads.

And then peace came.

But still they talked about the war. The enemy was banished, but the threat of the enemy was ever present. They were told that they still have to 'work hard', to 'live hard', 'to be on the lookout', for the enemy never slept, so Mr. 'Imaginary Someone' wasn't asleep . . . (Maybe I got it . . . maybe it was just the fault of 'Someone' . . .)

We were sitting on the terrace of one of the cafés on the *piazza* (Tiyana, me, the other girls with colourful faces, and the dapper boys) when, Tiyana said to her friend, with an annoying intensity in her voice:

"*Why,* on earth, did you say hello to her? Do you know *who* she is?" She blew her cigarette smoke right into his face. (I thought, 'Here we go; a little theatre will start!')

He said:

"She is a journalist." (A label!)

"I am not asking you what her profession is. I am asking you—do you know *who* she is?" (More labels needed!)

"No, I don't know." I detected both: caution and a question in his answer. (And I thought, 'Here we go; now we will have a dramatic crescendo!)

In a quieter voice, full of conspiracy, she whispered:

"She is *one of them* . . . too."

(And I started turning around in a sincere attempt to catch a glimpse of *them* . . . if not *all of them,* then, at least, one of *them,* at least, Mr. 'Imaginary Someone', at least one glance, to see the contours of him, to have at least a slight notion, to have at least a supposition . . .)

These were regular conversations and they meant:

"But look at *us.* Look how beautiful, how clever, sophisticated we are. Look how honest, strong and brave, the best on this planet Earth—we are. Look at *us;* the entire world and everyone in it envies *us*, for we are the best and the strongest; they all want to be like *us*, but they can't, for *we are* the chosen ones and nobody else can come close to *us*; nobody can disguise themselves and pass as *one of us*."

Tiyana went to church every Sunday (but not because she searched for God). To go to church was the new trend of this new society. She never believed in her 'devotion' but was rather devoted to showing off—showing off where she belonged, to emphasise her distinction. What was deep down, she was never aware of. Annamaria was often overly proud of Tiyana's dull proclamations.

Well, that was the way they talked, and I could not understand a word. I could not recognise *them* . . . me, poor little Lora . . . it seemed to me that all of *them* looked the same; *they* talked the same language, *they* acted in the same way . . . It seemed to me that *they* were all the same; the citizens of this beautiful town where *their* ancestors lived before *them*.

It was smart and good if you were able to recognise the differences and single out the enemy, publicly, loudly, for others to see how good you were in uncovering *them,* and that you were *one of us* for doing it.

Lots of people, when hearing that I came from Australia to visit my grandparents, would ask me:

"Who are your grandparents? Tell us who your family are, so we know who we are dealing with."

When I would say who my grandparents were, some people would say, "So, well, you *are one of us,*" and some would say,

"Yes, you *are one of us* . . . but you know, your grandfather . . . he never was clear about anything . . . he never took a side. He kept quiet. One who is not with *us,* certainly is against *us*. He still has not proved his loyalty; we do not know what he really thinks." (They must always know other people's opinions).

What I thought was this part of the world looked like some sort of a sanatorium (infectious ward!), paranoia dominated streets and their homes.

I wanted to ask (but I did not, governed or cautioned by a strange feeling): 'What about tolerance? What about the human right to be different? What about respect for others, the ones who wish to be different?' I understood there and then that it was a process in time. When I went to kindergarten, I was taught to accept and respect our friends, regardless of our differences. More than that—they told us to like the different ones even more, because of these differences we were able to learn more, to know more, to become richer . . . or we got it wrong in Australia . . . or was it just me, poor little Lora, unable to grasp some deeper meaning . . .?

Upon entering my room, with a worried expression on her face, Grandma asked:

"What are you listening to, dear?"

"The radio."

"Yes, yes, but what station? Please, change it, on this station they talk rubbish . . ."

"But Grandma . . ."

"Don't, honey. What if the neighbours hear you; it would be bad. In the neighbourhood, they do not like Marko anymore."

I switched off the radio.

On the other radio stations, they were singing songs about the state and their leader. I could not bear to listen to that. It was the same with television programs. Some programs we listened to very quietly.

Everybody had the right to ask, 'Who are you?'; 'Which political party do you belong to?'; 'Who did you vote for?', for they needed to know 'who they were dealing with'.

There were so many police officers on the streets. At any time, without any apparent reason they had the right to ask for your identification card. They told me that I must carry my passport at all times.

On our way back home, Tiyana said:

"Did you have a good time?"

"I did," I lied in a quiet voice and hurried towards the corridor. She followed:

"Give me back my suit."

I thought that she really must have been nuts believing that I had a good time in her skimpy *Chanel* suit.

I found Grandma worried. She said, I was out the whole day.

I gave Tiyana back her little *Chanel* suit (the highlight of her day!), after which she left our apartment without uttering a word to me or to Grandma.

"What happened, Lora?"

"I am tired, Grandma. What is wrong with this country?"

"Well . . . it is an unusual place, my child, isn't it?"

And for Tiyana, she said:

"I do not know what's wrong with her. Something is wrong there; but she was always like that. She had always pretended to live a life of high society; she used to spend unreasonable sums of money, and I never knew where it came from. One of the neighbours told me (and the neighbours knew it well; they knew everything) that she was seeing an older gentleman, a German man; the other neighbour said (maybe that one had better insight) that she was trafficking expensive goods from Italy. I do not know if either is true. Annamaria pretends she does not know, does not see anything; her father is not here, but regardless, even if he were he would not be able to do a thing. I really do not know where and when a mistake was made . . . maybe children are just born the way they are and there is nothing much to change, not even with good upbringing."

"Grandma, why is there a need to change somebody?"

"What do you mean, Lora?"

"Well, if she is the way she is, you should accept her just the way she is. Maybe it would be the easier way to live, for everyone. I do not believe that Annamaria is pretending 'not to see anything wrong'; I think she has accepted Tiyana the way she is. I do not like her particularly, but she is the way she is. We can accept her or not, but no one should strive to change her. It isn't good trying to change someone according to your own needs and wants . . ."

Grandma nodded her head while following me to my room.

When I was in my bed, she sat next to me. She held my hand in hers, and I said:

"Grandma, I do not understand anything here."

She smiled:

"My sweet child, I do not understand, either. Many of us don't understand. Many pretend they do understand, and many have just come to realise what has been happening here. But it is too late now. It is too late." She repeated it, looking at her wristwatch, "It would be better to go to sleep now."

"I am not sleepy, Grandma. Talk to me about Barbara."

I saw a little smile dance on her tired face. A barely detectable little smile coloured by nostalgia. I saw shadows dancing in her eyes and in her quiet voice, she whispered:

"My, Barbara," then she squeezed my hand tighter.

I said again:

"Grandma, talk to me about my mother. I came here wanting to know all about her. It seems to me that I knew so little about my mother."

"What do you want me to tell you about Barbara?"

"Tell me what was she like when she was a little child; what was she like when she was a young girl, a teenager and a young lady. Tell me about her and Dado. Tell me everything until the day she went to Australia."

She looked at me silently. I said:

"I know about her and Dado. She told me everything. But it was not enough. I want to know more about her, about them. Tell me everything from the beginning, what was she like, what did she love, what was she thinking . . ."

After a deep sigh, Grandma wiped her teary eyes:

"Barbara was herself from the very day she was born."

3.

"We had only her. She was our pride and joy; we wanted her to be the way we wanted her to be. But she wasn't that way. (And it happens like that).

We never took her seriously enough.

Why was she so different to the other kids? I can't tell you, she just was.

Why was I constantly trying to change her, I did not know; I can say I know now, but it is too late, I can't do anything about it anymore.

She was an extremely sensitive and nervous child. Her reactions were quick, jumpy and sharp, from the very beginning.

She liked to play with boys. She never liked girls; she would say that 'girls always make things complicated'.

She grew up with Dado. They went to kindergarten together, then to primary school. They shared everything, she would bring him home very often; winter days they would spend in her room playing games or watching television in the living room. We never had anything against their friendship. Or, maybe sometimes, Marko would say that he wasn't from 'the best family'. We hoped Barbara would continue the friendships we cultivated for many years. But she never liked our friends' children for they were 'average and boring', as she would put it. She would say that she never learned anything from them. She would say they were so neat and predictable, that they gave her a skin rash.

At that time, I never believed that a child could be 'different'. I always thought the right upbringing was everything. As Barbara grew up, she was more and more her own self. She did not respect any 'traditional recipes' as she used to call my advice. Whatever I would say, she would think about it and then ask:

'And why is it so?'

There was no answer which would satisfy her.

When she was a teenager, I would find her sitting in her room often apathetic, and in a foul mood.

'What happened, Barbara? Why such a bad mood?'

She would say:

'I don't know, Mummy. But this is not—it.'

'What is "it," my child?'

'I don't know, Mum, but you do not understand me.'

'What do you mean, I don't understand you? You tell me what you want me to understand and I will try.'

'Never mind.'

I would blame puberty. Sometimes, I would blame genetics—Marko's brother was never happy. I tried to avoid the truth, the truth that Barbara was not happy, so I would blame Dado as well.

'Maybe he had a bad influence on Barbara. He was always quiet and gloomy.' Then I thought 'it will pass'.

She was an exceptional student. The best in her class. Even though she rarely studied. But she read a lot. She read many books; every day she was with a new book. For a child of her age, those books were far too serious and demanding. All of her free time, if she was not with Dado, she spent with a book. At school, they told me she was 'too smart'; they told me she had 'a long and a sharp tongue.'

She was obsessed with *the truth.*

For her, the truth was a sacred thing. She used to say that everybody lied. Teachers lied, parents lied, neighbours lied, politicians, salesmen in the shops—they were all liars. Only, my Barbara, was telling the truth. She was so obsessed with the truth, that her majesty, the Truth, had a very bad impact on her relationship with teachers, friends and her marks at school, as well.

'Davor is the only one who understands me.' Barbara would claim when she answered the question, 'Why do you insist on the truth even if it could harm you or somebody else?'

She was a rebel. Because of Davor, she ended up interrogated at the police station, twice. She would defend the weak, and she was always ready to attack the oppressor, even though she was petite and of a thin, gentle frame, she had frail nerves . . .

I used to tell her:

'Barbara, you are not going to change the world; things are the way they are, and they were always like that and always will be.' She would answer:

'But we need a better world. Look around, Mother, where does all that lead us? Lies and corruption dominate our world; we admire those who came into power sucking the blood of the weak; we appreciate those who obtained their wealth by stealing it from others or deceiving them; we adore anorexic women with silicon breasts and aspire to look like them . . . everything is a lie, rottenness; I do not want to be part of such a world!'

'But, Barbara, the world was always like that and it always will be; you are not going to change anything.'

'Maybe I can't change anything, but I do not want to be a part of it. So, do not ask me why I don't choose, as you say, 'better people' for friends. Who are these "better people"? Stella? Is she "better" only because her father is a surgeon? You know, these "better people" talk only about what they just bought or where they spent last night.'

'But, what else should girls your age talk about?'

'Mother, you do not understand me.' She would turn her head to the other side; she would reach for a book and end the conversation.

She would say Davor was the only one who understood her. I was fond of Davor, ever since he was a little boy. I knew his father since our school days; he used to be a good friend of mine. His father was creative as well, at home he played the piano, and he carried a guitar to school. He never finished college; he got into real trouble with one of the male teachers; he left college that same year and never graduated. He was really, really talented. He played so beautifully, and his voice was even more beautiful. He was a very good young man; he knew how to cultivate a friendship. He got married very young as Davor's mother was already pregnant; she was in the last year of college. Poor soul, she died young; she died while giving birth. He went to Germany; so, Davor, a tiny baby, stayed with his grandmother. Whenever he came back, we talked about kids and other things. He told me he was doing 'God knows what' in Germany. But I think that he did . . . not so honorable things there . . . he always opted for the more difficult choice, but he was a distinguished piano player, he was such a good guitar player . . .

Davor and Barbara loved each other since they knew each other. Marko would say that 'Barbara needed a better friend' and I would defend him, 'Davor is a good child.' Marko would say, 'Nobody really cares about that child. He is growing up with two old women, how can they raise him properly?'

When the husband of Davor's grandmother's sister died, she moved in with them, thus there were two grandmothers raising Davor. I would often invite him to have lunch with us, or bake a cake and invite him; I had so much tenderness for that child. Barbara loved him so much, and when they were little kids they were like brother and sister. Barbara was only completely happy when Davor was around. When he would leave, the sparkle in her innocent eyes would leave as well; the exhilaration in her voice would cease. There weren't any games that could hold her interest any longer.

When she was a bit older, she used to fix motorbikes with Davor and go to rock concerts.

At that time, Marko was openly against their friendship, and I would hide that she was going out with him. They were fifteen. I would say to Marko that Barbara went to the library to borrow a book, and then I would rush to the window where I would hang a red towel. The red towel was a signal—time to come home. I never told her I was lying to Marko about her whereabouts. I told her that this 'red towel' was our secret and nobody needed to know about it, not even Davor. She would take her secrets 'to the grave' . . ."

When Grandma said, 'to the grave' she started crying again. She hugged me, I hugged her and we cried together. I told her, sobbing:

"Grandma, it is so painful to lose your mother. To lose a mother full of love, full of sweet sadness . . . to lose a mother full of sweet mystery and the sweetest words . . ."

She kissed my hair and pressed my head against her bosom. It must have been very difficult for her too; I couldn't even imagine what it was like to lose a child, but I thought the hardest thing was to lose a mother. Grandma didn't say a word, she only held me tight against her bosom. Much later, she said:

"Now you are the only one left."

With all of Grandma's love, I felt utterly alone in this world. That is the feeling when your mother dies.

4.

"What happened between her and Davor, I had never found out. On that particular day, I came back home and the door to her room was locked. I called her name, 'Barbara, Barbara', knowing that she was locked in her room. But a response never came. A fear rose in me; this icy fear rushed to my face and all my hair stood up. The feeling of utter horror, known only to a mother when faced with something out of the ordinary . . . something extremely unusual . . . I started yelling, 'Barbara, Barbara, open the door!' I was yelling so loudly that all the neighbours came out. In all this commotion, I saw Marko coming; he broke the door and we found her with her head slumped against the desk. The entire room smelled of alcohol, and on the mirror it was written, 'Farewell Davor', or something like that. I knelt down on my trembling knees and started crying and calling her name at the same time.

She did not regain consciousness; we did not know what had happened; we did not know if she was still alive. We took her to the local hospital where she was treated immediately. Time dissolved.

She came back home worn out and frail; she didn't talk to us; she just had an uncertain smile on her pale face. That day, Marko went to see Davor; he never told me what they spoke about. He never said a word.

Barbara, never, ever, asked about Davor again.

All her friends from university, her friends from the neighbourhood came to visit, everybody visited, except—Davor.

She didn't ask about him then, or ever again.

All that happened in autumn 1981. That same year, she enrolled into Law School, and for the winter holidays, she went to Australia, to visit Aurelio.

Aurelio called wanting to know what happened to Barbara. He invited her to come to Sydney; he offered to pay for the plane ticket. Aurelio loved Barbara, even though they never shared the same views about the world and people in general, but they had a similar sensibility for other things. Their differences never diminished their closeness. She was never close to Annamaria, but her relationship with Aurelio was entirely different.

When she decided to visit Aurelio, we readily supported her initiative.

She left in February 1982.

When she left, Davor disappeared, as well. I never knew where he had gone; we never saw him again. Some neighbours said they saw him coming home two or three times per year. Somebody told me he went to Germany, went to his father, but I had never seen him again.

Marko and I were enthusiastic about her going to Australia. We thought it would be fun to be with Aurelio. He was a funny, charming character who loved an easy, comfortable life and good parties. We thought that was precisely what Barbara needed at that time: a sea change, and a bit of fun.

Shortly after she left, her first letter arrived. She wrote that she was lonesome. Her letters showed much distress. Her thoughts were so deep, disturbing and full of profound pain; still, I could not understand her. I thought that this distress and pain were because of her lost love, that she was grieving for Davor.

Now, I do not think so. I think that she was born this way. I think her life ended exactly the way it was meant to end. I think there were no choices. All my life, I tried to understand Barbara, and help her to the best of my knowledge. But there was no understanding; there was no help. She lived in a world where I never belonged and was never able to visit, or to understand it. I think now that only Barbara and Davor, only the two of them, lived in some sort of an ideal world, 'The World of Truth', and the rest of the world never counted for them.

Now, when I think about my unfortunate child, I ask again and again—'Why?' Barbara had all the predispositions to be a happy person. She had a loving family; we were reasonably well off; we could provide her with a very good life. She had friends who loved her; she went to the best schools; she was one of the best students. She was writing, nobody stood in her way; we bought her an electric typewriter, at that time only a few reputable companies had electric typewriters.

We thought we gave her all we could have, all we had known. We thought, we gave her enough love and attention. But Barbara was never happy. Over and over, I asked myself—why?

Auntie Zlatka paid me a visit a short while after Barbara went to Australia. She enquired:

'Any news from Barbara?'

'No, it looks like all is well.'

She was quiet for a short time, then she said:

'I have a friend who knows a woman who reads from a coffee cup; let's see what is in store for Barbara. Apparently, the woman is very accurate; she came somewhere from the East; she has olive skin and, sort of Oriental eyes, but she is not a Gypsy.'

I said:

'Zlatka, I am a psychologist, yet I can't figure out what kind of future Barbara longs for. Do you really think I would go to a Gypsy woman? You know that this kind of thing is for naïve people, not me who believes that we hold the keys to destiny in our own hands, and so does my Barbara.'

When she left, I thought to myself, 'Maybe we should go, just out of curiosity.'

A few days later we paid her a visit, 'just out of curiosity'.

We entered an overcrowded room with old furniture. She said, 'Sit down.' We sat on the little old sofa to which she pointed with her hand. She was seated in a chair at a little round table.

Yes, she had a sort of Oriental shape of eyes; she had dark, smooth hair tied up at the back of her head with a red scarf. I could not figure out her age. Her nose was long but straight, profile almost noble. She had long slender fingers, her movements were very slow, delayed. Very strange kind of sparkle shone in her dark eyes. Her eyes looked to me like the eyes of a conman, or someone who could penetrate into the unknown. I just wanted to get up and leave the room when she addressed me with her lingering voice, hoarse from nicotine:

'Tereza . . . sit down . . . I am going to brew some coffee now.'

She left the room. There was a stiffness in the air. Or was it simply anxiety? On the table and on other pieces of furniture there were many ashtrays, jam-packed with cigarette butts, and half-smoked cigarettes. On the other sofa, a cat was snoozing; it seemed that the smell in the air was the smell of cat excrement. I said to Zlatka:

'We should not have come.'

She just winked at me, putting her index finger across her lips.

The woman came in carrying a tray with coffee cups on it. She said we could call her Zelda, but I suspected Zelda was not her real name. Later, we heard that name again; she was widely recognised as 'the one' when it came to fortune telling.

In complete silence, we drank our coffees. When we finished, she showed us how to 'turn the cup upside down'. She told us to wait for figures to form out of the sediment and left the room. Zlatka and I were sitting silently in that room, both filled with strange apprehension. When she walked in again, she came in different clothes: she had a bright-red *sari*, and her hair was covered with a black silken scarf. She told Zlatka to sit at the table, so she sat herself next to me and took my hand in hers.

She stared at me with her hypnotic stare and said in a coarse voice:

'Your soul is heavy with suffering.'

I thought she was playing a game. I never trusted fortune tellers, and while Zelda was staring into my eyes, I asked myself, 'How could I have been so naïve?' After all, I was a psychologist, she could not be a better psychologist than I to penetrate into my mind. I thought she would try to observe my face, my gestures, mannerism, or by the colour and intonation of my voice to assemble my apparent future, and to enter my 'soul heavy with suffering'.

So, there we were—both full of mistrust evaluating each other. The long minutes dragged, they felt like long hours while we stared into each other's eyes with my hand clasped in hers. When I asked myself for the second time, 'How could I have exposed myself to such nonsense?' she said:

'Your soul is heavy with suffering.'

'You said that already,' rushed out of my mouth.

At once, she changed her expression; she became so serious, her look was extremely stern. With a coarse voice, she said:

'You don't want me to repeat myself? Good. I will tell you now what you came to hear. This time you will hear the truth, nothing but the truth, without me repeating myself.'

Shivers ran down my spine from her mean look. She lit a cigarette and inhaled a few times, then she said:

'What is her name? Does it start with the letter B?'

I nodded my head and uncontrollably the name came out of my mouth:

'Barbara.'

'Barbara . . . remember Barbara . . . it was raining unceasingly on Brest that day, and you walked, smiling, flushed, enraptured, streaming-wet . . . Barbara is going to meet another man. Very soon. His name will start with T; he will wear a white mantle, so it is likely that he will be a doctor, if not, certainly, his field will be a medical field. Barbara will never forget a young man because of whom she had tried to take her own life; she will never stop loving him, but she will never meet him again. Yet, her daughter will meet him. Barbara is going to have a daughter; maybe she will name her with a name commencing with the letter L, I am not sure, for her father will want another name for his daughter. But when Barbara decides . . . anything she decides . . . it has to be her way.'

She fell silent while lighting another cigarette. My knees were shaking, my fingers trembling, I looked at Zlatka trying to figure out if she had told this woman something about Barbara, but there wasn't any expression on her face. The prophet of ill fate continued:

'She will get married in some far-away land . . . maybe she is already there . . . and, I see, she will never come back to this city. She will be very recognised for her work in several countries; I would say even continents, but the recognition will come after she dies. She will die before the age of forty.'

When she said that, I abruptly stood up, dragged Zlatka out of the woman's apartment, while she yelled after us:

'Oh, classy ladies, fine ladies, come back and pay! You want me to tell you your future, you want to hear nice things, you want fancy things to hear, you want to hear what you want to hear. You cheats, give me my money!'

Zlatka opened her purse, took out some money and threw it towards the apartment. She came down a few steps, collected her money, grumbling.

For days, I told myself that I didn't believe a word she told me. I repeated it to myself over and over being aware that Zelda told me facts she could never have known.

When Aurelio went to Australia, Zelda told Zlatka these exact words:

'There is nothing I could possibly say about your son. He can't escape his fate even if he came back home.'

Later, we learned what she meant."

5.

"One year had not yet passed since she left, she rang and simply said:

'Mother, I am going to get married.'

I fell into a deep silence; she thought that the line dropped, so she yelled:

'Mum, Mum, do you hear me?'

'I do hear you Barbara. But what are you talking about?'

'I am going to marry Ted, Mother.'

'Who is Ted?'

'He is a pharmacist. I work at his pharmacy.'

'Barbara, do you love Ted?'

'I think I do.'

'You think. Is it enough just to think that you love somebody and based on this premise make such an important decision as to tie yourself to them?'

'Mum, Ted makes me happy. He makes me laugh . . .'

I cut her short in the middle of her sentence:

'You have my blessing if that's why you rang . . . marry him, Barbara. If Ted makes you happy, if you think that this happiness will last . . . marry him.'

After that conversation, I cried bitterly. I could not understand why she made such a big decision hurriedly. I didn't know who Ted was, and if she really did love him. I knew how madly she loved Dado. She wasn't the kind of person who would be ready to love again so quickly. But she lived there, sixteen thousand kilometers away from home, and I really could not grasp what kind of life she had there. In Barbara's voice, I felt happiness and enthusiasm, and after all, all I wanted for her was to be happy regardless of where she was.

When I told the news to Marko, his hands fell on the table; he went pale and mumbled:

'She wants to marry Ted? Who the hell is Ted?'

'He is a pharmacist. She works in his pharmacy.'

'What do we know about Ted?'

'Absolutely nothing, Marko.'

'What does she know about Ted?'

'I do not know. Maybe she does not know anything either.'

We asked Aurelio, and he said:

'Ted is a very fine gentleman. He has his own pharmacy; he is some fifteen years older than Barbara.'

That was all we knew about Ted.

After that, we rang her and asked if the wedding date had been set. We asked her if she wanted us to come, but she said she didn't want us to have 'unplanned expenses'. We had unplanned devastation. We did not know who Ted was; did he genuinely love our daughter; what kind of life could he give to Barbara; we didn't know if we would ever meet him. As you know, in the eight years of their marriage we never met him. We saw him in photos Barbara sent, but for us he always remained sort of unreal. We would imagine who he was, what kind of life they had, what kind of relationship or conversations they had, what plans they had . . .They never came to Europe.

Barbara was of few words; she never liked talking about an uncertain future.

Then she had a child. We never knew she was pregnant. She said that this 'was not an important piece of information'. She said that a child would come regardless of if we knew about it or not.

I could not wait to get a photograph of our little granddaughter. She wrote:

'Her name is Lora. It sounds really noble. When she was born, I saw pride and sophistication in her eyes and thought that the name Lora would match. Ted wanted to call her Maddison, but I knew she was—Lora.'

Oh, Lora, my dearest little girl, you used to come to my dreams. At night, I would cry hiding my tears from Marko and pressing your picture to my bosom. I didn't know when I would be able to see you. We always waited for Barbara to invite us, but she never did. So, one day Marko called her and said that we were keen to visit them, but she said:

'Maybe next year, Dad; it is not a good time right now.'

She said that twice and after the second time, we never offered to come again.

Then one day, suddenly, she rang:

'Ted left us. Mummy, everything around me is so strange. Only Lora gives me the strength to endure. I am so tired. To soothe you, I can tell you that I was not really shaken by his leaving. There is some other kind of tiredness which crept into my body, into my heart. I am writing, Mum, and this is the only thing that warms my soul. Mum, I want you to come here; I want to be your little girl again. Come, Mummy; come, I want to put my head on your lap; I want Marko to be the strongest man in my world once again.'

Marko and I spent that night crying like two little children.

Barbara asked for our help, the first time in her life—openly.

It was the first time that we met you.

I was never as excited, in my entire life, as those days before our trip to Sydney. We had not seen Barbara for more than eight years; we had not ever met you. I was afraid of our meeting. I was afraid of what would Barbara look like. I was afraid of meeting my granddaughter I had never met before. You were so polite and such a sweet child. I was surprised, I did not know myself why I would be, for Barbara too had a kind heart full of compassion, why wouldn't she pass that onto her child? I was pleasantly surprised with Barbara's life, with her child. She told me about Ted. She said she respected him a lot; she said he tried to provide all she asked for, then she smiled and said:

'But the problem was that Barbara herself never knew what she really wanted.'

'Is it still like that, Barbara?'

'Yes, Mum, I am still like that. Still, I have not grown up. Still, I am a little child. Because of that, having a child was very difficult for me. Everything in my life was too difficult to cope with. Only my tremendous love for Lora kept me going. You know that I could hardly ever put up with responsibilities. You know how unpredictable I was. I could not be myself anymore; it was too difficult at that time. I thought that I had lost myself completely; I did not know who I was any longer. I could not write nor could I dream with my eyes open. Ted helped me a lot. He was a good father. One day he simply walked out. We never argued. It could be my fault that he left; I was always nervous, but it is my nature. I never knew if he understood that it was simply my nature, that he could not improve it with his efforts or his good will. He could not accept me the way I was; he could not love me the way I was. Peace and order were what Ted was searching for. I was not a person of peace and order. You know, we were just too different. When he loved me without a doubt, he put up with me and my sudden mood swings. Maybe he just stopped loving me. He left. He did not say a word, he just left a short letter and closed the door behind him, forever.'

I advised her to call him. I advised her to invite him and to talk about you, Lora, about your future. She did not say anything. I knew that she would not call him, she would never ask for his help. It seems as if she always opted for difficult choices; she chose a difficult life; it seems as if she deliberately chose illnesses and anxiety as if living like that, her characters would live easier within her head and in her stories.

When we visited the second time, she looked so tired; she looked as if she grew old quickly. There was that uncertain but fearful assumption in my heart, and I silenced that inner voice consciously. Barbara had dark circles around her eyes, and there was no shine in them. She was not a child anymore.

I asked her:

'Do you think, dear, that you are an adult now, completely grown up?'

She said:

'I grew old. You know, Mum, until last year, I was still that big child, never ready to grow up, and now, only a year later, I feel like a tired old woman.'

I did not comment on it, for Barbara used to be theatrical at times. She would put on a little theatre and drag us all into her plot, giving us, unconsciously, roles which she would reuse again in her prose. I never answered to her pathetic remarks, but I was worried because of her looks.

On that visit, we spent a lot of time with you while Barbara was writing.

Once, I asked her:

'Barbara, will you allow me to read some of your stories?' I hoped I might find what was troubling my little girl. She shrugged her shoulders:

'Better not, Mum . . . it is depressing, mainly. You would identify the narrator with me, but what I am writing is not a part of myself, it is pure fiction.'

'Even better. I'd like to see your imagination at work, please, Barbara.'

She would never say 'No', this word never existed in her vocabulary. She would simply say 'Next time', and I knew it meant 'No'.

I said to Marko that her appearance worried me too much, and he promised he would talk to her. He asked her out to dinner, and you and I stayed at home. Do you remember, we baked a cake together?

Upon his return, in bed, we whispered long into the night. Marko was retelling me their conversation. He asked her if she wanted to come back home. She said she did not belong there any longer. She never liked small towns; she was a big-city girl. She would say that only in big cities with its diversity and its inclusion she could breathe freely, small places were suffocating her free spirit.

We never talked about Davor again, but I think he was the reason why she never wanted to come back, not even to visit. Marko was very concerned about the state of her health. She defended herself telling him that she looked the way she did because she had exhausted herself writing the latest novel. He asked her how many novels she had written altogether. We were astonished—ten novels in ten years.

She said to Marko that she was writing the last novel day and night, that she slept very little; she said she ate very little; she said it had exhausted her completely. She carried so much pain in her eyes that it was painful for me to look at her. I asked her, did she still feel 'world pain', and she nodded her head. 'Where did that come from?' I asked myself countless times. Where did it come from; this unbearable pain in her eyes, in her bosom and in her bones? Did she carry it even before she was born, even before she was conceived? Where did she bring this pain from, the pain which had eaten her soul and her insides, the pain which had eaten my soul and was still gnawing at it?

I started looking for answers in Buddhism. I started reading books about reincarnation; I started studying biographies of the authors of 'world pain', all in the hope—that I would be given, at least, one simple answer to the questions which were unanswerable. But she was my child; I should have known her the best. And I did not. Nor did Marko, I believe now, neither did Ted."

Grandma stopped talking and wiped her tears with a handkerchief.

When she stopped crying, I said:

"That's the reason I came. To know who really knew Barbara. I did not know her really; I knew only one aspect of her personality; I knew Barbara, my mother. My kind mother, sometimes so kind and soft and sometimes like a she-wolf mother. She became the she-wolf mother after Ted's departure. She would tell me stories and poems off by heart; often, I would see tears and tenderness in her eyes, sometimes she would make a fool of herself, be my clown; she would do anything to make me laugh, to make me happy. When she was writing, she was not aware of herself or of anything, or anybody around her. She did not know if she existed herself; she did not feel thirst, hunger; she looked as if she was not breathing; all that was coming from her were the rhythmic sounds produced by her fingers on the keyboard. She would swing her head left-right and move her lips barely noticeably. I would come and give her a kiss before leaving, 'Barb, I am off to school'. Hours later, I would find her in the same position the way I left her. I would ask, 'Barbara, are you still writing?' Her eyes were red, she would say, 'I just sat down, sweetie,' completely convinced that she had 'just sat down'. Time ceased to exist for her whilst writing."

I went quiet, observing the pieces of the furniture in the room. Long ago, darkness had sneaked into the room and gave darker tones to objects; only grandma's face was brighter, for it was lit by a little lamp. Because of this shadow play, the light and dark, her face looked younger, livelier. Her eyes were shining; the shadows had softened the lines on her face and her hair had a yellow glow from the little lamp's light. Once again, throughout the room some unusual sweet scent spread, and in my grandma's face, I saw Barbara's image. I hugged my grandma, and through tears again asked her the same unanswerable question:

"Grandma, why did my Barbara have to die?"

That very question was tearing up her soul, she swallowed her tears squeezing my narrow shoulders.

She said:

"It is very late; we better go now and get some sleep."

As if she never said that, I continued with my questions:

"Did you know she was terminally ill?"

"I did not."

"Did you ever suspect?"

"I do not know whether I suspected it. I told you so many times, she was very stubborn. She never liked to be questioned; she never liked to be criticised. When we visited last time, I had noticed that she was too skinny, that she was pale and that she hardly ate anything.

She said to me, 'You always worry too much; you see what isn't there.' But I saw her pain on her face, I told her, 'You look like a victim, like a real martyr.' She gave me the same answer as before, 'You see things that are not here; sometimes you are so pathetic, do not worry, I will not die.' She knew she was going to die, I know it now. At that time, she was preoccupied with topics of the Soul, whether it existed or not, and if it did exist, where did it go when one died. I thought she was writing about it. I was afraid of the truth; I would often hear a ringing in my head, the voice of the ill prophet called Zelda. Barbara was obsessed with the character of a woman she was writing about. She told me that the character of her new novel was going to die; she asked me if I believed in 'the return of a soul'. I told her I never believed in reincarnation."

I interrupted:

"Do you really not believe in it?"

"I do not know anymore, Lora. I would like to believe in it, but it is so hard. It is so hard to believe in something you can't see, you can't touch. We were raised that way—we did not believe, we did not teach kids any religion. We believed that reality was only that which could be seen by the physical eyes, only that which could be sensed by our five senses. The sixth sense for us was always—a superstition.

Superstition was only reserved for naïve people, for little kids and fools. Beyond this, I struggled to believe. Now, I would like to believe that there is something more. I would like to believe that Barbara exists somewhere, in some other form—my mere wish that she just exists. I would like to believe that out there, where Barbara exists now, there is more peace and harmony for her tortured soul. I would now like, my dear child, that that belief gives me wisdom and patience, the knowledge that I will meet her again. But I do not know how to believe in it. Priests, I never visited, for their stories were too simple for me. It looks like we humans always search for something complicated in order to believe in it, as if difficulty itself gives it credibility. Simple things look too easy to obtain, hence they never appear as the right answer . . ."

She fell silent again. She stroked my hair and asked after a short silence:

"In what do you believe, my child?"

I was silent for a long time before I said:

"I don't know, Grandma, what I believe in, for Barbara never taught me to believe in the invisible. To me, as well, all those stories sounded simple, naïve, almost ridiculous. I had girlfriends who attended Catholic schools. They were filled with prejudice and fear. Everything was based on fear, the threat of constant sin. I know, it is so hard to come to the truth. I would often ask Barbara which path led to the truth, and she would say, 'It is a thorny path; it is hard to get through the forest of fallacies; it's a path of blood and tears.' I would ask her about God, and she would shrug her shoulders saying, 'I can't talk about God. I don't see Him anywhere, and yet, I see Him everywhere. You see the life around us, who created it? The Creator, but where is He? Are we Him, or is He all of us? Who created Him? I don't know who we are either. Who are you, Lora? This body? This blood? These desires, hopes and emotions? This ever-beating heart? This mind which is never still? Who is Lora? Show me exactly where is Lora placed in your body?'

She would confuse me. We knew, we were not just our bodies, made of flesh, blood, veins and bones. What is inside? Where is Lora? In her heart? Is she the soul? And where is this soul? Where is it located in my body? Where is it coming from and where does it long to go?

Tell me now, my dearest Grandma, where has Barbara's soul gone? You tell me now, Grandma, are we ever going to meet her soul again? Tell me, my dearest Grandma, you should know that, you should know how to comfort me . . ."

We stayed awake the entire night talking and crying. We cried the whole night for the first time since my arrival, and we could not say who suffered more: my grandma or I? Maybe she suffered more, for she said, 'The biggest punishment in life is to outlive your own child.' I never knew that, but I believed that the biggest sorrow was to lose your mother. For when you lose your mother, you know then there is nobody who will tell you, 'You are my heart and my soul; you are my sweet life.' These words were so strongly imprinted into my soul, and I thought that Barbara didn't have the right to love me that much, for her leaving left me utterly devastated.

6.

Dawn painted the room red. I got up and opened the window. The tree under the window was coloured in beautiful and unusual colours. It looked as if some eccentric painter played with the leaves: red, yellow, different shades of brown, deep green and grey. The sky was reddish and the red sun was coming out. I was not home anywhere anymore, for there was no longer my Barbara.

I looked at my grandma. She looked tired; much older than the previous evening. The lines on her face were deeper; the expression on her face rougher. Even her voice sounded rougher, hoarse when she said:

"Try to have some sleep now."

"I do not feel like sleeping, Grandma; I feel like wandering, like wandering through this world without ever stopping. I came here believing that I would find my mother sitting on this very bed, waiting for me. I did not find her here. I found only memories. Her memories. But even now I don't know much more about her, even now I still feel like I had never really known my Barbara."

While I was speaking, it looked to me as if somebody else was talking through my mouth. It was not me, at least not that 'me', the one I still believed yesterday that was—me. While I was in Barbara's world, me, or my 'I' had changed countless times; it cracked, changed, had been torn and shattered. My 'I', changed so many times, and I could not figure out of how many 'I's I was made of, and who were those little broken 'I's I had witnessed. At first, I could not find out who 'I' was any longer, but later, I understood that all those new 'I's made the new 'me'.

Why is it in human nature to evaluate, to criticise and to judge? But who is the one who can see what was happening with someone's 'I', and how that 'I' of yesterday was perhaps no longer the same but ever-changing.

Now I could grasp why Barbara was always telling me not to judge others; not to tell others what to say, what to do.

Now I understood why Barbara had only ever said when Ted left, "Ted has left". Nothing more. Not a word about his 'I'. She knew that his 'I' had changed, cracked, multiplied, faded, and darkened in all those eight years they spent together.

Now I understood why Barbara would say that she 'did not know' somebody, even when she actually did know them. She could not know when their 'I' had changed, maybe that very moment, and that was not the same person she knew yesterday.

She told me that her hometown was a place of prejudice. They talked about others all the time, all opinionated like 'Oh, I know him. He is a so-and-so. And his father was a so-and-so. And his mother was saying 'this and that', so what more can we expect from him?'

But a person learns new things daily. A person changes their 'I' daily, polishing it. Every new day was an opportunity to learn something new, something better through new experiences. The town people would remember something that had happened long ago, and comment: 'Once he said, "such and such" and he did, "this and that"' and "such" and "that" cemented his progress in other people's eyes. The people of the town would not allow you to grow and change your image, change your 'I', for they would say, 'but we know you are like that'. Barbara never wanted anybody to know her. Every day she wanted to be different from yesterday, a new person. She wanted each of her experiences to make her a new and better person, different from the one she was yesterday. I saw that with her every day, I would say: 'But you said yesterday . . .' and she would cut my sentence in half saying, 'It was yesterday, today is a new day.'

She would say that that was a freedom. To be what you wanted to be, every day. Not to repeat yourself again and again and behave in the way others were expecting you to behave. Just to do only what your original 'I' was telling you to do, in an attempt to change, to learn and to grow.

During one of her stays, Grandma told her:

'You have changed, Barbara.' She said:

'Of course, I have changed. It would be terrible if I hadn't changed, it would mean that I had not learned anything. Life itself changes us. Life changes us always for the better, even though sometimes it seems like it does the opposite. With new experiences, we gain new knowledge, and with new knowledge, we form a new 'I'. Every time my 'I' has been changed I've felt proud of myself. It would be horrible if I still had the same 'I' that I brought here with me many years ago. I have changed since then so many times, and my new 'I' is no longer surprised by new things, nothing is strange to my new 'I'. When I lived back home, it was unacceptable to talk in a different dialect; people would look at you oddly, but look at me now, I can't imagine my life without people from different places and with different accents. I learned that the world is so beautiful in its diversity. And the more diversity, the more 'I's, and all those different 'I's again melt into the same knowledge, into the same experience, into the same soul. Yes, mother, I have changed.'

I understood Barbara only now, only now when I came to her country and met different people with different customs. Everything was so different and my 'I' had changed already several times—it became stronger and wider, all encompassing.

7.

We stood at the window inhaling the fresh crisp air in silence. I heard her heavy breathing and I could say that I almost heard her slow and heavy heartbeats.

An older man came out of the building, and he looked up towards the windows. He could not see us. When he was sure that there was no one who could see him, he started looking through the rubbish bins. He took some things out and placed them into a plastic bag. At first my grandma did not see him, for her eyes were focused somewhere in the past. But when she noticed him, she withdrew herself quickly inside, and said:

"Get inside, Lora."

I stepped back and asked:

"What happened? Who's that man?"

She said:

"The Professor; we still call him 'Professor', for he was a professor at university. Both he and his wife were professors at the same university. They didn't have any children. They are retired now and after all these years working as university professors, their pensions could not afford them a decent life. They can't buy a loaf of bread and a carton of milk daily. Every morning, poor soul, gets up very early; he looks around assuring himself that no one can see him, and then he goes through the rubbish bins."

"He must have gone insane, otherwise why would he do that?" I commented.

"No, he has not gone insane, dear. Everything else, here, has gone insane. This is a country where retired people check rubbish bins every morning, otherwise they cannot survive."

"How come?"

"Because we were deceived and robbed by our own state. That's why Lora." Once again, she wiped away her tears.

"But why, then, do people not rebel against all of that? Why do they only whisper?"

"I don't know. People are afraid. When the new government came, we were all hoping they would bring a better life, now we know that they are even worse than one could imagine, and yet nobody rebels against them. Young people have been unemployed for years, lots of them go to foreign countries in search of work, for all that we have here is crime and corruption. There are so many murders, lots of people just disappear overnight; we already have the highest number of adolescent suicides; there is no future here. And people do not talk, they don't rise up, for they are still not ready for tolerance and true democracy. For centuries, we have been living here in fear, always led by someone's iron fist, and it is so hard to change that mentality which was passed down from generation to generation. I believe now that I do not know anything anymore. I've lived a long life, met many people, read many books and now, it looks to me that I know so little. I am astonished by everything, and nowadays everything is a mystery to me as if I had found myself at the beginning rather than at the end of my life." Then, in a lowered voice, she said: "And all of that does not count anymore; since Barbara passed away . . . nothing matters anymore."

We heard Marko coughing, Grandma said:

"You see, Marko is waking up. My Lord, the night has passed, we did not have any sleep. Lie down now, I am going to prepare breakfast and will warm up the living room, then I'll call on you if you are still awake."

She left the room, and I came to the window once again. I looked at the tree below the window asking myself: 'Does this tree have feelings like we humans do? Does it feel this difficult time and this profound but silent sadness which has been floating above the town?'

***

The next evening, I went to bed very early, the night had not fallen yet. My sleep was so deep, without any dreams. Through the Venetian blinds the first rays of sun woke me up. I opened the window to let the morning into the room; the mornings here smelt of Barbara's hair. While the sun was rising, it seemed as if I heard quiet music.

There was complete silence on the street. Everything was at a standstill, just like on a beautiful postcard. Out of the building came the Professor. He looked up again. I didn't know if he saw me or not; he took a plastic bag out of his pocket and started filling it with some items. I felt sorry for him. The peace on the street was broken by the sound of a moving car. The car stopped in front of the opposite building. It was a grey Mercedes, a two-seater. A man came out of the car. He was alone. He opened the other door and took a big bag from the seat. The man was slender, tall; he had longish black hair. He wore black jeans and a black leather jacket. He locked the doors; he took the bag and with a light step headed towards the building. I looked at his shoulders, they moved slowly as he walked in almost slow motion. He walked so carefree as if his mind was totally free.

I looked at the car once again. On the bumper, there was a big round white sticker and in the middle of the sticker was the black letter D.

A thought had occurred, 'It means Davor.'

I knew, it was Davor.

Quickly, I put on my track suit and tided up my shoes.

Grandma and Grandpa were still sleeping. I heard them snoring while passing their room. I looked at the clock—it was six o'clock. I ran down the stairs. My heart was beating quicker, I felt a strange excitement in my bosom. I knew it was Davor. I ran into his building and climbed up the stairs to the first floor. The first door on the left was half opened; there was a dim light in the corridor. 'He entered here,' I thought.

I quietly returned to our apartment. Passing by grandparents' room, I heard their heavy breathing. I entered my room, Barbara's room, and opened the suitcase. At the bottom of the suitcase there was a manuscript. I took it and ran down the stairs again. I met the Professor carrying his plastic bag. I said, "Good morning". He said:

"I hurried this morning; I have already been to the shops."

I swiftly crossed the road, there was a light on in one window. I felt an immense excitement not really knowing—why. I felt like Barbara.

I came to the door and stood there for a while. I wanted to ring the bell, but I just kept my extended finger in the air. I did not dare.

What would I tell him? I did not know yet.

I pressed the buzzer. First shortly, then the second time I pressed it with more determination.

"Oh Barbara
It's rained unceasingly on Brest today
As it was raining before
But it isn't the same anymore
And everything is wrecked
It's a rain of mourning terrible and desolate
Nor is it still a storm
Of iron and steel and blood
But simply clouds
That die like dogs
Dogs that disappear
In the downpour drowning Brest
And that float away to rot
A long way off
A long long way from Brest
Of which there's nothing left."

SATYAM

He opened the door (as if he opened a new chapter of a book). A weak light shone on his face (as if the weakness of the light was hiding him from me). His face was yellowish (because of the weak light). His eyes were big. Maybe they were the most profound eyes I had ever seen. He looked extremely tall to me and his height increased my insecurity.

I was squeezing the sheets of papers in my hands; he ended the silence:

"Are you looking for someone?"

I didn't say a word.

"Who are you looking for? I have just arrived from a long trip and haven't even had time to put my bags down; I am so tired."

I mumbled:

"Are you Davor, sir?"

"Yes, I am. What do you want so early? Who are you, young lady?"

"My name is Lora. May I come in?"

"This early, Lora? Fine, come in, then."

He let me in. There was a heavy smell inside, one of stale air. As if he had read my thoughts, he said:

"I will open the windows right now; it has been a long time since this place was aired."

He opened the windows and offered me a seat. I sat on the chair inhaling the crisp air; he said:

"Would you like a cup of coffee, Lora?"

"Yes, please." I said. I never liked coffee, I liked tea. While he was preparing the coffee, he glanced at me several times. He probably could not grasp what I wanted from him. He said:

"I haven't done much for this market for years."

"What do you mean?"

"Are you a musician?"

"No, I am not. I used to play the violin, but it was a long time ago."

He placed two cups on the table. Putting a cup in front of me, he said, "Here you are Lora," then he sat on the chair holding his. His movements were slow like the movements of someone who belonged to some other reality where everything was moving much slower. Daylight already filled the room; he was sitting opposite me, I was looking at his face.

His skin was olive, his eyes as black as olives. He had a mole on his face, and it gave him a younger appearance, giving him a special charm. I could not define his age; I could not remember if he was older than Barbara; he looked young. He looked like someone who was approaching their thirties. His hair was black and smooth; it reached the middle of his neck. His hair was well trimmed, of equal length. He looked cultured, well-manicured. His fingernails were narrow and long, nicely shaped; his fingers too, were long and slender like the fingers of a real guitarist. Who knows if he was still a guitarist, or if it was just a distant past. (And I wondered, how distant the past could be measured only by memories?)

And those black olives on his face, those warm eyes, were framed by long dark eyelashes, and his eyebrows were thick but narrow as if he was controlling their fine line with tweezers. His teeth were rather big; the two front teeth were slightly overlapping. Because of it, his upper lip looked fuller. I saw incredible peace in his eyes; there was peace in his movements, and then this peace was transferred onto me just by being aware of it. (I said that before—it looked as if he transported me into some reality of slow motion).

That peace seemed to me like a long-lost love, or like a love found again. The peace stood between us, and it was surreal like a distant past, measured only by memories. He was silent; he waited for me to start. I said:

"I am Barbara's daughter."

He showed a little smile. Nothing moved the peace on his face. He asked:

"Which Barbara?"

"Barbara Milich, or Donoghue."

Once again, he smiled gently and said:

"You are Barbara's daughter. I heard she got married; I heard she had a daughter. So, you are her daughter. You don't look like Barbara. Tell me, how is she? Is she here, I haven't seen her for ages?" (and the word 'ages' echoed . . . ages, ages, ages . . . it echoed like a long-lost love or like a newly found love, like a past which was measured only by distant years, only by memories . . .)

"She is not here. She died."

Only then, he shuddered. I saw a jolt on his face; his eyes widened, then he squeezed them while repeating my words in dismay:

"She died."

"Yes," I said quietly.

"When did she die? How did she die? Where did she die?"

"She died three months ago. She passed away from cancer which rapidly spread through her body. Her illness was short; she died quickly. She died still beautiful. She died in Sydney."

A somber silence fell between us. It looked as if Barbara's own death stood in between us paralysing our gestures, words and thoughts. Then, Davor stood up (he was still moving slowly in his own reality) and he turned his back to me. Maybe he wanted to hide the tears in his eyes. He went to the window and leaned against the windowsill. After some time, he came back and sat at the table. He lit his cigarette offering me one. I refused, I didn't enjoy the coffee either. He started his sentence with a voice that sounded very different to the voice I heard before; it had the ring of a voice that came from the past:

"I haven't seen her in nineteen years. We grew up together. Nineteen fucking years I have not heard anything about Barbara. Just vague rumors. Now you come saying that she has died. I haven't even been here for the last five years. Last time, I just came for a day. I came today to see an agent, I want to sell this apartment; you've come early in the morning telling me that Barbara died. How did you find me? How did you know I was here?"

"I didn't know you were here. I was standing by the window when I saw a car with a sticker which said—D. I thought, 'This must be Davor,' and I came to see if I was right."

A little smile escaped from his lips, he said:

"I live in Germany."

Then after a short pause, he continued:

"What do you know about me? You said, you thought—that must be Davor. What do you know about Davor, Lora?"

I put the manuscript on the table. On it, it was written *Letters to Ted*. I said to him:

"Ted is my father. Those letters were written to him. But, I think they were written to all of us. Barbara left them to me. Maybe to you, too, Davor."

He asked:

"Did she continue writing?"

"She lived for me and for her novels."

"She could express herself through words so beautifully; she was so talented."

I stood up, leaving *Letters to Ted* on the table. I said:

"I'd like you to read it. I think I owe it to Barbara."

I headed towards the door, he followed me; he opened the door for me and said:

"Come sometime in the evening, I'll read this today."

When he said a short goodbye, our voices sounded different to how they sounded before.

When I entered our place, my grandma was already up and was very surprised to see me come in.

"Where have you been, Lora?"

"The mornings are splendid here. The air is so crisp . . . everything smells of long forgotten memories."

Grandma smiled and said:

"Come and sit down; I have already prepared breakfast."

I could not wait for the evening to come. The hours dragged carelessly; the minutes adhered onto the membranes of my patience (the membranes of my patience were fragile; my fingers were nervous). My heart beat in a different rhythm, an unknown rhythm, provoked by Europe (or just—provoked). I felt as if I were going to a first rendezvous. (Accordingly, I thought that was the way I would feel if I were going to my first rendezvous. I was absentminded and anxious not knowing the reason for my worries.) I was impatient and excited the entire day. Completely absentminded. I did different things in an attempt to shorten my day, but regardless of it, the hours dragged slowly. Grandma noticed my uneasiness, therefore I said: "I am so muddleheaded today." I never said why, so grandma searched for the reasons and excuses for my moodiness. On that day, she hugged me more than usual. Pleasant were here caresses; the caresses of Barbara's mother. They filled me with security; they protected me from my own thoughts. I was thinking about Davor the whole day. I wondered how he felt whilst reading Barbara's *Letters to Ted;* I wondered how he felt whilst reading those shared memories written by his former beloved. His first love. I wondered if he had a wife, a family; I wondered how these letters would echo in his soul. What would they move? I was keen to know who Davor was. Did he carry Barbara within him into his world?

A red evening was descending in the sky. I liked those evenings particularly because of the strange nostalgia which was announced by its colour. The colour of that evening was the colour of Barbara's dearest dress and the colour of her voice.

I said to Grandma:

"I am going for a short walk. I'd like to be alone."

I didn't want to mention Davor; my inner voice told me to keep it a secret. I approached his building stealthily. I looked up at the window; Grandma was not there. I did not enter his building, I went down the road. Mulberry trees lined both sides of the wide road. How did I know this? How did I remember this name—mulberry? Perhaps the sweet scent announced its name. When I turned my head, and looked at the window once again, Grandma was standing at the window; I waved and hurried my step. That intoxicating smell of the mulberry trees smelled of Barbara's last words. I sat on the bench, which could not be seen from Grandma's window; I inhaled the sweet scent of the mulberry leaves or branches and counted the minutes. The hands on my wristwatch moved slowly; the scent was intoxicating just like someone's bosom, just like the bosom of my mother when she was breastfeeding me. After fifteen minutes passed, I slowly went back looking at Grandma's window the whole time. There was no one at the window; I ran. (While I was running the scent of her milk was still following me.) I ran until I reached his house; I ran up the stairs to his apartment. There, finally I stopped running. I sat on the stairs to calm my breathing, to calm my heart and to get out of my nostrils this intoxicating scent which followed me. I thought about Barbara, she would wait for him like this—seated on the steps, waiting for hours, as his grandmother wouldn't tell him she was waiting there. She would sit and wait for Davor to open the door. I felt a soft hand on my head; I knew that Barbara's soul entered the corridor and sat next to me gently caressing my hair. The corridor smelt of mulberries, or of mimosas or of Davor's long-forgotten-love. I nearly cried, but I did not; I needed to be calm. When I was completely calm, I stood up and pressed the buzzer.

His measured steps were echoing, bouncing off the concrete floor; I heard the key unlock the door; I saw his yellowish, tired face; he looked as if he grew older that very afternoon (perhaps older from reading). His eyes were red and there were dark circles around them. They looked as if they were not Davor's eyes any longer, the same black olives framed with long thick lashes that I saw before. The sparkle was gone from his eyes, the sparkle which was given to distinguished souls. Again, his voice was different when he said:

"Oh, Lora, you came. Come in for a while." He talked while following me:

"I was driving the whole night, even today I haven't had any sleep, I am exhausted. I just wanted to fill the bath right now and then straight to bed."

I said nothing. I was disappointed. For him the most important thing was to fill the bath, to get some rest. And I was waiting impatiently the entire day, full of anticipation. I was waiting to hear from Davor what was he going to tell me upon reading Barbara's letters. But Davor said that he was tired from a long trip; he was tired from the sleepless night. Not a word about Barbara. About the road which smelled of mulberries or perhaps of acacia . . .

I turned around and headed towards the door. I muttered:

"So, well . . . then, I suppose . . . goodbye . . ." I felt some strange pain in my chest . . .

He reached me at the door:

"Can we have breakfast tomorrow morning; I am so tired right now, the reading of her letters exhausted me completely."

My mood changed from a simple sentence. He had read Barbara's letters.

I said:

"When should I come?"

"Come early. I am going to bed early this evening, so by eight I will be awake. Come after eight o'clock."

Then he closed the door (as if he was closing a chapter of a book . . . the chapter which he would reopen and read again only for me). There was complete stillness. Yes, the door of his apartment opened and closed some other world; a world of a different reality. He kept the keys in the palm of his hand. Would he allow me to enter through that door and show me a world known only to him?

I sneaked out of his building looking at Grandma's window. I remembered the red towel which Grandma used to put on Barbara's window as a signal that it was time to get back home. There was nobody at the window, neither Grandma nor the red towel.

That night, I slept poorly. I woke up countless times. I dreamt of Barbara. She came and said:

'That's all I had left to you, my sweetheart. Wealth, perhaps, would not make you happier, though freer for sure. Nourish this friendship with Davor, for there are only a few souls like his. Tell him that I am sending him my love; tell him that I am waiting for him. I am waiting for the both of you, my dearest, because both of you belong to me.' These were the words my late mother was telling me in my dream. She came with a wreath of fresh daises on her head, and her eyes were bluer than ever. She had hands made of clouds, so light and tender. When she touched my cheek, I knew it was her hand, only her hand was that tender, the hand made of clouds. When she touched my cheek with her lips, I knew they were her lips for only Barbara's lips had the scent of mimosas which spread throughout the room waking me up. I jumped from my bed, searching through the room, calling:

"Barbara, Barbara, where are you?"

The moonlight lit her picture on the desk and her eyes shone. I could not figure out had the picture come alive, or had Barbara's eyes shone for real.

I fell asleep again, but Barbara came to my dreams again; she touched me again with her tender hand, the hand made of clouds; she kissed me with her soft lips which smelled of mimosas. I saw her once again walking down the road lined with mulberry trees, escorted by light wind which played with her hair and carried the sweet smell of acacia.

After that dream, I dreamt of Davor and Ted, and I did not know which one was her husband. Both of them were floating; each of them on one cloud, and as they were floating away they became smaller and smaller whilst Barbara was standing on the ground with her hands stretched out towards the sky calling their names.

The strong smell of coffee woke me up (that smell reminded me of oil on canvas hanging above Barbara's desk; reminded me of the lillies in the hands of barefoot children . . .)

I entered the kitchen and found Grandma standing next to the stove.

"Good morning, Grandma."

"Good morning, Lora, did you sleep well?"

"I did."

"Do you want to come with me today?"

"Where are you off to?"

"I need to go downtown to pay some bills. We can go together; we can walk down there."

"I don't feel like walking downtown. I'd rather walk along the coast to fetch some fresh sea air."

"I don't like it when you go out by yourself. There are some spooky characters out there. There are many armed men around; I don't like it when you go out all by yourself."

"There is nobody there in the morning. A few people, jogging. Grandma, I am a big girl, so don't worry, I don't like it when you worry too much about me."

"Still, I'd prefer if you came with me. We can go to a café to enjoy some good coffee."

I delayed my answer, for I could not tell her that I was going to meet Davor.

"I'd rather go to the cinema with you, this afternoon. They are showing an Australian film today. I'd rather walk along the seashore this morning. I like that smell, it evokes something special within me, it evokes Barbara within me . . ."

Grandma agreed:

"As you wish; we can go to the cinema in the afternoon."

I asked her:

"When are you going downtown?"

She said:

"Right now. I have a few things to do, so the earlier the better."

She went out before I did. I left the house fifteen minutes past eight. My grandfather Marko was still in his bed. Grandma brought him breakfast in bed. He ate slowly and dedicatedly as if he were reading some pleasant prayer.

I put on a pair of black jeans and black skivvy. I put on Barbara's coat which hung in the wardrobe. After nineteen years, it was fashionable again. The coat was made of grey tweed, the pockets and the collar were made of black velvet. It reached down to my knees. I gathered my hair in a little ponytail and tied it up with a black ribbon. I looked at myself in the mirror. 'Who are you?' asked the reflection from the mirror. No, no, no, I didn't know who I was but at that moment I could not care less.

Dressed like that, I pressed the buzzer next to Davor's door.

He opened the door with a little smile:

"Good morning, Lora."

Entering the apartment, I asked:

"Did you have a good sleep?"

"I slept like a baby."

It was obvious that he had a refreshing sleep. His face was relaxed, he was freshly shaven, the smell of his cologne spread throughout the room. He said:

"I just got to grab some cigarettes and my keys."

We walked out of his building and headed towards his car. I looked at the window, and he asked:

"Are you afraid someone might see you?"

"Something like that . . ." I said.

"I know, it wouldn't be good if they see you with me, particularly Marko; you can get in trouble, you know that."

Then he stopped and said:

"I got to go back; I have forgotten something."

When he came back, he was carrying the manuscript in his hand; on it, was written *Letters to Ted.* We were silent the whole time he was driving. Music was coming out gently and unobtrusively, just like his cologne was gently and unobtrusively coming from his direction. Davor, with his index finger, was rhythmically tapping against the steering wheel.

We were driving up the hill, towards the highest part of town. There was an old castle there, a church and a historical centre, with its beautiful but rundown buildings. We could see Davor and Grandma's buildings from here. We were walking along the narrow, little streets when Davor said:

"There was a nice café here many years ago. I hope it is still there. From the terrace, you can see the entire town; you can see neighbouring villages and islands. The view is stunning, you'll like it. Have you been here before?"

"No, never."

We found the little café; it was open. On the pebbled terrace there were four round tables. The view, sincerely, was breathtaking. You could see the city, the port, the islands and little villages at the foot of a big mountain which was rising high above Barbara's hometown.

"I haven't been here for years. I thought it might not be here any longer. It's beautiful here, isn't it?"

We were sitting there silently while looking at the panoramic sight of the city, both dedicated to our own thoughts. I saw by the melancholy in his eyes that he was searching through past memories. He said:

"Barbara and I were regulars here. Everybody used to know us."

The waitress came out and he continued:

"I don't know anybody anymore; you see this little girl . . ."

I protested:

"She is not a little girl; she is a young lady. She must be my age."

He showed a little smile. We ordered our breakfast.

From inside of the café, a woman with long blonde hair came out. She came straight to the table and said:

"Good Lord, it is you."

Davor looked at the woman then he smiled:

"You are still here, I just can't believe it."

Then he stood up and hugged the woman. She said:

"I looked at the two of you through the window and I thought you must be tourists, as I have never seen you before. Then, nearly at the same moment, I recognised you and said loudly, "My Lord, this must be Davor. Our own Davor. You could not deceive me even with a different haircut."

Davor said to me:

"This is Klara. We went to school together. Klara's father owned this café, and we all gathered here after school. My band played here years ago, you remember Klara, don't you? Where's the old man?"

"Do I remember, my God? Those were the times!" (Her voice was coloured with tones of longing for the past). "Where's the old man? Still here; pain in the neck. He knows everything best, the same story as before. I married Tony; do you remember Tony Vesely?"

"I certainly do. When did you marry?"

"You see, this young girl who brought you your breakfast, she is our daughter. We all work here. Tony went down to the fish market; he'll be back soon. But what about you? We heard you were a big fish in Germany. Well, old buddy, you don't remember us anymore?"

"What big fish? I am a studio musician, what kind of a big fish can I be?"

"Did you ever marry?"

"No."

She was looking at me; Davor didn't say another word. Then Klara said:

"Well, then, you enjoy your breakfast while it is still warm."

"Thank you, Klara."

When she left, Davor told me:

"I thought people had forgotten me. Funny thing is: when you return, after only a few days, it seems as if you have never left. But nevertheless, my life over there is so different to the one I had here; over there is my real life, here, only the memories remain.

"And Barbara, is she only a memory?" I asked. His eyes were soft with sorrow and his voice was soft when he said:

"A painful memory." Once again, he fixed his gaze somewhere in the distance towards the high mountain and repeated it as if he was saying it for the first time: "A painful memory."

Out of the box, he took a cigarette and extended the box towards me. I said:

"I don't smoke. Barbara smoked too much, therefore I would not touch a cigarette in my wildest dreams. She nearly set the entire house on fire twice when she fell asleep with a lit cigarette.

I found her surrounded with a pile of papers, head leaning on her shoulder and a half-smoked cigarette on the papers. I was always in a total panic fearing she would burn the house down. She started everything with a cigarette; she ended everything with a cigarette. No thanks, I don't want to be a slave."

Davor said:

"I started smoking first. Back then she was against smoking. The whole year she was grumbling about my smoking. She used to say that she didn't like when I was 'just like the others'. But those were the times when one needed to prove their bravery and masculinity by smoking. She started much later than I, but when she started, she did it 'properly'. She did everything 'properly' with zest and dedication, there was no middle way for Barbara."

"Did you read all her letters?"

"Twice. Yesterday."

"What do you think?"

"I think she was extremely unhappy, that's what I think."

"Was it really exactly the way Barbara said it?"

"Exactly as she said it."

I said to him:

"Tell me more about Barbara."

"Yes, I will. It seems as if I was the only one who really knew Barbara. Or, at least, I knew her best. Barbara had a very complex personality, it was obvious even when we were little kids."

2.

He fell silent. He put out his cigarette and combed his hair backwards with his long, slender fingers. Then he sighed deeply and once again reached into his pocket and took out the box of cigarettes. He took out one and he tapped it against the table, then took it in his fingers and started squeezing the top.

He sighed again and said:

"I didn't have a mother. I was a quiet, introverted child. I had Barbara. From the very beginning of my life, I knew that Barbara was going to be the most important, the most influential person in my life. The love we shared was not some sort of a wild, uncontrollable love of youth. The love we shared was as old as we were. It was complete and self-sufficient. Only Barbara could understand me; only I could understand Barbara.

She should have been a happy child. From the outside, it looked as if she were. She was the only child of a very influential family; I can say, the most influential family, for her father was the most powerful man in the city. He was Chairman of the Supreme Court. Marko Millich. I could say a lot about Marko Millich. The judge. He sentenced many, I don't know whether he was fair or not; but to me, I certainly can say that his verdict was solely based on his emotions.

A day without Barbara was a lost day for me. I had a grandma who was a bit nuts; she would never tell me that Barbara called me, that she knocked on the door. Hours later, when I went out, I would find Barbara sitting on the stairs waiting for me. I would go back to the apartment calling my grandma an old witch, telling her how much I hated her, threatening to tell my father, when he came the next time, how nasty she was . . .

Every time I found Barbara sitting there with her bottom and her hands frozen, waiting for me for hours, I would hit my grandma with a storm of wild words and accusation. Barbara would whisper:

'She told me you were not at home, but I knew you were. Just out of spite, I was waiting here.'

She did many things 'out of spite'. Only I knew what kind of spite it was. It was spite against stupidity, lies and hypocrisy. Even as a child she fought spitefully against lies and hypocrisy. She would say:

'Isn't it so, Dado, that we'll always tell each other the truth, only the truth and nothing but the truth?' I would agree knowing of what importance the 'truth' was to her. When she was a bit older, she would say that she 'could die for the truth'. My Barbara, my truth-warrior. But she was of a gentle build, tender and of frail health. Every time when she would wait for me for hours in the cold corridor, because my grandma had told her I was not home, she would get ill. I would tell my grandma that I would run away and that she would never see me again. I would threaten her, saying that I would run to Germany, never to come back. When Barbara was ill, I was always at her place reading to her, first picture books and then books, and later, I would take my guitar and play her favorite songs.

I think, the first time I proposed was when we were about five. We 'knew' that we were meant for each other and that we would get married when the right time came. We never worried about that. But as I grew older, I started to worry about Marko. I knew that he never really approved of our friendship. Who was I? A little boy from the neighbourhood without a mother or father. A little boy who was growing up with two grandmothers. The same way my grandmother turned Barbara away from our door, Marko did to me, countless times. But I never told that to Barbara, my pride would not allow me; I was ashamed. But above all, I was afraid of Marko. I kept that for myself knowing that if I told Barbara, she would tell him whatever was on her mind . . . it would ruin our friendship. When Marko would find me at their door, he would say:

'You, again? You want to see Barbara? Not now, she has more important things to do.' Then he would close the door. I never sat in front of their door waiting for Barbara. Because of my male pride. Or, could it be that I was never as strong as Barbara. Nothing was more important to her than to 'show the truth', if not to someone particular, then to the neighbours:

'Davor's grandma won't let me in!'

I heard Marko, countless times, telling his wife:

'Why is this child here again?' When he would meet me in the street, he never ever greeted me back. I knew why. We were—nobody. Marko was always surrounded with 'people of importance'. 'Someone Important' was Marko's friend. My father was a labourer in Germany; my grandmothers were simple women, and my mother died. As a child, I could not understand why Marko never liked me. Later, I understood. Barbara was mildly aware of the silent dispute between me and her father. But she loved him very much. Later, again, I understood that even though she loved and admired her father, she quietly rebelled against his authority.

I can't say what was going on behind closed doors. But she always rebelled against any authority. Marko had authority; his word was always the final one, and no one talked after him.

But that was not the way to treat Barbara. He never understood. In their house, rules on 'how a girl from a respectable family should behave' were very clear.

Barbara was like the wind. She was so free. Nobody could catch Barbara and tame her.

She would say to me:

'You promise me, Dado, that everything is going to be just the same when we get married. Promise, that we will stay best friends. I can't listen to anybody's orders; I want you the way you are—full of understanding and patience, always ready for dialogue, always ready to accept my point of view.'

I would reply:

'Well, that's me, why should I change?'

'Maybe we all change when we get married.'

'What are you talking about, Barbara?'

'You are the only one I can really talk to; only you can understand me. Why do adults always think they know everything best? Why does Marko think he knows everything? Even when he doesn't have an answer, even when he hasn't seen something, he pretends he knows. Dado, please, do not say that you know everything. I hate those who know everything, those who give wise advice. My soul is untamable; there is no advice or recipe for my soul. My soul is as free as a bird.'

She could tell me anything. I understood her utterly for Barbara was I, and I was Barbara. We had the same desires, the same thoughts, the same joys and the same sorrows. What would you call it in English—soulmates? We were soulmates to each other. It was enough for us—just to be in the same room. I would play my guitar, she would write in her little black diary and we did not need words. We were complete. Time stood still. That was the first and only time in my life when I touched Timelessness. Many times after that, in vain, I searched for Timelessness. I can't count now, on how many doors I had knocked; how many eccentrics I had to meet, how many *mantras* I had changed, all in the one and same hope that this could lead me to Timelessness once again, that Timelessness would bring me back to Barbara . . .

When we were fifteen, we were inseparable. At that time, I felt like a real man; I would do anything for her, whatever she wished for. She had very different desires to other people. She would sneak out of her apartment in the middle of the night while her parents were sleeping, she would call beneath my window, or she would throw pebbles at my window. She was in her pyjamas and dressing gown, softly calling: 'Open the window.' And I would open the window for her to climb up into my room. Then she would lay her head onto my shoulder and say:

'Wake me up before four.'

She would say:

'All I want is to wake up in your arms.'

She was a fashion pioneer in town. She would dress completely differently from other people. Months later, everybody would wear what she had been wearing before, but she, already, was wearing something new. When we used to go out, she would put on my jeans. I wore jeans three times bigger. But she would roll them up, tighten her belt around her tiny waist; she was as slim as a porcelain doll, and on top of all that, she would put on stiletto heels. When our friends would see her, dressed like that, they would look at her speechlessly as if asking:

'Barbara, are you aware of what you are wearing?'

Because of Barbara, I was everything that I am and everything I was not.

Because of her, my calm nature would easily change. I broke a policeman's nose, I got myself into a bitter argument with her teacher; because of her, I smashed my guitar to pieces when she left the concert . . . because of her, I played the guitar, I tattooed her name on my bicep, I wrote poetry, enrolled into university; because of her, I wanted to be better, I wanted to be 'Somebody', somebody worthy of Barbara.

Often, it seemed to me as if she didn't belong to her family. Barbara was not a social snob, she was an intellectual snob. While her girlfriends were judging others by their family background, their material and social status, or their looks, Barbara would evaluate people by how many books they had read. She would say, with her nose turned up:

'I don't want to talk to her, she hasn't read two books in her entire life.'

She read a lot. She wrote superbly. She was always carrying her little black diary and a pencil as she could not afford to 'miss out on something important.' After school, we would go to a café all together. We would all sit around the same table, but not Barbara. She would sit all by herself and she would write. If anybody asked, 'What's with Barbara?' I was quick to defend:

'Mind your own business, leave Barbara alone.'

She always told me that with me, she felt so confident and secure; jokingly she would say:

'More secure than with Marko and the whole police station.'

She would say:

'With you, I can be anything. I am not just *this* Barbara; I can be whatever I want to be, and I can show you all my faces, because you understand and love all of them.'

I loved all of Barbara's faces.

Sometimes, she would be like a little girl. A capricious little girl, and everything needed to be the way that little girl wanted. Everything was the way she wanted, for I loved her moodiness and sometimes even provoked her to show me all her colours.

When she was the 'truth warrior', my name was—Satyam. Often, I would think that she did not have any mercy (or brain!) when she was grabbed by the role of 'truth warrior'. She would say whatever was on her mind and what she was feeling without any hesitation—straight to the point. She would say:

'How come, you don't get me, Dado? The truth is above everything. The bitterest truth is better than the sweetest fallacy.'

Sometimes, she would be completely disappointed with the world. Miserable because of it. Then she would say:

'Something is not quite right. It often seems to me that I am in the wrong place at the wrong time. It seems to me that I was forty when I was born. Without you, I would be absolutely lost and sad.'

'And right now, how sad are you?'

'Right now, I am so sad that I think this place is not my real home. It often seems to me that I have found myself here by mistake, or by some sort of a whim. Maybe even, by some sort of punishment. If it were not for you, for your love and understanding, this place would be cold and dull. Everything is so stupid, so superficial. Dado, there should be some "better world". A world of Truth and Justice. I do not see justice around us, at least not as a judge's daughter. The world is full of lies and injustice. Why does it hurt me, I can't answer, but there should be a better world somewhere.'

I would promise to take her to that 'Better world—The World of Truth.'

So, off we went in search of the 'World of Truth'. But not together. Each of us went to our own 'World of Truth', or lies, I don't know . . . They took Barbara away from me, and I was banished to my 'World of Truth', Marko passed the judgment."

He stopped. I was looking at his lips. He had them pressed tightly together, he must have had a bitter taste in his mouth, like he had bitten into a freshly cut lemon. He grabbed both my hands and kissed them; at the door there were two women watching us. When I looked towards them, they disappeared like ghosts.

I was teary, he gave me his handkerchief. I wiped my eyes and blew my nose in it. He hugged me and whispered something into my ear, something I did not understand. I felt strange, in Barbara's old coat, with Davor's handkerchief in my hand and his arm over my shoulder, once again, I did not know who I was.

When I stopped crying, I said to Davor:

"I do not know who I am."

He just looked at me with a hint of pity in his dark eyes, and said:

"Do you think I know who I am? Do you think that anyone ever knows who they are?"

"I don't know anymore whether I came here to find Barbara or myself."

"You will find yourself through finding her. That's why I want to talk to you about Barbara, so that you can learn more about her unique and sorrowful soul. I never figured out if she was sorrowful by her own choice, or whether it was inherited from her own past that she brought into this life. We will never find this out. You tell me about Barbara, the mother.

"She was 'My Mother'. She would always say 'I am your Mother', as if she alone was astonished by that. What I can tell you about Barbara-mother is that she loved me with a very possessive love. She never wanted to share me with anybody. Not even with my father. I would meet with Ted secretly."

"Did Ted love her?"

"I was eight when they separated. They never argued. I think he loved her, but he never understood her. Now, I think that she was 'too heavy', too complicated a person for Ted. Ted cherished simplicity. He could never have it with Barbara. I remember that in only one day she would change her mood several times. Ted used to follow her, asking:

'What's up Barbara?'

Without any comment, she would sit at her computer. She constantly led her internal dialogue, she was often unreachable, unavailable; she forgot often to make dinner; she forgot to sleep, to eat . . . only I could bring her back. My voice would bring her back to this reality. When I was hungry, she was hungry too; when I wanted to go out, her legs needed a stretch; when I was sick, she would lie in my bed next to me . . . and now she lies in a grave and I do not know any longer how to call her back . . ."

Again, I was crying; Davor's eyes were looking somewhere far, maybe to Germany.

"No one was indifferent towards Barbara; people loved her or loathed her. She had a strange urge—the urge to leave. Who did she want to punish—the person she was leaving, or herself, I never knew.

I woke up drunk. Next to me was the body of an unidentified woman. It was not Barbara. Upon realising that, my hair stood up in a surge of horror. 'What happened?' I asked myself. In a panic, I started shaking the woman. What if Barbara hears about this? The young woman stood up and started dressing herself. I was cursing. How did this happen? What if Barbara hears about it? I asked myself over and over.

She showed me her little smile and said:

'You see, Barbara, Davor is not only yours. Hey, Davor, what will that eccentric girlfriend of yours say when she hears about us? . . . as you know she will hear about it, this town is far too small for secrets."

I was beside myself. I jumped out of my bed; I pushed her out with my hands and kicked her arse with my foot:

'Get out, get out!' and she said:

'Don't scream, your sweetheart might hear you. She might hear you, and you know, she is ill tempered.' As I said before, they loved her, or loathed her. I screamed at her, in her face, then she left. I sat on the floor, in the corner of my room and cried. I knew that everything was going to crumble.

That year Barbara had enrolled into Law School. It was her father's wish, not hers. She wanted to study literature. They told her nobody lived from writing. But that was not the reason why she did not pursue it, the real reason was the literary contest where she had not won first prize, but second.

That year, I had enrolled into University to study to be marine engineer. Barbara enrolled into Law because of her father, I enrolled in engineering because of Barbara.

It was my birthday that day. Barbara came early that morning; she came with a wrapped present in her hand. I was sitting in the corner of my room completely numb and ready to meet my fate. I knew she would not forgive me. Not Barbara.

I remember her shoulder blades, they were trembling as she left my room, my apartment, when I told her that some other woman woke up in my bed this morning. Her present was lying on the floor; I kicked it a number of times with my foot; I kicked anything that was in my way. I smashed my guitar once again; my guitar, the second biggest love after Barbara. I tore all the posters off the walls, and smashed the framed picture of me and Barbara onto the floor; I pushed my fingernails into my eyes wanting to dig them out from their sockets. On that day, I could not find peace anywhere. I drank the entire day. I was torn between the desire to call her, and my self-imposed ban to do that. I was afraid of her voice; I knew it would be cold; I knew it would not be the voice of *my Barbara* anymore. I could not even dream what kind of vengeance was waiting for me! She would never forgive, not Barbara, so unconsciously she assigned the worst punishment one could think of. She wanted to run away to death.

The next morning my grandmother woke me up. I was exhausted, the hangover; the entire night I was vomiting from the excess of alcohol and the biggest shock to which my whole body was exposed. I said to her:

'Get out of my room. Leave me alone, I don't want to come out of my room today.'

She said:

'There is someone at the door who wants to talk to you.'

'Tell them to go to hell; I don't want to talk to anybody.'

Then she said:

'It is Barbara's father, he wants to talk to you.'

A rush of fear paralysed me. It was not just the plain fear of Marko Millich and the judgment he might pass. What had Barbara done? I was trembling like a little leaf in the wind. I was shivering like a madman without any common sense. My heart was jumping in my chest like a wild beast; I heard loud tones in my ears; an indescribable heat rushed to my face. 'What had Barbara done?' I don't remember how I came to the door. For the first time in my life, Marko Millich was standing at my door. He looked so unbelievably tall. He looked like a giant; a very, very angry giant with black smoke coming out of his nostrils. He had wolf-like eyes when he looked at me. In his eyes, I saw hatred and threat intertwined like two snakes hissing at me. He did not wait for me to utter a word. He came very close to my face, and grabbed the collar of my shirt. He pulled me closer and in a hushed voice said:

'There is no place for you in this town anymore. You better find a new address for yourself, and preferably very far from this town; you know who I am, and where my power can reach. If you choose to stay, I will do everything to stop you in all your endeavors. So, pack your bags and leave as soon as you can, you little nobody. If you try to call, or to see Barbara once again, I will be your judge, jury and executioner, do you hear me? Go as far as you can, and forget Barbara's name and address, forever. Pack your bags today.'

Then he turned his back and left. I still remember his eyes.

Everything was broken within me. I could not cry again, for this was far too serious for trivial tears. I knew that I would never come back to this town. The town where I was born, where I had spent my childhood and youth. The town where I had my friends and my first and only love.

I put a Long Play record on the record player; the day before, I smashed my guitar.

Music was all that I had left. I could take it with me, in my soul."

He lit his cigarette once again, looking at the sky. The sky had changed; it cracked with greyness here and there. Grey rugs were dragging across the sky; the trees were bare, leafless now; underneath our table was a little curled up kitten which reminded me of myself. I felt that Davor was so close to me, as close as Barbara was. I took his hand, the one which was not holding a cigarette, and took it to my lips. He only said:

"My, dear, child."

We were immersed in our own thoughts. He was smoking and still looking at the sky when he said:

"Barbara's eyes had the colour of this sky."

"What happened next?"

"I will tell you later. There are too many curious eyes around. It is too cold now."

He called the woman; he paid; then hugged her, and she said while extending her hand towards me:

"I want to shake hands with your girlfriend . . . come again."

Davor did not say anything, we just left.

Gentle music played as he drove. Again, he tapped his index finger against the steering wheel. He said:

"I will take you now to a place where I haven't been for some good twenty years. You will again see the entire port and the gulf, but from a different angle."

We came to a very beautiful, little town with old, charming buildings. He told me that the buildings were built in times of the Queen Maria Theresa. He gave me a short history of this beautiful place, about the tourism that started there more than a hundred years ago; he told me about European tsars who visited those beautiful villas to enjoy the good climate and stunning sites. He behaved like my protector, like my own father. He opened the door for me; he held my coat; he pulled my collar up and blew warm air into my cold fingers.

We sat in a very old restaurant in the middle of a park. It was a rather stunning park, with fountains and statues of little, chubby angels. The place had huge windows, you could see the whole park, the street and then as he said, the entire gulf. I could clearly see the whole town, for a strong wind started blowing, and it took away the smog, clouds and mist. He pointed out where my grandma and his buildings stood.

A group of young people were sitting at the near-by table. They were too loud, showing off. They pointed their fingers towards Davor, whispering; then a young, tall and slim woman walked to our table. It was Tiyana.

She said:

"What are *you* doing in the company of the distinguished Mr Davor? Sir, I am Annamaria Millich's daughter; you used to be my mother's close friend. She has pictures of you, your records and she would be very happy if you only call her and tell her you're in town . . ."

Davor interrupted:

"Say hello to your mother," then he looked at me and asked: "What would you like to drink, Lora?"

"Hot chocolate, thank you." Davor went to get us our drinks, and Tiyana sat in his seat:

"For Christ's sake, what are *you* doing with Mr Davor?"

I did not say a word, for I did not want to talk to her. She persisted with her question, and I kept my silence. When Davor came back, she was still sitting in his seat. She started again:

"Mr Davor . . ."

He said:

"I am not a mister. I am just Davor."

"Oh sorry, but I do not feel comfortable calling you only by your name. I am a well brought up girl; here, we address people with 'sir'. I wanted to ask you, sir, is it really true that you used to play with U2? I heard you were doing things with Tom Waits? Do you really know all those people?"

Davor said:

"Do you like myths? To elevate somebody to great heights, to worship icons? I am not a distinguished one. I am only doing what I know how to do best. Can you excuse us now, for you interrupted our earlier conversation? See you later."

She stood up with a fake smile on her face and spoke loudly so that everybody could hear her:

"Certainly, I'll see you later, Davor."

With a straight back, she walked to the table where her friends were seated.

"My God, who else should I meet here today but Annamaria's daughter! Annamaria was just like that—pushy and arrogant. She and Barbara could not stand each other. Barbara liked her brother . . . what was his name . . .?"

"Aurelio." I said.

"Oh, yes, Aurelio. He was a strange fellow. Who knows where he is now. I do not believe that he stayed here while the country was at war. He would never soil his fine suit". Then Davor giggled a little.

"Aurelio died."

"He died? Really? Not in the war? Aurelio and the war?"

"He died in a car accident. I never met him; I was not born yet when he died."

"Barbara couldn't stand snobs. Annamaria was a snob. When she used to cross our path, Barbara would say, 'There is that stuffed turkey, let's cross the road, I don't want to meet her.' You could not talk about anything else with Annamaria but her clothes and her apparent beauty. I met her daughter now, and funny it is how much she looks just like Annamaria. When I look at you, I do not see Barbara. Only sometimes underneath your timid smile, something strong appears . . . maybe Barbara pops up."

The waitress brought us a cup of hot chocolate and a glass from which a very strong smell was spreading. It could have been whiskey, I did not know. Davor lit his cigarette and after few puffs, he said:

"So, what happened next?"

3.

"Then I learned that the world has different ways to kill a man. No, that was no longer just a bullet, or a car hitting a body that lifelessly hits the ground. I learned of a more sophisticated death.

The death of the soul.

'I do not want to go anywhere,' that was my answer, I knew it. But this answer was not in accordance with Reality. Barbara was not mine anymore. This town had changed its name; it was not called Home any longer. I was not vibrating with its rhythm anymore; I could not recognise its sounds and its colours. The sky was just blackness, and I thought:

'Doesn't matter, anyway, I do not exist anymore.'

That day, Igor came with a very worried look on his face. His eyes were bigger than usual, his face was redder. His speech was different when he said:

'What happened?'

'I don't know, you tell me.'

'Where is Barbara?'

'I don't know, you tell me.'

'I heard she is in hospital. I heard she drank a fistful of pills and a bottle of cognac. I heard she barely survived. I was told she had written some sort of "Farewell Davor" letter. What happened Davor; what is the truth?'

'I don't know. It must be so. This morning, her father came to see me . . .' I hugged Igor, saying:

'Goodbye, my friend.'

He looked at me with a disturbed look:

'Hey, don't you be silly now. Cool off. Maybe this is not true at all. Why "goodbye". Look, I'll call Teresa, she will tell me what happened . . .'

I packed my suitcase that afternoon. I decided to go to my father's. I did not call him; I did not tell him I was coming. Looking at my big suitcase, my grandmother asked me:

'Where are you off to?'

'Mind your own business!' I said and slammed the door.

She yelled through the window:

'That was the way your father left.'

I could not care less. I walked the street which was not mine anymore (I could not hear its sounds; I could not smell its fragrance). For the first time in my life, I did not look at Barbara's window. My legs carried me on their own accord, heavy like a zombie's legs; my soul crouched somewhere unknown within me and went numb, astonished. I thought that it had gone numb forever.

I did not catch a bus; I did not stop a taxi. I passed by my University building when someone called out my name, 'Davor!' Then I thought—it was not my name anymore.

It was not raining that day. It was supposed to be an ordinary day. It was to others. People were sitting at café tables out in the weak sun; they read their newspapers while sipping their afternoon coffees. On the empty tables, seagulls were pecking little crumbs. Someone yelled, 'Davor!' Then, for certain, I knew it was not me.

The railway station was a huge, grey and repulsive building. In front of it, there were unshaven taxi drivers with their hands in their pockets, and cigarettes hanging from the corner of their lips. It was an ugly picture, and I did not want to be a part of it.

I never liked railway stations; I never liked travelling by train. I never liked those changing images through the window, changing without any meaning or purpose.

The woman at the counter asked, 'How can I help you?'

'One way ticket to Düsseldorf.'

'No direct line, you've got to transfer . . .'

'I have already transferred . . .'

'Beg your pardon?' she asked, confused.

'Nothing, nothing. I will transfer . . .'

The train started its journey.

I tried to avoid thinking about Barbara. The sound of the iron train tracks was rhythmically repeating her name. I opened the window and cried into the wind.

'What will happen to Barbara?' That's what hurt me. What will happen to me, did not matter; I already wanted to punish the traitor. By the worst method I could think of. Marko was the judge, and I was the executioner. And the punishment read: Kill his soul.

I changed trains four times. Dirty stations, the stench of stale urine and exhausted passengers. The night trains were full of small thieves. The distinguishable stench of railway stations. Scenes changing without apparent logic.

I tried not to think about Barbara. The sound of the iron train tracks was rhythmically repeating her name.

'Where is Barbara now?'

While scenes were changing, I saw her face in each of them; in the whistle of the locomotive I heard her voice, it was calling Davor. We never said goodbye.

The train carried me further and further away from Barbara; it took me so far that I thought,

'We will probably both die not seeing each other ever again.'

When the train brought me to my destination, a light on the horizon announced dawn. I called a taxi and gave the address to the driver; I could not utter a word of German. He was driving around for a long time; it seemed to me that we passed by the same places. I asked him in English where he was taking me, and I could not understand his answer.

I rang the doorbell. Once, then, once again. I rang several times. A woman opened the door. She was young; her fake-blonde hair was uncombed. I asked her about my father. She looked at me suspiciously. She spoke fast while gesticulating. I could not understand anything. She shut the door in my face. I rang again. Then my father opened the door in his dressing gown. He was very surprised when he saw me:

'Davor, how come?'

We stood at the opened door. Then my father gathered the edges of his dressing gown together, and opened the door wide, saying:

'Come in, son.'

He walked me into his living room, then he went into some other room. I heard him talking with the fake blonde. I heard water running; I heard her dressing. She left without a word. Father made us a coffee. After we had our coffees in silence, he made breakfast and sat next to me. Only then, he repeated his question:

'How come, son?'

'I came to stay with you.'

'How come you did not call?'

'I didn't have the time to call.'

'Something quite big happened. What?'

'Nothing happened. I just came.'

He did not believe me; he knew I never came unannounced.

'Is Grandma fine?'

'She is fine.'

'What about Uni?'

'Still at the same place.'

'Where is Barbara?'

'Barbara's at home.'

'So, everything's just normal then.'

'Just like always.'

'I am so surprised by your sudden visit. How long are you planning to stay?'

I ate in silence. I was hungry. Father had a new place. It was a colossal apartment. The building was brand new and luxurious; you could see a well-manicured garden from the window. The furniture was brand new; white was the colour that dominated. The armchairs and the sofa were made of white leather, the side table was made of dark, almost black wood with little white details, while a black and white piano stood in the corner of the room. The kitchen was big and modern, all in pearl-white marble. The bathroom was made of marble too. In the living room, rare paintings adorned the walls. I looked around, he came behind me and asked:

'Would you like to have a shower?'

I said:

'It is so nice here,' he nodded his head. I felt uncomfortable. I asked him:

'Are you going to work now?' It was six o'clock in the morning.

He sat next to me. On his wrist was an expensive watch. He turned his palms up, showing them to me, and asked:

'My hands, how do they look to you?'

His hands were white and soft. His fingers long and slender. The fingernails well shaped, cut finely; they looked perfectly manicured. I understood his question, so I smiled:

'They look like a gambler's hands.'

'I see, son; you'd like to stay here. Life in a foreign land is not an easy one. I do not know the reason why you want to stay. The reason is not the need for a better life, nor is adventure, you were not a born adventurer. I will not interrogate what made you come here; maybe one day you will be ready to tell me. But, as I told you, life here is not an easy one. Not for a foreigner, and a foreigner you will always be. Even the second, the third generation, we are all foreigners. You will be the Foreigner. So, be ready to be considered less intelligent, less worthy, certainly not the best company. You've got to understand that you won't be able to associate with who you'd like to, but rather with second-class citizens and loners. Are you ready for that, Davor?'

I said nothing, therefore he continued:

'Well, if you are ready, let's continue. Your chances to amount to anything will be three times harder; you will not become Beethoven. What kind of work could you possibly do here? You have not graduated yet, you just commenced university. Even if you had your degree, nothing would change. At least, not for the first few years. You do not speak a word of German.'

He hugged me; he ran his fingers through my hair. He sighed and started again:

'I thought you would be spared of such a life. It's a dog's life. I thought I would secure you a good life over there. I thought you would live *your life* there. Here you do not get to live *your life*. I thought you would go to university, you would have fun with your band . . .'

'I thought so, too. But these times are gone.'

He continued as if I hadn't said anything:

'You were all under the impression that I was a labourer. But I am not. I could not be a laborer, Davor. I could not dig roads, clean the streets or public toilets. I could not work on building sites, curse with labourers, take the morning coffee on the pavement and eat a greasy pie wrapped in a sheet of old newspaper. I grew up in a city, went to college. I grew up with a piano, playing classical music. So that I would never do things like that. Do not ask me what I do, and what I have been doing all these years. I don't want you to be a part of my world, which means, I will never introduce you to any of my "friends" nor to any women I know. To you, I will remain what I was all these years—a caring father. You will enroll into a college to learn the language first. I want you to enroll into university after you learn German. There is no need for you to work, I will provide everything. You must obtain your degree, otherwise there are only two choices left and none of them is where I'd like to see you. I dreamt of your future. It is so difficult for me to see you here now. I see indifference in your eyes; I do not know what happened, but it would be best if you took a shower now, and then have some rest, you are tired.'

I didn't care what he was doing. Wherever I looked or touched, was brand new and expensive. Everything was signed by the finest designers.

That was my new reality. It looked bleak. There was no more Barbara, nor the father I knew before. He was 'Someone Else' too."

4.

"I hardly remember the first five years of my life in Germany.

I drank. Constantly and heavily. During the day I slept, and when night came, I went out, just like my father. He did not ask me anything; nor did I ask him. Someone else took care of our clothes and domestic duties. I noticed a woman coming three or four times during the week with a basket of washed clothes.

I enrolled into a college for foreigners to learn the language, but I attended it rarely.

There was plenty of money, all the time. Just like the absence of my father—all the time, plenty of absence. Sometimes, I would not see him for weeks. I do not know whether he believed I was studying, but he pretended he did.

On one occasion, he said:

'When you conquer these emotions, you will succeed.'

I never wanted to conquer 'these emotions'. I loved to suffer and I suffered a lot: for my home, my friends, even for my grandmother, but the most I suffered was for Barbara.

They exiled me to Germany; I heard they exiled her even further—to Australia. I heard she got married; I heard she had a child. I heard she had married well, she was happy. But I never believed that she was happy. Not after all that happened. I was never sure what happiness was. I know, one can find some sort of peace. But I never believed that she was happy. When all was well in Barbara's world, when everything was the way she wanted it to be, when she had my undivided love and understanding, there was still, within her, that special 'touch of sadness'. Just like in a fairytale, when the thirteenth fairy touches the child with her magic wand. The inborn touch of sadness. I already lived in a foreign country and knew that in someone else's land you couldn't be happy. Maybe if you had forgotten everything. If you had forgotten yourself. I could not forget myself, even though I tried drowning this image of myself in alcohol.

And boy, could I drink! I would drink anything I could find. I was never selective of any drink or any company. My company often consisted of the same kind of losers, just like me. Men and women from the fringe of society, mostly immigrants who didn't have the gift of forgetting themselves. Sometimes, I would befriend the same kind of Germans who would claim, even dead-drunk, that they were finer and more sophisticated people than 'us'. Drunk, they would say they belonged to the Chosen Clan.

We would gather in some dingy holes where the light was dim and the waitresses angry and gruff. They used to play 'good music' there, music which portrayed the feelings of a lost man. The sound of that music was hollow, the singer's voice cracked from alcohol, nicotine and shouting. I would go there almost every evening approximately at the same time, sit (approximately) at the same table and lose myself in the music and alcohol, and let myself be guided by them further and further away from me. I could not stand my own voice, that was the reason why I spoke rarely. At the beginning, my 'mates' tried to lure me into conversation; I would shout them a drink, a few times, just to be left alone. Even when I was surrounded by people, I would never speak.

The first three years, I drank every night and all night. I would come home at dawn—sober or just tipsy. Satan had nested within me, and he drank through my mouth while my brain stayed absolutely alert and sober. My battles against Satan were of little strength; I would lose those battles easily. Sometimes, I would stay at home, for I had decided to change everything, to break the bad habit for good. But I didn't have the needed strength. I had only my guitar. When I sometimes stayed at home, sober and alone, I would tear my soul to pieces with sounds of my guitar. My guitar became an indivisible piece of me, only music gave real meaning to my life.

I would always see her looking at me from a distance. Barbara.

I thought she witnessed my regret which was obvious in my self-destruction. I thought the more self-harm I did to myself, the bigger my regret. More sincere. When I was more drunk than usual, I would say loudly:

'You see what kind of loser I am; thank Heavens you are saved from me.'

I thought that there was no salvation for my soul; I was waiting for death. But death does not come so easily. It can't be waited for.

After several wild years, I was not so sturdy anymore. I would easily get drunk, and I would fall asleep wherever and with whomever was near. Pub owners would force me out late in the night, or a policeman in the park would tell me to leave when I would fall asleep on the park bench. They used to push the baton into my ribs: 'Identification card! Identification card!' Ah, bloody pigs, they knew everything about everyone. I thought that only my country was full of policemen who pushed their batons into your ribs. I thought a man couldn't even get properly wasted.

Sometimes, for days, I would lie so sick and exhausted in my bed, only gathering strength for sinking deeper.

I would think, 'I will end up like this: ill, drunk and with the blues in my soul.'

Nobody had ever called me. Nobody had ever written me a letter. Only my old buddy, Igor. At that time, I lost my last illusion—about friendship. I used to have so many friends, I could not count their number. I would ask Igor:

'Are friends still asking about me?' He would say nothing. I would ask him:

'What did people say after I left?' He would change the subject.

The death of my soul was supposed to happen in three acts: with Barbara's and my exile brought by Marko's sentence, then, with my alcoholism and self-destructive ways, and the third—with the death of my father.

That was meant to be the third act, the last assault of fate.

(But it did not happen that way.)

I told you, Lora, how Marko cast me out, and I told you about my self-destruction.

Listen to this, now.

One morning, not particularly different to any other morning which I faced after a night of total drunkenness, I found my father's body in front of our apartment. Blood was still gushing out of his temple, but he had left his body already. The expression on his face was a gruesome one, therefore I thought the last scene he had seen must have been disgusting or terrifying. That was the time when I would get drunk easily and my hangovers would last for hours, but I sobered up instantly. I knelt next to his body and started shaking him:

'Father, Father, it's me. Look at me—Davor.' I screamed while pulling him closer by his collar. His red blood was streaming down his white jacket. That scene awoke another one, long forgotten: white snow, a dog barking, hunters and a shot. A dead rabbit was lying in the white blanket of snow and the blood coloured the snow with a wide circle of red. Once, I went hunting with my father. He shot a rabbit. For me, it was an utterly disgusting deed. He said:

'C'mon, be a man, do not turn your eyes away.' I had always turned my eyes away from violence and death. This time I could not turn my eyes away, for this time in my arms I was holding my dead father's head whilst crying. A siren was heard, police officers came. They interrogated me briefly, then they let me go: a drunkard like me always had an alibi.

The next day, I found an article in the daily papers. Only from that article did I learn who my father really was. I was not surprised: all these luxuries and money, where could all that have come from?

I was twenty-four years old, and my father was forty-four.

I dressed him nicely; once again, for the last time, in his favorite white suit; I put him in a lacquered casket, upholstered with red velvet; I put the lacquered casket in a long black hearse, and I brought him back home. After five years, it was the first time I came back home. Everything looked the same, only I was not the same as before.

I clearly remember my reunion with my grandma. I rang the bell and when she opened the door and saw me standing there, she started to shake as if she was having a seizure. Her fragile legs shook uncontrollably, and she started wiping her eyes with the tea towel she was holding in her hand.

She mumbled:

'I thought I would never see you again.'

When I entered inside, everything looked just as I left it. For a moment, I had the feeling that I had just come back home from school. The same smell of Grandma's kitchen; the tick-tocking of the old clock on the wall; the checkered, two-toned tablecloth which used to irritate me when I was young; so I would hide them from her so that she always had trouble finding them. Coffee-percolator as always, ready on the stove; the curtains pulled apart; I could see a pot-plant on the balcony.

I did not look at Barbara's window; she was happy in Australia.

Grandma asked:

'Aren't you going to sit?' Only her voice brought me back to reality.

I said:

'You sit down, Grandma.' She lifted one eyebrow and asked:

'Son, what's wrong? Are you in trouble again?'

I said:

'We are both in trouble, Grandma. Dad has died.'

She put both hands on her heart. She whimpered like a wounded animal. I hugged her. What a rare gesture of tenderness to share with her. A wailing sound came out of her, and it sounded as if some fragile mechanism was broken. I feared that nobody would fix her again. And that was true, I found my grandma lying on the kitchen floor just a few days after my father's funeral. There was a kitchen knife and two halves of an apple lying next to her. Igor helped me with both funerals. It seemed to me like we had never been apart. Some things simply resist the cruelty of time. I did not see anybody else. When I was about to leave my home again, Igor said:

'Why don't you stay? There is always place for you in the band; you don't have to go back there.'

'I have to.' I said, and once again I left my hometown."

5.

"In the days of my self-destruction caused by alcohol and feelings of guilt and remorse, I thought it was the beginning of the end for me.

My father's death marked the end of that chapter and the beginning of a new one.

That was when I stopped drinking.

The following year, I studied a lot; I played a lot. I was accepted into the Conservatorium of Music. Was it a miracle, or were they really aware of the rare gift they later talked about? In the Conservatorium, they talked about my 'absolute pitch'. I could play any instrument or piece of music; in a symphony orchestra I could discern every note; I could hear every, almost unnoticeable, little error.

But my life changed because of Brenadette.

Beautiful Brenadette. Surreally beautiful, like some Brenadette had appeared from a long-forgotten fairytale . . .

My father died, my grandmother died, I played every night, all night long, and I studied during the day; there was strict order in my life. But I was lonely, eternally lonely.

I saw Brenadette in a library. I borrowed some books from the library, walked out and sat at one of the tables in front of the popular café, next to the library. From the library, out came Brenadette; at that time, I still did not know that was her name. Someone called her name, 'Brenadette!' and she turned her head to the opposite side, not towards the calling voice. (Later, I heard from her that she could not stand it when someone called out to her loudly in public; she said that was a 'scandal'.)

She carried two books in her hands as if she carried two cocker spaniels, with care and love (I learned cocker spaniels were her pets).

Brenadette was the most beautiful woman on this side of the planet.

She was nearly as tall as I was; she had very long hair, the colour of well-brewed beer; she had very fair skin as if she was made of the finest porcelain; black eyebrows and black eyelashes which framed her turquoise coloured eyes with little black dots in the middle. She had full lips like a child, and two dimples on both sides. Her look could easily hypnotise any fool. And not just fools, believe me. Her teeth were perfect too, as if somebody measured them and made them fit to perfection. Her body was the body of a mythic nymph. She was dressed to perfection. Everything on her was expensive, too expensive. She looked like a Million Dollar Girl. I was already used to the arrogant ways of German women, especially when they heard me pronouncing German with difficultly; I was taken aback when she came to my table and asked me kindly:

'May I sit?'

I nodded my head even though I did not want her to sit at my table. Carefully, she laid her books on the table. On one book was written Franz Kafka, and on the other *Bhagavad-Gita.* I knew who Franz Kafka was, but I did not know who *Bhagavad-Gita* was. She threw back her hair coloured like well-brewed beer, which smelled quite the opposite. Possibly, it smelled of the Mediterranean, and that was the reason I smiled. I did not intend to commence any kind of conversation with her (surely, I would stumble); I did not understand why she sat next to me, for there were empty tables around us.

She said simply:

'I am Brenadette.'

'Davor' said I.

She laughed loudly, showing her perfect white teeth. I did not understand what was funny; she said:

'This is fantastic. Can you repeat it once again?'

I said, again:

'Davor.'

Then she said:

'Aha, Davor.'

So, that was the first time Brenadette did not have to repeat her name. Moreover, it was the first time that she asked someone else to repeat their name.

She was christened as a Bernadette.

She changed her name to Brenadette. You ask, 'Why?' When I asked why, she laughed and said, 'There were too many girls with the name Bernadette. Not one Brenadette. I liked the look of confusion on people's faces. I liked to repeat it twice. "What?" always the same question. "Brenadette," the second time. "How come? Why not Bernadette?" "No, it's Brenadette." ' Always the same reaction. When she was asked, 'But why Brenadette,' she would reply, 'But, why not?'"

I repeated her name loudly with my whole mouth —"Brenadette," and Davor continued to recount his story.

"I imagined Barbara to be like her at that age.

Simplicity was always considered to be a virtue. I was in doubt—virtue or plainness? I liked complex women, complicated ones, with deep emotions and passion. I liked unpredictable ones; ones with strong personalities who knew where they were going. I liked capricious, courageous and independent women; the ones to be partners and friends. Alice in Wonderland or Princess and the Pea types were not my choice.

I loved Brenadette, she carried Barbara's strength within her; she carried Barbara's capriciousness and her unpredictability. But she carried Barbara's attributes quite differently; she carried them maturely and it seemed to me that Brenadette was all that Barbara was yet to become. She was wise and measured, careful in her movements like a cautious cat. She knew what she wanted; she knew what she did not want, and she governed her life by such knowledge. She belonged to the same world to which Barbara and I belonged: Satyam—The World of Truth.

She spoke her truth easily and plainly. She never really cared what her truth sounded like to others. Even her eyes looked like cat's eyes. With these eyes of hers, she would look one straight in the eyes as if hypnotising them, easily delivering her thoughts, which sometimes were as sharp as a sword. Just like with Barbara, nobody was indifferent towards Brenadette.

Very early on, she learned that the little human heart was full of envy. As I said before, she was not only beautiful, but she was an extremely intelligent woman, too. Yes, you can't find that often. A superficial glance of Brenadette indicated the complete opposite of her true nature. That was exactly what she wanted. She wanted to be evaluated wrongly. She had the luxury to choose and she made her own choices. She would say that her great looks and expensive image gave her the possibility to choose—everybody feared her. She looked too perfect for a mere mortal to address her. I felt uncomfortable myself when she sat at my table:

'What the hell could I possibly talk about with a woman like that?'

She looked powerful, self-assured, a little bit audacious, even dangerous; intimidating. She looked like total perfection, unreal. She looked like that little figurine on a wedding cake: everybody admired her, rare were those who really wanted her. Too much beauty, too much sweetness. What was hidden behind it? And those eyes of hers from which one could not hide any secrets.

Well, whilst she was sitting at my table, she said:

'You don't come to the pub anymore, do you?'

I looked at her suspiciously:

'You must have mistaken me for someone else, we do not know each other.'

She raised her voice a little bit:

'Really? We did not know each other's names until now, Davor, but we do know each other. At least, I know *you.* You've visited *The Bunt* regularly for the last few years. You used to sit, all alone, alone you would drink; you talked to yourself in some unknown language. I understood a bit later or my intuition spoke to me, you were reciting Prevert's *Barbara.* I did not see you all of last year, my poet.'

The Bunt and *Brenadette.* What could they ever have in common? A Million Dollar Girl and *The Bunt.* A hole on the outskirts of town where friendless visitors were regulars; the ones who stank of alcohol, sweat and solitude. *The Bunt*—the losers' last resort. Years ago, it was a pub where alternative music was played. It was opened till dawn, the booze was cheaper, therefore the place attracted a cheap clientele.

I did not say anything, so she spoke again:

'I still go occasionally, but you don't come at all.'

'No, I don't visit anymore.' She stared at me with an intense stare from which I felt uneasy, I said:

'I stopped drinking, so I stopped coming.'

She smiled, again:

'Can't you come sober?'

'No.' I said.

'Well, I come sober and I leave sober. I lost all hope that I would see you ever again.'

It all sounded so stupid and fake. Why would she hope to see *me* again? So, I asked her exactly that:

'Why would you hope to see *me*?'

'I have never seen that much sadness in anyone's eyes, or as much suffering in anyone's voice. What was her name?'

'Barbara.' I said quietly, and she nodded:

'I thought so.'

After a short silence, she asked:

'Where is Barbara now?'

'Nowhere, she lives only in my memory. She is someone else now, someone I do not know anymore.'

She looked at me speechlessly, I saw compassion in her eyes. Then she said while her eyes were fixed on her long fingers playing with the pages of a book:

'You won't ask me what I was doing at *The Bunt*?'

'I won't.' I said while I looked for a waiter. I waved to him. When I saw him approaching, I extended my hand and said:

'It was my pleasure, Brenadette.'

I was just about to cross the road when I heard her voice:

'Davor!' I looked back and saw her waving with my books in her hand. Yes, she had confused me. I came back to her table and sat there again. We both laughed.

Later, she told me that she was looking for me everywhere in the desperate hope to see me again. She said she wanted to see me, for she saw the eternal sorrow in my eyes. She told me that 'only old and mighty souls carry that much sorrow'. She told me that 'only old and mighty souls have the privilege of great suffering'. She talked like that while gesturing with her hand around us:

'Look at these smiling people around us. They are happy because all their desires are fulfilled—they live in a wealthy country; they have enough food, enough beer, sex and festivals. They have automobiles that carry them to their picnics. They have huge altars in their living rooms—televisions which control their thoughts and their lives. The biggest suffering for them would be if somebody took away their holiday this year. The suffering of the average well-fed citizen! They don't care about other people's business, for their own business is taken care of by Someone Big and Sacred . . .'

I was listening to her words without interruption. It was as if Barbara was talking through her. But, I was confused by her image which was in opposition to her thoughts. She had an expensive wrist-watch, thick gold bracelets and chains, rings with real diamonds—it all spoke to her valuing something else other than 'the suffering of one's soul'.

Later, I found out why she was a regular at *The Bunt*. Every Thursday, Thomas played at *The Bunt*. Yes, Thomas, the unshaven one, deprived of sleep; the one whose clothes were stained all over, never pressed; the one with messy, dirty hair.

She told me she visited every Thursday. She would come there dressed in an old pair of baggy jeans, an oversized jumper and a pair of sneakers. She would gather her beautiful hair, the colour of well-brewed beer, on top of her head and cover it with a big woolen beanie. She would sit dressed like that next to my table and look at Thomas. He looked at least fifteen years older than he was in his old worn-out, but too small, coat with his eyes fixed on the past. Only his music was alive, everything else was dead for Thomas, long ago. His hair was dead, his teeth were dead, his look was dead, outdated, but Brenadette came anyway, every Thursday, to see him.

It seemed to me that Brenadette was Barbara; I was Thomas.

She was born there, in the same district, just around the corner from *The Bunt*. It was not an affluent part of town; her childhood was not a happy one. But she had Thomas, so life was good. Since the day he was born he was 'a star'. The star of the street, the star of the school and the brightest star in Brenadette's sky.

She had to start working early. She grew into a rare beauty. But she said she felt like everything around her was 'empty and cheap'. She never liked that feeling of emptiness and poverty, shallowness and triviality. Some tiny, inner voice, was calling, telling her to go elsewhere. That tiny voice would often whisper, 'there is a better life waiting for Brenadette.' And that tiny voice grew stronger and louder, 'Brenadette, Brenadette, life is elsewhere . . .'

She learned early on, that she possessed the most powerful weapons to fight poverty and banality—her beauty and her intelligence.

She was twenty-three and had numerous unfulfilled desires. Nobody she knew could fulfill her desires; they all belonged to the same world ('same shit') where she was trapped. The only difference between her and others was that she was aware of that 'shit' and was deeply unhappy with her life. Her friends were finding 'some other meaning to life', or they did not look for any. 'Some other meaning to life' was, actually, just evenings at pubs where they listened to music and drank a lot. Those who did not find any meaning in anything were still going to places where they listened to the same music and drank a lot.

Brenadette did not want to be part of such a world. She knew that there was a better world and that she belonged there (The tiny voice was telling her, 'Brenadette, Brenadette life is elsewhere . . .')

Was it chance or not, but she met Dieter. He looked like 'someone who might fulfill all her desires'. He was the wealthiest man in the region. He bought her expensive presents; he took her to places Brenadette had only seen on postcards before, places to which she would never have been had she never met him. Dieter was forty-seven years older than Brenadette. He had a wife and two married daughters, both older than Brenadette. Regardless, she told him one day:

'I don't want to be your mistress. Marry me, Dieter.'

I guess Brenadette was not his first mistress, but she was certainly his last. I guess she was so irresistible even to Dieter, who was rich, not only in his wealth, but in his experiences too . . . with her eyes, with her body of a nymph and with that singing voice whose rhythm echoed in one's ears forever . . . with her unusual desires, with her surreal stories always on the edge of reality . . . where would he ever find another Brenadette . . . where would he ever find so much laughter, so much spontaneity and sincerity . . . So, when she said, 'I don't want to be your mistress. Marry me, Deiter' . . . all that could have been saved with one word, with one decision.

He divorced his wife, maybe not lightheartedly; they split their wealth not lightheartedly, but regardless of it, he was still the wealthiest man in the region. After Dieter's divorce, after he split his wealth in half, they booked their wedding. But first, she went to see Thomas. She thought it did not matter anymore, for they grew up together, they stayed together too long; she matured and he did not; he was not ambitious at all. Or, at least they didn't have the same ambitions any longer, as she put it. She said:

'Thomas, I am getting married to someone else.'

She said she could never forget the expression on his face. Nor the colour of his eyes which she had never seen there before. And because of that new colour in his eyes he became someone else for the rest of his days.

She married Deiter; only three years later he passed away. She was only twenty-six when she became a wealthy widow, the wealthiest in the region.

At the same time, approximately, we started the pilgrimage to *The Bunt*.

When I met her, she was thirty-two, but she looked like someone approaching twenty. Often, I would ask her:

'How did you preserve your beauty?'

'There is some deeper meaning to it.' She would say. For her, everything 'had some deeper meaning'.

Everything important about life, I learned from Brenadette. All the important people, I met at Brenadette's. She loved life and cherished it like a rare gift; she loved people; she laughed so often with a ringing and contagious laugh. She loved travelling and wandering around and beautiful Brenadette could afford it easily. But I sensed always that there was, within her, that special touch of sadness, the same one Barbara carried within her, the same one seen in those whose soul yearned for 'something else', for 'something sacred', something big, pure and timeless. Whose soul yearned for a lost love, or a lost God within.

She never tried hard to be perfect. She never tried to control herself or any situation, that's why she looked perfect to me. The way she behaved showed that she knew only 'the best' belonged to her, not by mere chance but because of her intelligence and capability to materialise her desires. In each of her sentences, there was a gap for a question or for further clarification. There were no 'big mysteries'. She was not afraid to open up to another person, for she was exactly aware of who she was. She never had the need to dominate people, nor was she afraid that others might dominate or reject her.

In her trying times, she knew how to console and support herself knowing that everything had its time to flourish, time to pass. The end of her trying times, she would wait with patience and with some sort of unusual feeling that 'even this will pass'. She knew that everything was ever-changing, and like a rare collector, she collected memories and stuck them into her soul like flowers in an herbarium, to keep them there for eternity.

That day, when I met her, the day when I had forgotten to take my books from the table, she gave me a lift home. She said:

'How bizarre! I met you in *The Bunt* and here we are—we are almost neighbours. Davor, tell me more about yourself. Who are you?'

I invited her to come up, and when she saw the place, she said:

'What a beautiful, sophisticated place.'

'Nothing here is mine. I mean, I inherited it all.'

'Inherited? From Barbara?'

'No, from my father.'

'Who is your father?'

'He is nobody anymore—he died. I inherited this apartment from him and a big fat bank account. You asked—who was my father? He was the uncrowned king of the underground.'

'How exciting!' She said and sank deeper into the sofa.

'No, it is not exciting, it is sad. I grew up believing that my father was a labourer in Germany. I didn't have a mother; I grew up with two grandmothers; I saw my father once, rarely twice a year. I was an insecure and quiet child. Only now can I understand why Marko hated me that much. He knew who my father was.'

'Who is Marko?'

'Barbara's father.'

'I see.' Said Brenadette.

She sat at the piano and started playing. I took my guitar trying to follow her, but she played very badly. I agreed when she asked me to give her piano lessons. She started with three times per week. She never paid for her lessons; after each lesson, she used to take me out for dinner. Sometimes we would go to the best known, the most expensive restaurants in town, on other occasions we would visit cheap eateries on the edge of the town where sausages and sauerkraut were cooked, and where they served cheap beer on tap.

When she took me to the expensive restaurant of her choice, I would feel like a very important person. Everybody knew her; everybody wanted to say hello, to shake hands with her. I met her friends, too. It was a cast of extremely wealthy, extremely arrogant, all-knowing pure-blooded Germans. Jokingly, she told me that she saw the blue blood in their veins. They would rarely address me. If they really had to talk to me, then it would be in short, clear and simplified sentences—the way we usually address the less intelligent, or little kids. I never belonged there; but I never really tried. I never tried for a few reasons. The main reason was I never truly wanted to belong to such an exclusive group which looked down on all others; then the other, equally important, reason was they would never accept me whatever I tried. They knew 'where I belonged'. Exclusivity was given by birth. With my name and the accent I had, I felt better when I stood alone, just observing them silently.

'Why do you say that? Do you really feel like that?' Brenadette used to ask me.

'Yes, I do feel like that, but I don't care. My talent can't be taken away from me. What my soul needs, theirs has never even heard of. But one thing was strange, it was silly to think why such intelligent, educated people, you said, "blue-blooded nobility," can't accept that a sophisticated and talented person could be born anywhere else. Or, was it some evil spell cast upon some nations, so we always consider them to be ignorant, servants or barbarians? So, what about an individual? The Nation above the individual? Always the same ". . . Ahh, you come from *there* . . . well, maybe you are not all the same, after all . . . it happens sometimes . . . someone might be a bit better". They put you into this little drawer and never let you out of it in their minds. I don't want to associate with people, Brenadette; the human mind is so limited, so fickle; I like to be just with music.' "

Carefully, I touched Davor's hand and asked him in a quiet voice (full of incomprehensible anticipation):

"Was Brenadette your wife?" (But I wanted to ask something else; I did not know how to form that question, but it was for certain different to the one I asked).

"No, Brenadette was only Dieter's wife and nobody else's. When I would ask her:

'Brenadette is there somebody special?' She would mysteriously smile and say:

'There is . . . there is always somebody special in my life.'

Nobody knew who was Brenadette's 'special someone'. Some thought that I was her 'special someone', her piano teacher; but I never really knew who it was. She had many friends, many admirers; sometimes she would be out of the country for weeks. She would go shopping in Paris; she frequented fashion shows in Milan, and theatres in London. On such occasions, I was not with Brenadette, 'someone else' accompanied her.

The connection between us was music and *The Bunt*. In our youth, fate touched us in the same place (in the region of our heart, by our own choice). We took that as some sort of secret sign, an undisclosed language of destiny of our intertwined lives, while telling and retelling our past, playing the piano and eating the most expensive meals, without champagne."

That answer did not satisfy me (for the question was wrong). I knew Dieter was Brenadette's only husband. But what I wanted to know was — were they very close, did they hold hands, did they dream about their future together, were they lovers? (Were they lovers? That was the right question I wanted to ask, but I could not utter it. I feared the colour which would colour my fair cheeks; I feared my voice, but was it because of Barbara or because of something new and unexplainable?)

"Did you love Brenadette?"

He smiled while looking straight into my eyes. (That look of his was exactly what I feared, the look which could colour my fair cheeks red, could colour my eyes with shame and nail them to the table.) It was a long, long look of his, and I felt as if my ears were burning. I knew I was red all over my face. Even my neck started to burn. (But nevertheless, I asked him!)

He said:

"I never stopped loving Barbara." He continued looking me in the eyes without blinking. I said to him (in a voice which sounded as if it would start singing):

"Please, do not look at me that way." (For he was just looking at me 'that way', with a look which could read everything, each of my hidden thoughts and each of my presentiments).

"The more I look at you, the more of Barbara I see in you. I feel as if my soul was made of numerous, multi-coloured petals, I feel like some sort of rare flower. Each time I tell you one of my numerous stories, which my soul is made of, I feel as if I am breaking off one of the multi-coloured petals and letting it go in the wind, giving it freedom. It looks as if this flower was made of 'petals of secrets', and telling you my secrets I am taking off the burden of those secrets which I never shared with anyone, in the foolish hope that one day I would share them, somewhere, sometime, with Barbara. And that flower became frozen in my strange inner wasteland, it almost became frozen in my own soul, making it damp and tired, too tired for the soul of a freedom-wanderer . . . and here you are, young, pure and beautiful, and I am opening up to you with ease, spontaneously, the way Brenadette used to open up to me. You are asking me, did I love Brenadette. Certainly, I did."

6.

"But those were hard times for love. We both belonged only to ourselves, or to somebody else for a long time. I don't know how much you know about alcoholism; you are still young and pure, but someone who drank as much as I did, could not stop that habit in one day, with one single decision. My battle lasted for years, and I still don't know whether it ceased. Each time when I got into some sort of crisis (most often an identity crisis) I would reach for alcohol, once again. I would think in such moments:

'Anyway, everything is wrong.' I would think:

'Only one more time; just today. Just one, or two drinks . . . I won't get drunk . . .'

I hid the fact I was drinking from Brenadette, for I feared I might lose her friendship. I had only her, and deep down I believed that she was an incarnation of some demi-goddess. This 'last' drunkenness (each 'solid' drunkenness was 'the last one') was liable for two very significant events. I will tell you in no particular order."

(I closed my eyes. I could sense the pleasant fragrance of his cologne; the unpleasant smell of alcohol; the sophisticated fragrance of Brenadette's perfume; the smell of Germany; the smell of Davor's cigarette; the timbre of his voice; the timbre of Barbara's voice and the smell of her bosom; the smell of mulberries . . . even the smell of my childhood came uninvited . . . I did not want the smell of my childhood at that time, nor the smell of Ted's pipe . . . I just wanted the smell of a long forgotten or found again love

. . . I wanted the smell of Davor's voice, which was painting these pictures . . .)

"I was seated in some cheap eatery, without even knowing its name, I just stumbled into it. I carried a few books underneath my arm; it was raining heavily, each and every rain reminded me of Barbara. There was a tavern, and the smell of cooked cabbage coming out of it. It smelled of warmth; it smelled of home; it smelled of all that I once had and lost, and knew I would never have again. I wanted to have all of that, at least for a moment, so I walked into the tavern where I sincerely just wanted to eat the cabbage, but I had ordered a carafe of wine—I said I would eat a bit later. The entire afternoon I drank, totally convinced that it was my last drunkenness; convinced that I was drinking 'for the last time, today'. There were some people there, indifferent and casually engaged in a light conversation. I envied them on their light conversation, for that was the way good acquaintances chatted. I envied them while they were checking their watches, for it was time to go home, where dinner would be waiting for them, a wife, who never ceased to grumble; where their favorite program was on television; their dressing gown was waiting, a pipe . . . I sincerely envied them in that moment for all that I never wanted to have, never wanted to be. They belonged somewhere; this was their tavern, their beer, their town and their life. Mine was non-existent anymore. I was building something fragile on legs of glass; some sort of life which was often knocked down, and every time one of the little glass legs, which held the illusion of my world, would crack, I would enter any tavern, I would order a cheap wine and would think, 'Anyway, nobody cares anymore.'

Precisely at that moment, I had the impression that all the guests of the tavern had heard my thoughts. There was dead silence. It seemed to me that all of them were looking at me, for it was written on my forehead as if on a big screen, '*Anyway, nobody cares anymore.*'

When I lifted my eyes, I noticed that nobody was looking at me. All the eyes were on the entrance door. And there, at the tavern door, an Angel stood; a creature which confused them all and left them speechless. I could not discern whether I was tipsy, totally drunk or hallucinating. There was an Angel standing at the entrance door and with its light legs started walking towards me and in a human voice, the Angel said:

'I have been looking for you the entire day.'

She lifted me up, with one arm I hugged Brenadette's shoulders, she held me around my waist, she paid the bill and walked me to the car.

While I was still drunk, it seemed to me that she cried.

The next morning, I got up with an unbearable headache with feelings of shame and regret. The only thing I could remember was that Brenadette appeared in the tavern like some sort of Angel of Salvation and took me home. I did not remember the rest: how I found myself in my bed dressed in my pyjamas. I didn't know what the time was, she opened the door of my bedroom and walked in, dressed only in my bathrobe. She just sat next to me without a single word. When I opened my mouth, wanting to say something, she placed her hand over my mouth. Stillness filled the room just as melancholy filled her eyes.

She looked different; she looked like some other Brenadette. She said:

'I used to go out and search for my father. Every evening, I would drag him back home; he would stumble and I would help him get up again. We comforted each other saying that 'from tomorrow everything was going to be different' knowing that was not true. My furious mother was waiting at home, insulting us with very imaginative names. I always thought that she drove him down that road. She was a heartless woman, and I had never learned anything good from her. Or perhaps, I had—I learned that I never wanted to become like her. Such little love was in her heart . . .' She was crying. It was the first time I saw a very different Brenadette, fragile and crying. I took her in my arms consoling her by kissing her hair, her face, and her cupid-like lips.

After she told me the whole story of her life, I loved her even more.

She told me she was 'desperately looking for love'. (And I, Lora Donoghue thought: Maybe we all are just 'desperately looking for love') She found love—Thomas. She told me that only Thomas knew how to give her everything she ever missed out on in her life. When she finished school and found her first job, she moved out of her parent's house. When she was leaving, her mother told her:

'Go, it is about time you got off my back. If only I'd be so lucky and that bastard croaks . . . I have had enough of you both.'

She said that a new Brenadette was born (by that time she had already changed her name.) She said she was so young and could not really treasure true love. (There I quivered, I got frightened—does true love come when we cannot really treasure it?)

She thought she could find love again, and again . . .

All she wanted was money, believing that money would buy her freedom. She bought freedom with money but the price of her freedom was the price of her true love.

She never loved Dieter; she loved his money and all she could buy with it. She respected Dieter, for she learned from him the real value of money, she learned how to speak properly, to read the right books; she used to travel with Dieter and learned a lot about this world and its history; she met important, influential and respectable people. Dieter was the first person to tell her about the evolution of human souls through reincarnation; he took her to the Theosophical Society; he introduced her to the works of Madame Blavatsky and Rudolf Steiner. All these stories and scriptures had immediately found their place in her unsettled soul. He taught her what real spirituality was; he took her to the most interesting and intriguing seminars; he was able to unmask charlatans. In these circles, too, he was very influential and respected. She became more than his wife— she became his disciple. That morning, I had learned so much more about Brenadette; that morning I had become Bernadette's disciple. (And what about me, Lora Donoghue, whose disciple was I, Davor?)

She told me:

'There is something strong and big within you, something which propels you forward, but this small, frightened Davor is holding onto his memories like it is the one and only reality which doesn't let him encounter a new reality. Your memories are keeping you at bay, which you should have left a long time ago. That's why it seems to you that your boat is sinking. Davor, the past no longer exists. The past is only in your memory, and memory is very selective, you are choosing only the moments to which you emotionally bind yourself to. When you understand that memories are selective; when you understand that the past really doesn't exist anymore, you will start to live again. Free that enormous creative energy which lies suppressed and hidden by your self-pity. You do not belong to your hometown anymore; you do not belong to Barbara, nor does she belong to you anymore; you do not belong to the past; so, look at the world. The world goes on, the sun still shines and the seasons still change, wake up Davor! Start the journey of discovering yourself, and when you discover who you really are, then be who you are. There is no one on the other side of the door; no one is looking through the keyhole. There is no final judgment Davor, be yourself. Just be, Davor.'

That's how she used to speak to me and I would kiss her wide forehead from which her thick hair fell onto my bare chest. (That picture which he painted by his words . . . 'and I would kiss her wide forehead from which her thick hair fell onto my bare chest' . . . was so alive, so real, and it awakened within me a sudden rush of unknown, but intense, feelings.)

'How can I be who I am when I don't even know who I am?'

'Well, firstly, you've got to find the answer to that question—who are you? When you know who you are, only then can you live your authentic self.'

'And how can you know—who you are?'

'Oh, it is difficult. We often sympathise with our ego which is not the "real self", which leads to total misunderstanding and inner conflict. We cling to some image of ourselves even when it is negative, just like you when you identify with the image of miserable, lonely Davor, with Davor the loser, and you completely meld yourself with that image. And this identity of yours is so strong and alive you can't escape its grip. For to escape from the grip of this false image projected by your ego needs enormous energy and knowledge, and you do not know how to obtain this energy and knowledge.'

I looked at Brenadette with an open mouth:

'So, how can I obtain this energy and knowledge?'

'It is a tricky road, you've got to travel slowly and patiently. Look at yourself. Who are you now? A puppet on a string whose strings are pulled by an invisible force. But this force is not invisible, it is your force, your own thoughts, your own mind has created it. It is the lack of knowledge of who you really are. And to know *who you really are* you can know by -*knowledge*. By *learning*. But not by the *knowledge* and *learning* you are familiar with. There is a different kind of *knowledge* and *learning*. The knowledge and learning you already know does not bring purity. The knowledge found in books cannot free an imprisoned mind, it only imprisons it more. Regardless of the amount of knowledge we acquire, it won't bring us the knowledge of the Sacred and

Timelessness. It won't bring us the Truth. Davor, we are on the same path—we are searching for the Truth. If we want to come to the core of life, to the essence of life, what kind of knowledge do we need? Countless books have been written about it; countless universities have been established, but still, it is very hard to find that knowledge. The way to find this knowledge is through *silence*. The silence in your own heart. Observing yourself. With a different awareness. Mathematicians, scientists and analysists gave us the numbers, names, formulas and shapes. Organised religion gave us dead idols and a rigid code of conduct. But man is not any happier. For we, deep down, we long for something pure and immeasurable. Sacred.'

She continued:

'You have come to the end. So, let's start from the beginning. It is time for *knowledge*.'

And we started our journey to *knowledge*. I went with Brenadette everywhere. She taught me that 'spiritual people' were not necessarily 'saints', nor were 'people of knowledge' really all that knowledgeable. We visited every *ashram* we knew of, where we were received suspiciously and with distrust. In some of these places, we found such rigid rules, more rigid than those they wanted to break free from, claiming that the 'outside world' was not a world of 'free people'.

On one occasion, we came to the 'Temple of the Soul'. The presence of my beautiful Brenadette stirred so much envy that these 'spiritual' people decided not to let us in.

On another occasion, we went to a two-week seminar. Brenadette came in her usual style, full of luster and life, and the monotone voice of the woman at the reception desk said:

'You will be required to dress in simple clothes whilst here, we are modest and simple people.'

Brenadette said:

'We are neither modest nor simple.'

But later we saw it was quite the opposite—they were neither modest nor simple. They would constantly recite the sentences of an old, almost senile man; every meal they started by quoting him, and every meal would finish in the same manner. Some of the followers would entangle themselves in their simplicity, and they simply did not know what they wanted in clumsily faking simplicity. Lustful eyes of the 'saints' would rest on the bosom of beautiful Brernadette, whose sentences always were simple and clear.

After these kinds of 'seminars', 'residential retreats', 'cleansings' and 'rechargings' in various monasteries, *ashrams*, 'houses of light', Brenadette would tell me, smiling mischievously:

'Thank Heavens we escaped from that *mad house*.' But regardless, we would always go back to the same places. They all knew Brenadette from a long time ago, and never tried to 'teach' her or change her. It was known that Brenadette did what she wanted to do. She had the right to follow her own rules and pose her own questions. They would say:

'Well, we all know the way she is.'

They would welcome her with open arms, for these places were very dear, and not only did she pay generously, but she brought her wealthy friends, too.

'Why do you take me to these places if you do not believe in their doctrine and teachings?'

'I use only what I want. In this vast forest of rules and fallacies I am trying to find the essence, or just little crumbs of knowledge or truth, which have been covered with their rules. More than that, I'd like you to learn which way *not* to behave, how *not* to think. I'd like you to understand what the truth is and what is a fallacy; I'd like you to penetrate into the emptiness of the majority of these, so-called, "teachings" —to recognise manipulation, thirst for money, power and respect. I want you to recognise that those who want to lead others are not able to lead themselves, and how freely people give their souls to be led astray. Places like that are full of "lost souls" wandering from one *guru* to another, from one organisation to another, and all that those *gurus* and organisations do for them is brainwash their minds and empty their pockets. I want you to understand that there is no "better world" than the one we live in. The world we live in is perfect; everything is organised in the best possible way. The problem is that people don't know how to relate to this world. When you learn the rules of how to relate to the world around you, you will enter the World of Perfection.'

We would meditate for hours, or would sing in a totally unknown language the same verse over and over. I would ask Brenadette:

'How was it?'

She would say:

'I nearly died of boredom.'

But she did not really think that. She did not think at all, for she already knew that a thought alone floated on the surface of reality. But for her Reality was Elsewhere.

Some time later, we met a man called Charlie. Charlie always wore blue jeans and a black jacket with *Ray Ban* glasses on his nose. He talked very little, for he said 'he knew very little'.

We met him at Brenadette's house. Well, we never knew how he had found himself there, he had not been invited.

It was her birthday. I bought her a cat, she said:

'You are mad, why have you bought me a cat when you know that Dax can't stand cats.'

'Teach him, considering you were able to teach me to love things I never even liked, you will be able to teach Dax to love a cat.'

The big salon was already full of people I did not like. I had told her the day before that I'd rather take her out for dinner instead of attending her party, but she said:

'Fine, your invitation to dinner is accepted, but you are expected to come anyway.'

So, I came. I sat at the piano. Zoya was waving at me. She came with her two long-haired, annoying and spoilt daughters. (Well, that was exactly what she was proud of when she said: 'You know, my daughters are so spoilt, they do not know how to do anything. Can you believe it, not a thing; they don't even know how to boil an egg, my sweet princesses'). Yes, the 'Princesses' were impudent (disrespectful and insolent; they just rolled their eyes constantly), they did not say a word, but Zoya talked instead. She talked non-stop and my ears hurt from her high-pitched voice. She said:

'You know, we are fifth generation genuine Düsseldorf folks, can you believe it, an old family. Fifth generation!'

This simply was not true; she was the daughter of Russian migrants. Her husband was a well-known plastic surgeon in the city, and that was another reason why her daughters did not speak with 'commoners'. He would always come much later than them, but anyway, they really did not need him around. He said:

'We have travelled all over the world, all of America; my wife always accompanies me on my travels, I like to show off what a beautiful woman I have.'

Whatever he used to say irritated her gravely, so when he said that, she exploded:

'If you repeat that once again, I will spit on you.'

A hushed silence fell onto the stunned guests. Her husband resembled a man who had just learned that he had a terminal illness. All eyes were fixed on the poor 'ill man', and from their gaze his hands started to tremble. Uncomfortable silence, uncomfortable little coughs. Brenadette came to the rescue and in a playful manner, she said:

'You will spoil him! My, God, I nearly misunderstood you; I thought for a moment that you said you would spit on him. Isn't it funny? But instead, you said you would spoil your very generous husband!'

I started to bang the piano keys dramatically playing Beethoven. Brenadette burst out laughing; she hugged the red-faced Zoya, then everybody started laughing. The room was full of loud, laughing people, mixed with the crescendo of Beethoven's symphony, and the tension ran out of the room like some dirty, invisible river which was carelessly created by Zoya, for she could not control the river's flow (of course, for she could not control her own tongue like a silly child who can't grasp the meaning of each word, so it plays with words carelessly, just for the sake of playing.)

So, I wanted to say the guests were important and esteemed town elite, and they held brainy conversations.

There were three men I could not stomach: Brenadette's lawyer, her doctor and some jerk—some sort of an artist and fashion designer. All three were young, modern men, very interesting; I assumed, humorous and certainly rich and unmarried. They were Brenadette's close friends.

I never claimed a right to Brenadette (but I was certainly jealous of all three of them).

That was our non-verbal agreement. We were good friends, intimate friends, but free people. Nobody could have claimed any right over Brenadette; she belonged entirely, solely to herself. So, I knew that she would be 'mine' as long as I respected the fact that she was firstly and solely 'hers'. These three young men knew the same.

When she would go out without me, I never asked her with whom she went. She would only say:

'I'll call you when I come back from Paris. I am going with friends and I do not know when I will be back.'

I would say:

'Have a good time Brenadette, and call me when you return.'

This was the only way I could have kept our friendship going, our dinners together, our visits to *ashrams* and 'houses of light'.

These three men did not belong there. They belonged to some other world.

I was seated at the piano, playing quietly when Charlie approached. He brought a chair and sat next to me. (He smelt of Persia, or like someone I could play music with, or someone I could talk to for hours.) We started playing together. When we finished, we were both in some sort of ecstasy. I looked at his face, at his eyes, and then I recognized him:

'You are Charlie Phill!'

He laughed:

'I answer to that name, too.'

"What else do you answer to?"

'Karel Filov. Crazy Charlie. Charlie the Best. Or simply—Satyam.'

'I read you went to India. How long did you stay there?'

'Seven years.'

'When did you come back? What are you doing here in Germany?'

'I came back last year. I run some seminars here.'

'Are you still playing?'

'Yeah, doing something new.'

We started playing again, he said:

'You are good.'

'Do you really think so?'

'What, you lack self-confidence?'

'Yes.'

'Come to my seminar tomorrow.'

I took Brenadette with me. She said:

'Why didn't you tell me it was the famous Charlie Phill?!'

'Don't you know your guests?'

'He was not my guest, he came with someone. There were some other people I had never seen before. But I did not know that it was Charlie Phill himself. The hero of my youth—Charlie Phill. He was Tomas's idol, too.'

'He was the idol of an entire generation. I had his poster above my bed. If only somebody told me back then, that one day I will sit at the piano together with Crazy Charlie!'

7.

We came to Charlie's seminar. The hall was completely full of people of different ages and from all walks of life. When he came out, people started cheering, applauding ceaselessly. After the initial commotion, the crowd fell silent; Charlie was standing there looking at the crowd. He started his talk. His sentences were short and clear. There was complete silence, you could hear only his voice; he sipped water and sporadically cleared his throat. When he started to talk about the mechanical nature of the mind, it looked to me that he was looking straight at me. He talked about the mind which lived mainly in the past and kept our energy tied to the unreal, which was in fact, the past, hence we were all living unaware of the only reality we have—the present moment. He said, while seemingly looking straight into my eyes, that we were prisoners of our own thoughts, that the mind was just one inconsistent, illogical river of thoughts which carried us in its current, and we were powerless to resist its might. He talked about the mind which was not creative and positive, but he said there was something higher within us, something we were not aware of because of the constant chatter of the mind: its past memories and its anticipation of future events because of which we were losing the magic of the present moment. The magic of the moment lasted the entire time he spoke. We were silent, the idea he wanted us to grasp was floating above our heads. We were enchanted by the magic of the present moment and the total experience of us in it. We were all a part of that magic, we felt it genuinely and we lived for that instant whilst Charlie was taking us there with his hypnotic voice full of rhythm. I once again felt like the old Davor, I felt like a child who never cared about time, for it never really existed. There and then, I understood that time did not exist. I understood that time was made by the mind. Higher intelligence did not know anything about time, that was why little kids were always surprised when they were told it was lunch time. For they know that 'lunch time' could be only measured by their hunger, not by time. This natural measure of time belonged only to kids, because adults had broken this natural rhythm by trying to equate it with the time written on the wall clock.

His talk lasted for a long time, I really could not say how long, but I had found this crack between time and the mind, and I enjoyed exploring this new dimension. A loud applause broke my state and brought me back to the room. Charlie held his hands on his chest in a prayer position. After his talk, a lot of people gathered around him; it was not possible to come close. I looked at Brenadette, she was sitting on her chair in silence. I said:

'Not bad.'

'Not bad at all.'

We were sitting next to each other, I was holding her hand. When she stood up, I stood up, too. We walked towards the exit when we heard his voice calling my name:

'Davor!' I turned back, he waved at us signalling to come back. When we came, he hugged us both and said:

'This was my last talk for today. You are invited to Gertrude Mahler's, too.'

Gertrude Mahler was a renowned science-fiction authoress. She was wearing a dress of the same colour as her hair. Purple. Her dress had a plunging décolleté, and her large breasts were on display. But, I dare say, the quality of her large breasts did not match her age. Her perfume was too strong, just like the squeeze of her masculine hand. She extended her hand to me but not to Brenadette. She just looked at her quizzically, for too long. As always, Brenadette was indifferent.

When we entered her extravagant house, a group of people were already gathered in the big living room. Nobody was introduced to anyone, all the people gathered around Charlie; he said he would talk about his stay in India.

Brenadette was talking with a tall man. He looked familiar to me, as if I had seen him at least once before. On the big wooden kitchen table, there was a variety of delicious food. I was hungry, so I came to the table. I noticed a figure standing on the other side of the table—it was Thomas. He tried hard to talk with his full mouth to a young woman who was so tall and skinny that it looked as if she could be blown away if a light wind came through the window. I came to him and said:

'Hey Thomas, how are you doing?'

'Well, there is plenty of good food, good booze and great girls. I am doing great, old buddy, what about you?'

'I am OK. Are you still playing at *The Bunt*?'

'Every Thursday, I think it's Thursdays that we're in *The Bunt*. Did we play together sometimes?'

'Never, but I know you from there.'

He did not understand that we had never met before; he tried to hook me up with the tall, skinny woman. He said:

'This is my friend . . . we used to play together . . . it was quite some time ago.'

She did not say anything; she was only changing the position of her legs, giggling.

I said:

'We actually never played together. I know you through Brenadette.'

He looked at me with an astonished look. He asked:

'Who is Brenadette?'

'I think she used to be your friend.'

'I have never met anyone with that name.'

He went out onto the balcony. Brenadette was still in deep conversation with that man, there were too many people around Charlie; I think some of them were journalists, for they were writing notes on their notepads.

A young woman came to me, she looked similar to the one Thomas was talking to, very tall and very skinny, one could be easily concerned about her health after a brief look at her; she whispered into my ear:

'A handsome man has to have dark hair, olive skin and a prominent nose,' she started to caress my forearm and continued:

'Smooth skin, hairy forearms, slender fingers. What's your name Dark Eyes?'

'Davor.'

'That sounds so great! Davor. But what does it mean?'

'It means—leave me alone.'

She pulled at her mini skirt which barely covered her little bottom, she twitched her nose, took a sip from her glass and with the lazy walk of a bored cat, sauntered off.

I woke up the next morning in an unfamiliar room; there was somebody's head on the pillow next to mine. I knew by her scent, it was not Brenadette. It was the girl with the lazy walk of a bored cat.

'Oh, no! I got smashed again.' I muttered.

I got up and went home leaving her fast asleep. After I had a shower and something to eat, I called Brenadette. She was very angry with me. I knew the reason she was angry with me was not because I had spent the night with an unknown girl. There was another reason. The next day when we got together (she did not want to see me the same day), she said:

'Were you sober, or were you drunk when you spoke to Thomas about me?'

'When did I talk to Thomas?'

'You, idiot; you are a real idiot when you are drunk.'

'What did I talk about with Thomas?'

'You were forcing him to remember me, while he repeated many times that he had never met me, never heard of me. You were talking so loudly, both totally smashed; you were great entertainment for all gathered. On your insistence, in the end, Thomas finally said:

"On that day, when he came for her cheaply-sold-soul, she had died in my eyes forever; so, I don't know that name anymore."

When he said that, I left the party. Don't you know, Davor, that I do not tolerate things like that? You can't do that to me. Who gave you permission to talk about me? Who gave you permission to talk to Thomas about me?'

I was absolutely aware of how much I had hurt her, I said:

'Brenadette, I never wanted to hurt you. You are the last person in the entire world I would ever hurt. Can you forgive me, Brenadette?'

She said:

'Go now, Davor. You're no longer the person I believed in.'

Once again, I decided 'I will never ever take a drop of alcohol again.' I had disappointed Brenadette; I never wanted to, but I did. I did not know how to fix it. We stayed friends but she stayed aloof, distant, she was not the same Brenadette. I asked her numerous times the same question:

'Brenadette, how can I fix my mistake?'

She would shrug her shoulders and say:

'You must not drink Davor, never; alcohol has completely wrecked your brain.'

In order to gain something in life, first you must lose something. I lost Brenadette's friendship but gained Charlie's.

I did not remember when I gave him my phone number that evening, but a few days later, he rang:

'I'm doing something new, I'd like you to give it a go.'

And I sure did 'give it a go', he said:

'You are almost better than I am.'

From Charlie, I learned everything that needed to be learned about music. I learned from him, as well, 'how to live in the present moment'. And how we lived! Yes, we did. We travelled the entire world; we played the biggest concerts you could imagine; we lived hard, we were everywhere—on magazine covers, on TV; the *paparazzi* were chasing us all the time; women were crazy about us; we drank heavily; we experimented with various drugs or, on the other hand, we had periods of 'complete cleansing'. Charlie would put us all on some of his programs 'for total cleansing' where we cleansed our bodies, our thoughts, minds and hearts. We cleansed ourselves with food, with deep rest, with meditations, with chants, by visiting holy people and sacred places. He told me:

'Don't stop now, this is the pinnacle of your creativity! Later we will take different paths.'

Yes, later, our paths had parted.

I lived for two years in America, another two in London, then I came back to Düsseldorf, again.

I was too tired. Those were four hellish years. I just remember them in glimpses.

I remember our Australian tour. The first concert was in Sydney. It was a warm, starry evening when we landed. They told us it had not rained for days. When I got up the following morning, torrential rain was pouring as if the sky had opened. I thought of Barbara. I went out and wandered around the unknown city, rain poured over my shoulders, in every woman's step I hoped I would find the rhythm of her steps. I would run after some of them thinking for a while: 'There she is, fate has finally decided to bring us back together!' I looked for her the entire day; I searched for her on different beaches, throughout parks, in cafés. I searched for her on the streets, on big avenues; I searched buses, trains and I asked street vendors if they knew a woman named Barbara, if any woman named Barbara was their customer.

But I did not find her. It was not a friendly rain; it was not a warm rain, it was unknown, torrential rain and in its thunder, I had finally realised the real distance which had stretched out between me and Barbara. I sobered to the truth that time did exist, and I understood that time had put an unbridgeable gap between the two of us. Like a little mouse's heart, my heart was trembling knowing that time had decided to never bring us back together in this lifetime. I consoled myself by thinking I might meet her again in some future lives, that she would be mine again, exactly the way I knew her; that we would be once again one soul. Only with Barbara, I was whole, the same soul, completely me. With a broken soul and broken hopes, I came back to the hotel where Charlie was waiting for me: 'We were looking for you for the entire day,' and I answered, 'I don't believe in your theory about nonexistent time anymore.' When the concert started, I imagined her standing in the crowd; I imagined her as the young and beautiful girl she used to be; I imagined her as a fifteen-year-old girl who was anxiously waiting for her idol to come onstage—for her Davor. I came to the centre stage, and yelled:

'Tonight, we are playing for all the Barbaras in this world.'

Charlie gave me a disapproving look; I had never told him about Barbara. Anyway, he would always say that my memories got in the way of my creativity, and I knew just the opposite—my memories enticed my creativity.

I came back to Düsseldorf. I opened my studio. Big concerts and all the travelling never did me any good. My wild ways have ended, it looks like I really have stopped drinking, it's been a good few years now that I have not touched any alcohol; I sleep a lot; I read a lot and I have created some sort of peace within me. Then you came and plainly said that Barbara had died. I read her *Letters to Ted*. Now, I am back to the beginning and I am asking myself—is Marko Millich aware of what he had done?"

"Do you hate him, Davor?"

He was silent. Once again, his voice sounded as if someone else was talking:

"I stopped hating a long time ago. I don't hate Marko. I don't hate the injustice done to me and Barbara; I don't hate life for writing such a fate for me. Simply, I do not hate anything, anybody. Marko did not only seal mine and Barbara's fate. It all reflected onto his own, as I know Barbara had never come back since she left."

I said:

"You are not happy, are you?"

"I don't know what happiness is. I do not know who is happy either. With a little bit of brain and a little bit of heart, it's not easy to be happy. I am at peace and that is good. I can't say that my peace is deep and permanent, but I am much more peaceful than in previous years. You know, once I was sitting with Charlie in the room, each playing our own melody on a guitar when Charlie said, 'Do you know why I took you into the band?'

I did not know, I never really believed that I was exceptional. Charlie said:

'That very evening when I met you at Brenadette's, that evening when I heard you playing the piano, you painted with your music all those pictures of sadness you carry within you. You paint pictures with your music; you build an atmosphere of complete madness. Now, I am going to tell you about your sweet sadness which you believe you carry within you because of one woman. The way we inherit our genes, the way we inherit specks of our personality, in the same way we inherit the sadness of our ancestors. You inherited your sadness; you won't find a remedy for it no matter where you wander to. You inherited this sadness from your great-grandmother on your mother's side. Go and find some relative of your mother's who might tell you more about it, but knowing about it won't bring it to an end. This sadness will follow you until the end of your days. Who knows, you may carry it into yet another incarnation, this sadness has seeped into your bones, into your breath, into every cell of your body. And only because of this, your music is what it is. Only because of this, there is all that hysteria around you. Your sadness is what makes you untouchable, your sadness is your charisma. Without it, you wouldn't be anyone special; maybe a bit more gifted than others and that would be all.'

When I heard that, I did not like it. I did not want my great-grandmother's sadness. I wanted my own sadness. My sadness for Barbara. Barbara was coursing through my veins. But with time, with travelling back to my childhood through my memories (which happened often when I was alone) I understood that I was always sorrowful, only in Barbara's company the sadness was not there. With Barbara I was Davor. Without Barbara, there was only my great-grandmother's sadness within me. Later, I read my sadness as a consequence of losing my 'saviour from sadness'. I thought—if I had inherited this sadness from my great-grandmother, if Barbara was my 'saviour from inherited sadness', then everything was the way it was meant to be. Then, even Marko was just a pawn, just an obedient soldier who followed orders on how to make my inherited sadness course through my veins eternally. There was no saviour. I had my inherited sadness; what had Barbara inherited?"

"A talent." I whispered. Tears were rolling down my cheeks, Davor hugged me (I liked his embrace). He was so close to my heart, I felt as if I had found again, a long-lost friend (or someone's long-lost love). It looked to me, that I, too, had inherited someone's sadness, perhaps Barbara's sadness, her sadness for her lost love. I had always felt her sadness. Sometimes, she would be silent for days, I could not figure out where she belonged at those times. I did not know with whom she spoke; I did not know was her talent ripping her soul apart or was it something else. That 'something else' was seated next to me looking at the palms of his hands on which, it seemed, a destiny was never written. Then, I already knew, that neither would I ever get rid of that sadness, which was glued to my soul on the day Barbara's soul left her body.

When Davor spoke again, I could not understand him. He spoke in a language unknown to me. Upon finishing the incomprehensible sentence, he said:

"Let's go. It's late."

EPILOGUE

When we sat in the car there was no more Brenadette, no more Charlie, no more of Davor's concerts; there was no more Düsseldorf and London. We were driving home, it was late. I was thinking about my grandmother. She must have been in a total panic. When she saw me at the door, in a heavy voice, she said:

"For Heaven's sake, Lora, I have been sick with worry."

She talked about the war, about drunken soldiers; she talked about men who raped a twelve-year-old girl, a nineteen-year-old, and an old widow . . . She retold me horror stories about people who, in this war, were transformed into animals. She cried liberated from the agony (of waiting), for I was alive and she begged me not to go out alone in the evening hours. She talked about armed men, about bombs blowing up night clubs; she talked about late night telephone calls, about threats, begging me never to go out in the evening hours alone.

"I wasn't alone; I was with Davor."

She thought I had gone crazy because of the pain for Barbara; she cuddled me, consoled me. Once again, we spent a sleepless night while I told her about my encounter with Davor. She did not say anything. She did not protest; never uttered a word. She did not ask how he was; she did not smile. She accepted it all; she was happy that I had returned home; she was happy we had locked the door.

***

Ted's letters never arrived. I called him. He wrote frequently. I was told that letters often went missing at the post office, that they were stolen. Out of Ted's ten letters, two arrived. I went down to the post office to inquire.

There was a man in the post office who wanted to send a newspaper, and the teller serving him was screeching like a wild bird:

"You can't send this newspaper out of the country. This paper spits on our country. It has been writing filth about our president. I shall call the police; you must be one of those nostalgic pigs who longs for the old regime; otherwise, you wouldn't be reading a paper like that . . ."

Everybody in the post office was staring at the man who was nervously turning around. Somebody yelled out:

"Yes, I know him! He is the nostalgic pig who longs for the old regime. I know everything about this worm. He wants to send this filth to Germany. He must be some sort of spy working for a foreign secret agency; we do not need those types around here in our country. Let's call the police!"

Another person yelled:

"There is too much democracy in this country, so anybody can do whatever pleases them. He wants to send this filth of a paper, the enemy's propaganda!"

More and more people started gathering around the man, and there were more and more threats. I could not understand what they were yelling; I ran out of the post office. I did not care about Ted's letters anymore, he would phone me anyway. While running out of the post office, I ran into two men. One of them grabbed my hand and said:

"Where are you off to?" What a relief, when I saw Davor's face.

"There are people there in the post office gathering to lynch a man for wanting to send some newspapers to Germany."

Davor's friend asked:

"Was it the TB Herald?"

"How do I know?"

"Of course, what else? This is real madness."

Davor said:

"Igor, this is Lora. Lora, my friend Igor."

We shook hands, Davor said:

"Lora is Barbara's daughter."

Igor looked at me silently, Davor continued:

"Barbara died."

Igor nodded his head; he knew already. Then, Igor said:

"I am going to get Tena; we need to bring the file. Wait for us *At Pippo's.*"

Davor nodded his head and put his arm around my shoulders. Igor yelled:

"I'll be quick; it all depends on Tena . . ."

We walked slowly with his arm around my shoulders (I wanted this walk to be a long, long walk . . .)

We walked up the hill and reached a house where it said, *'At Pippo's'*. We walked into a dark room, full of smoke. When we sat down, Davor said:

"In eighteen years, I have been back three times. The first time, when my father passed away. The second time, Igor called me to collaborate on his new CD. He was the only one who always visited me. He stayed a true friend. Lots of people had forgotten me. Those who did remember me rather didn't want to. I never knew why. I met my school friend Ivana once at a party. We spent twelve years at the same school. She did not want to say hello to me. I came and asked:

'How are you Ivana? Do you remember me? Davor.' She said:

'I do remember you,' and walked away.

Those who never knew me before wanted to meet me, get to know me, shake hands with me, or to get an autograph. But those who knew me, walked away. They never pardoned me my success. There, I understood, it was too small, too suffocating of a society for me. Friends could not pardon if you grew out of your own environment (*Why him?*). They talked behind my back, they said I was arrogant, that I was always too ambitious and calculating, they said that my fame was bought by my father's money, they said I was average, that I was below average, that I was a poofter, that I was a criminal just like my father was, and that music was only the screen I was hiding behind. They said I was an alcoholic, a junkie, that I lived off old rich women . . . Well, later I lost the desire to come back. They never really offended me for nobody really knew me; nobody knew how I was surviving. I grew out of a small-town mentality. I didn't even laugh at petty souls like I used to. I could not find anything any longer which tied me to this town. There was only the memory of Barbara, but nobody ever mentioned her as if nobody remembered her anymore.

I missed diverse characters, I missed free people, I missed several different languages on the streets, I missed Black men, Puerto Ricans, I missed authentic ideas and thoughts and opinions said freely and loudly.

Then a war started, which pulled me even further away from my memories. War was never a civilised creation. That same year, Igor came. He said he was called to the war. He said that there was not a single idea (neither small nor sacred) which could turn him into an assassin. He ran away like the majority of young, urban men did. He played the bass guitar exceptionally. He did not want to replace it with a gun. It was not a part of his mentality. He said to me that some of the 'big rockers' became 'small nationalists', they shrank down to their nation, they sympathised with the herd. Some of them, instead of rock songs started singing nationalist songs with their hands over their hearts and with a pathetic tear in their eye. Igor spent that entire year with me. After a year had passed, he wanted to go back, as he said, for him, it was impossible to live in a foreign country. He said:

'I am going back.'

'What if they take you to the army?'

'I belong there with all my soul and my body; I can't pretend that I live here; here I am disintegrating slowly but surely. What if they take me to the war? I won't go; what can they do? They can take me to military court, but there is no way I am going to the war.'

He went back home.

And me; I am here for a third time. I came to sell my grandma's apartment."

2.

Igor and Tena came, Igor said:

"Are we ready to go?"

I asked Davor:

"Where are you going?"

"To the reputable agency which has a 'roof for every head' " he said theatrically with well-felt cynicism and mockery in his voice.

"May I go with you?" I felt best when with Davor. He took my hand and off we went.

We came in without knocking. There was a table right opposite the door and an unpleasant woman was seated there. The air was sour; from her the smell of anger and agitation was spreading throughout the room (or was it just her body's unbearable odour?) Hostile was her look, and with tension in her voice she barked at us:

"What do you want?"

Igor said:

"We want to see Lubo."

"You can't call him Lubo, to you he is Sir Lubo. Do you have an appointment?"

Igor spoke again, Davor was looking at the tips of his fingers, precisely into his fingernails:

"May we see Lubo . . .?"

She interrupted:

"You can't call him Lubo, he is Sir Lubo to you. Do you have an appointment with Sir Lubo?"

Igor spoke once again; Davor was speechless, still looking at his fingernails:

"We do not have an appointment booked, but we'd like to see him today."

The phone rang. The bitter, angry woman said in an unkind voice:

"You can't see him today, for you do not have an appointment."

She swatted her hand in our direction and then picked up the ringing telephone.

"Hello, *the agency which has a roof for every head,* what do you want? No. No, you can't. No, you can't see him without an appointment. No, you can't make an appointment right now, not over the telephone, I have some clients here right now, call sometime later."

She scoffed. She ducked down, opened the last drawer and took a sip of a dark, oily drink from a hidden glass. Once again, she looked at us and asked:

"What is it that ain't clear to you people?"

Igor said:

"We came to see Lubo . . . and we will certainly see him today."

Davor was still peacefully looking at the tip of his fingers, at his nails, and I could not grasp what was happening. I could not believe (even when they explained it to me) that this arrogant, uncivilised woman was the owner of this agency. Who comes to her? Who was ready to pay for arrogance and hostility? As I said before, whatever happened here in this country was so strange to me, often I felt awkward. Such an agency in Sydney would not last more than three days. Who would come in ever again?

Each time the telephone rang, the unkind woman gave the same answer:

"No, you can't come without an appointment first. What's wrong with you people, in which language should I speak to make you understand? Sir Lubo is in court; no, he won't be here today. Call some other day."

Each time she finished a conversation, she would open the lowest drawer, take her little glass, and take one little sip of that dark, oily drink of an intense smell.

Igor sat down, Davor sat down, and Tena sat down. I remained standing, for there were no more chairs. I was standing there observing them all. The room was filled with unpleasant silence and the sour, angry odour of her body which increased by each minute. Davor seated himself comfortably in a black leather armchair, no longer was he looking at the tips of his fingers, but his seemingly absent look was resting somewhere towards the ceiling. Igor could not conceal his nervousness; he drummed his fingers against the table, and that was the only sound in the room. Tena was turning the pages of some file she brought with her. Stealthily, I looked at the agitated and unkind woman (I felt sorry for her, it would be very sad to carry so much anger within her!); she was sitting and staring at the three of them as if just her unfriendly stare could make them go away.

She was approaching her fifties even though she tried hard to hide it with excessive make up and fine clothes. She had a fashionable haircut, but her makeup was far too heavy. Like the majority of the people in this town, she was well-dressed. As if that was the only thing that really mattered — what kind of clothes you wore (but, what about kindness?). Her look did not match her behavior. She looked like a pampered lady, but behaved like a tipsy, immature young man (who thought nobody could find out he was tipsy). I concluded that a woman like her should not be working with people, for she lacked people skills, she had no charm nor diplomacy. It was obvious she was anxious, displeased and deeply unhappy (she did not even try to hide that).

It was so obvious that the poor woman never got any attention or respect. But, hey, her sharp tongue was quicker than her slow mind.

Davor started to hum some melody. That only agitated her more:

"What, do you intend to camp here? Sir Lubo won't come today. He went to court, to another town; he'll be here, possibly, tomorrow."

Now it was Davor's turn to talk; he spoke softly still looking towards the ceiling:

"I would not agree with what you have said, just as I would not agree that Lubo is a Sir. Real Sirs behave differently."

Redness hit the uneasy woman in the face, rage painted red spots all over her face. Some strange excitement came over me. I could not guess what would happen next. I did not know who Lubo was, and whether he would ever present himself. I could not figure out how long we were going to wait (for the phantom Lubo, unreachable without an appointment).

Then someone knocked on the door. The uneasy woman nearly screamed:

"Coooome in!"

Two people came in, I assumed they were husband and wife. They had an English accent, I recognised it at once. They told her they had an apartment in the old part of the city and wanted to sell it. I could not understand what was the role of this angry woman in the agency and who was the famous phantom Lubo. She was doing literally nothing, she asked the same question:

"Have you got an appointment with Sir Lubo?"

"No. It is necessary to make an appointment?"

"It is necessary, we have a lot of work here, and we do not see clients daily" (Lie, lie, lie!)

"Well then, when would Sir Luu . . . when would he be able to see us?"

"I can't tell you. He is not here right now. Leave your name and a telephone number with me, and we will call you back. Don't ring or come again, wait for our call." (More than a lie. A lie and haughtiness!)

In superb English, Davor said:

"It would be better for you to look elsewhere. They took my money in advance, they did not do a thing for me, and now, Lubo has been hiding from me."

The couple looked at us in dismay. They said, "Thank you" and left. The woman at the desk started yelling at us loudly, the door to the other office, which she defended with her body and life, had opened and at the door, was standing a scruffy, bearded man; suddenly, he smiled and opened his arms:

"Look, look, isn't that Davor? I would not recognise you if I met you downtown. Are you waiting for me guys?"

Davor stood up, he did not take his extended hand:

"What's up Lubo? Are you hiding? You have been hiding for the past two years? You took my money in advance and what have you done? You have gone into hiding."

Lubo was smiling while swinging his head from left to right. (As if he wanted with this gesture to announce that Davor was impatient, ignorant, a little fool.)

"Oh, calm down, my old buddy, Germany has changed you completely. All of you, migrants, think the same — that everybody is after your money. You do not know the situation in our country. The war destroyed a lot. The courts are overworked, they can't process much. The apartment was in your grandmother's name, I had to sign it over to your name . . ." While he was saying that there was a stupid, little smile trembling on his lips, the smile of a liar. He blamed the state, greedy people in the government which robbed the country; he blamed nationalism, unemployment, poverty and everyone's (but not his own) gluttony.

Davor stopped him:

"Listen, I gave the Power of Attorney to Igor; where is my file, can I see it? This woman did not even want to talk to Igor. She said she would speak only with the owner, then I came and she said you were in some other town today . . . but, can I see the file today, I'd like to see the Power of Attorney?"

He pretended he looked through some files; after a quick riffle through some papers, he said:

"Look, the last time I saw Igor he said that you gave up selling the apartment. Actually, what I did, I ripped the agreement in half, as we agreed not to sell it . . ."

"Who did you agree with?"

Once again there was a stupid, little smile on his face, the one which indicated he was lying:

"What do you mean with who, Igor? With you. You know Davor, Igor drinks quite often, he tends to forget things. I met him downtown, and he said that you had changed your mind regarding that matter; he said I could throw away the agreement . . . yes, that was what he said, therefore I ripped the Power of Attorney . . ."

Igor was laughing, Davor said:

"You said Igor was a drunkard, and you, you are a fine gentleman? You are a real professional, no doubt. What you want to say is that you, a professional gentleman, was approached by a drunk man in the street, he informs you completely drunk that I had changed my mind, and you, simply rip in half my Power of Attorney. Is that what you want to say? Is that professionalism?"

(I thought—it is not professionalism, it is some sort of crime!)

The unpleasant woman barked once again:

"Lubo, don't get stressed, tell them to get out of here."

Igor exploded:

"You've said too many lies already, shut your mouth."

Lubo said:

"Well, well, do not insult her now."

Davor said:

"Are we insulting you fine people? You don't think you were insulting us with all your lies? Listen, Lubo, everything you've said was a lie, two years you have been lying to me. You took money in advance and told me you needed it for some expenses; now tell me, what were your expenses? Nothing has been done, the apartment was not signed into my name, it was not sold, so where has my money gone?"

"Well, I placed an ad in the papers . . .I went to court several times . . ."

"Show me!"

"But, Igor said that I can stop the process, because you had changed your mind, my friend . . ."

Davor came very close to his face and said through his teeth:

"I am not friends with your kind."

He turned around and walked away, we followed.

We sat in some café, Igor was extremely agitated but not Davor. He said to Tena:

"I don't think you can do anything more. This country is a mad house. We shall make an agreement that I allow Igor to live in the apartment for the time being."

Later, they told me that empty apartments were freely taken by war refugees and soldiers; once they moved in, nobody was able to get them out.

I asked:

"What is happening here?

"Chaos is happening: robberies, frauds, deceptions, murders . . ." and Davor added:

"And because of it, it is high time we went back home Lora."

Davor said that he was going back tomorrow.

He said he had had enough. And I wanted to go back, too. To Sydney. Even though there was no Barbara waiting there for me.

REMEMBER BARBARA

Tired, I greeted the morning. After all that had happened, I was not closer to myself. There were a multitude of little broken 'I's within me, and each of them had tried to take a central place, each of them tried to win this battle and to silence all the other 'I's. It was an exhausting battle. While standing in front of the mirror, looking at Lora's face, the face of 'Barbara's Angel', I asked myself yet again, 'Who am I?' I was not any closer to myself even after I had learned more about Barbara.

I knew I did not want to stay any longer in 'Barbara's world'. It was not even Barbara's world anymore. Everything had changed. It was not the same city anymore, those were not the same people as before. Even Barbara would not be able to find herself here again. She must have been aware of it, therefore she never went back. Even their memories had been forbidden. They persuaded people that it was different to what they remembered. Davor told me:

"I believed I was a Slav till yesterday, now they say I am not. I can't speak on behalf of others, but I know that through my veins courses a dark, vehement blood which makes my soul restless, wandering; it pushes my soul to create something out of nothingness, to create music out of silence, to create light out of darkness, to create more pain from pain itself . . . in order to touch absolute purity . . ."

That was the morning we were supposed to say goodbye. He said he would leave early. Thoughts about Davor made me restless. I had a role model. A hero. I wondered whether I would ever find someone like Davor. I would not compromise. I would not do what Barbara had done. Oh, how naïve I was, the circumstances were different, and Davor was not mine, neither was I his. I never felt Barbara's pain of parting. I never felt her pain, the pain of a migrant on the other side of the world.

Even though I was going back to Sydney, I did not know where my home was. I was to partly continue to live Barbara's destiny, she lived within me, through me.

The door to his apartment was open. I entered the kitchen; Davor was making his coffee (and that aroma of freshly brewed coffee, I knew, would always take me back to this apartment).

He asked without turning towards me:

"Would you like a cup of tea?"

"Yes, please."

I sat and we drank coffee and tea in silence.

I was first to break the silence:

"Where are you going?"

"To Germany." He said with a smile.

"Is that where your home is?"

"No, Lora. I don't have a home. This is not my home anymore, but there, too, I am a stranger. But, I do what I love doing. I have several exceptional friends and the majority of people I know respect me. As for the rest, I do not care. I do good things . . .when I create, I think of people who do appreciate my work . . ."

"Who are you going back to?"

"I am going back to my music."

After a long silence (in which I tried to guess his thoughts), he said looking through the window:

"I don't know whether it is true that we love only once. But I was a man of one love. I loved your mother for the entirety of my life. I'll tell you a simple truth that I grasped in these days upon meeting you. Man is never dead. I don't know whether the soul continues to live or we live through our descendants, but there have been few days now that I sense Barbara's presence around me. I go to bed and she comes; she sits next to me and we talk about our past. They are only memories perhaps, but so alive, I can hear Barbara's soft, whispering words . . .then I look at you, I see one of your gestures or the movements of your hand, and I see Barbara in you . . .Where are you going, Lora?"

"I am going back to Sydney. I don't know where my home is either. I was born and bred there, but with some unexplainable threads Barbara tied me to this land. But this mentality is not a part of me, I can't understand this hatred around us, the division of the same people; I can't understand the local values, everything is vastly different. Barbara taught me to be free; my school taught me to be free. In my country, there are so many different kinds of people, so many different backgrounds and customs, and this is something we are all proud of. Sydney is the world in miniature; you can find everything in my city, every race, every nation. If I pronounce anything wrongly, just one letter, here it is a catastrophe, they correct you all the time, just about anything; they lift their index finger up in condemnation, or they put it across their lips. It all puts some sort of invisible weight on my chest, and I feel like I can't breathe freely here . . ."

Davor just nodded his head silently.

"I have had enough of hysterical saleswomen yelling; I've had enough of rude bank tellers who have never said the phrase 'thank you'; I've had enough of little thefts while getting my change back; I've had enough of undelivered letters by the postman; I've had enough of whispering, telling little fibs without reason; I've had enough of fake smiles, or the fear I see in the eyes of kind and meek people. I've had enough of all the lies they serve daily in their newspapers and on television. Here, everything is one big lie, Davor."

Davor said:

"Will you leave *Letters to Ted* with me?

He was waiting for my answer while I was silent.

"I could make a photocopy and send it to you."

"Would you agree if I photocopy it and send it to you? I just have one translator on my mind. I could translate it and publish it in German first."

"Do you think that someone would publish it?"

"Quite positive about it. I'd like you to send me all her manuscripts . . .I owe it to Barbara. To make her immortal. We always joked about it, I would say 'Barbara, you are immortal', and that meant that she was so different from the others, that she was original, one of a kind."

I was speechless; I did not know what to say, I did not know if I had the right to give her manuscripts to anybody. He took my hands in his and said:

"Do you trust me?"

"I do." I said truthfully.

He took a piece of paper and wrote his address and telephone number on it.

"So, that'd be all. Take care, Lora."

I stood up, Davor hugged me. I smelt his cologne, I felt shivers down my spine . . . for he smelt of long-forgotten memories, he smelt like a long-lost love or a love found again, he smelt of mulberries, tobacco and coffee . . . he smelt of a very unique smell—the smell of Davor . . . the squeeze of his hand had weakened, and he said while looking into my eyes:

"Love. The love for a man or a woman. The love for music or for the written word. The love for humanity, for knowledge, for life, for God . . . Love, Lora. Only love makes us colossal and strong. Only love leads to complete merging with yourself, merging of all those little broken 'I's into oneness. Love is that creative power, and creative power only comes from love. Love is going back home, the unity with God."

He kissed my forehead (I trembled). I kissed his cheeks (my lips were trembling). We went out together (I wanted to say something more, but I was afraid that my voice would tremble . . .) He sat in his car and said:

"I will wait."

I ran up the stairs and came back with Barbara's letters. While I was placing the manuscript in his hands, I felt as if I was placing it on an altar (the altar of long-lost love).

He honked to me while he was driving away; I saw his hand waving. The letter 'D' started to get smaller; Davor had gone, and it seemed to me that this time he had left this town forever.

When he disappeared around the corner, I knew that my time had run out, too.

EPILOGUE

Six months had passed and I had not heard from Davor. I sent him three postcards of Sydney, and I left a message on his answering machine twice.

I thought:

'That was how he disappeared from Barbara's life too, I will never hear from him again.'

I felt so bad, so guilty that I had given him Barbara's *Letters to Ted*. I felt sincere remorse.

I hadn't had the right to do that, I hadn't had any right, I should not have done it . . .

***

One year had passed and I knew that I would never hear from Davor again. But I was not angry or remorseful anymore, I found all sorts of excuses for him. I knew that he was tremendously busy, I knew that he was a known and sought-after musician, I enjoyed the memories. I told myself:

'Who knows where he is now? Maybe in London, or he could be in America, maybe he forgot to take my address and phone number with him.'

I did not reproach him for anything, Barbara had never reproached him either.

I lost all hope he would ever call, so I stopped thinking about him so often.

That day looked like any other day. No unexpected signs (as if we always wait for some 'unexpected sign of destiny'). The doorbell rang. It was a Monday, ten o'clock in the morning. I thought, 'It could be Ted coming for breakfast.' On Mondays, he would come for breakfast, after we would walk together to the pharmacy. I worked with Ted while studying Pharmacology.

I opened the door. It was the postman. He brought a little parcel. I walked into the living room, turned the parcel over to see who had sent it. It was Davor—from London. I opened the little parcel with trembling hands. It was a book. On the red book cover, in the top right corner, in golden letters was written Barbara Millich, and in the middle of it, in the colour of a very ripe cherry, the title as if embroidered, *Letters to Ted.*

I started crying uncontrollably, just like the day I learned my mother had died. Out of excitement, the book fell out of my hands, and a letter fell out of the book. It said:

Dear Lora,

Thank you for the postcards and your messages. I have been very busy, so I didn't manage to call you even though you are always on my mind. I was busy trying to get the right translator, then the right publisher. You must read the reviews, soon I will send them. We made it, my sweetheart. The publisher wants more, he wants everything she has ever written.

I have to finish an important and big project, then I will call again . . .

I did not read further. I took the book on which in golden letters my mother's name was written– Barbara Millich. Davor's last words echoed in my ears:

". . . the love for music or for the written word. The love for humanity, for knowledge, for life, for God. Only love, Lora . . ."

(And deep down in her heart Lora knew . . . she knew . . .)

About the Author

Branka Čubrilo is the author of seven novels and two collections of short stories. Branka's articles, essays and short stories have been published in many online and print magazines in various countries and languages. She has worked as a radio producer and presenter (SBS Australia), as well as an interpreter and translator for several languages.

Branka lives and works in a beautiful coastal, leafy Sydney area, with her daughter Althea and their cat Mia.

www.ingramcontent.com/pod-product-compliance
Lightning Source LLC
LaVergne TN
LVHW091035080826
845145LV00002B/505